CONDEMNED TO DEATH

The Burren Mysteries by Cora Harrison

CONDEMNED TO DEATH

A Burren Mystery

Cora Harrison

This first world edition published 2014
in Great Britain and 2015 in the USA by
SEVERN HOUSE PUBLISHERS LTD of
19 Cedar Road, Sutton, Surrey, England, SM2 5DA.
Trade paperback edition first published
in Great Britain and the USA 2015 by
SEVERN HOUSE PUBLISHERS LTD.

Harrison, Cora author.
    Condemned to death. – (Burren mystery)
    1. Mara, Brehon of the Burren (Fictitious character)–
    Fiction. 2. Murder–Investigation–Fiction. 3. Women
    judges–Ireland–Burren–Fiction. 4. Burren (Ireland)–
    History–16th century–Fiction. 5. Detective and mystery
    stories.
    I. Title II. Series
    823.9'2-dc23

ISBN-13: 978-0-7278-8442-8 (cased)
ISBN-13: 978-1-84751-549-0 (trade paper)
ISBN-13: 978-1-78010-595-6 (e-book)

All Severn House titles are printed on acid-free paper.

Severn House Publishers support the Forest Stewardship Council™ [FSC™],
the leading international forest certification organisation. All our titles that
are printed on FSC certified paper carry the FSC logo.

Typeset by Palimpsest Book Production Ltd.,
Falkirk, Stirlingshire, Scotland.
Printed and bound in Great Britain by
TJ International, Padstow, Cornwall.

For my daughter Ruth – always the first to read my books – and always ready to accompany me on explorations of remote places on the Burren and to lend a listening ear.

Acknowledgements

Many thanks to family and friends who continue to encourage me during the writing of these books; to my agent Peter Buckman who always reads them with promptitude and appreciation, seasoned with some wholesome criticism; to my editor Anna Telfer who delights me with praise and who spots any weaknesses; to the team at Severn House who turn my typescript into such a wonderfully attractive product; and to the professionals in the field of Brehon law who do all the hard work of translating from medieval Irish and thereby facilitate my weaving of stories about the O'Davorens of Cahermacnaghten.

One

Brecha Crólige
(Judgements of Bloodlettings)

Fingal (kin-slaying) is the most serious crime that can be committed under Brehon or Gaelic law. No fine can be paid, nor no recompense made by someone who has killed a member of his immediate family. The murderer is banished from the kingdom by being placed in a boat with no oars and sent to drift out to sea.

The body of the man in the boat with no oars had been washed up onto the orange sands of the beach of Fanore. Mara, Brehon of the Burren, with her seven law scholars flanking her, stood very still for a moment, looking down into the sightless eyes. The sands and the dunes behind them were crowded with fishermen and their families; with boats; with small canvas-covered shelters; with fires smoking beneath the long lines of herring and mackerel suspended from straight twigs resting on v-shaped upright ones; but everyone, including the small children, was very silent. Death by drowning was well known to this fishing community, but there was something strange about this death and it chilled even the experienced Mara to the bone.

Mara had been Brehon – judge and investigating magistrate – of the one-hundred-square-mile Kingdom of the Burren for over twenty-five years. She had imposed penalties for many crimes, including that of murder, but she had never had to impose a penalty for the ultimate sin in Gaelic Ireland – that of the murder of a close family relation. Brehon law refused to shed blood and ordinary deeds of murder were punished by a heavy fine and full declaration of guilt and repentance in front of the people of the kingdom. And since blood cannot be shed by the judicial process, then the punishment for *fingal* (kin-slaying) was left to God. The murderer was put in a boat with no oars, the boat was pushed out to sea and the man was abandoned to the ocean and the winds. It was one of the first laws that any young legal scholar learned at the commencement of their schooling.

The dead man was unknown to her, unknown to all, it appeared. Not a young man, a man in his fifties, she judged; though the hair was plentiful, the face was lined. Clothed in white linen, he lay there, judged by God and condemned to death. What had he done to merit this death and where had he come from to end up on this remote shore – these were the questions in Mara's mind, but as she gazed down at him, doubt crept in.

Was all as it seemed?

Mara turned and looked around. The body in the boat had landed in a small inlet on the southern extremity of Fanore Bay, right into a little sandy cove, well away from the main beach. The storm winds had died down, but there was still a strong breeze from the south-west and it was easy to see how the boat had been washed in by the tide. The position was right; it was the boat itself that puzzled her. Where had it come from? And what was the history of the man who lay there, quietly dead, half covered with seaweed, dressed only in linen, the skin of his face whitened by the salt spray, the tongue protruding, looking for water, the bleak sentence of death to be read in the position of the body lying within a boat with neither oars nor sail; a boat set adrift to be at the mercy of wind and waves. Mara looked out at the Atlantic Ocean, and then back at the grey stone of the mountains that towered above the beach. She could not have foreseen that this would occur within the few short days since she had last visited Fanore.

It was three days ago that Mara came to the seashore on the north-west side of the Kingdom of the Burren. She went there on midsummer's eve with her seven scholars, who were going to take part in a great fishing expedition. They set off early that morning, riding the eight miles from Cahermacnaghten on a path that wound between the mountains and then descended from Ballyiny to sea level. It had been a long time since Mara had travelled this steep narrow roadway and oblivious of the excited chatter around her she was absorbed in the beauty of the flowers. The hills rose high on either side of them, not gentle mounds covered with grass or heather, but vast chunks of exposed rock where the rain had carved the limestone boulders into thick bare slabs and terraces of stone and where each crevice and crack was filled with tiny plants. As Mara rode along behind her noisy scholars, her eyes were on the dark green ferns and on the flowers, noting where the intense pale sky-blue of the harebells contrasted so beautifully with the bright pinkish-purple of the daisy-shaped cranesbill blooms. The tiny rock gardens of wall rue and starry blossoms in white and purple absorbed her so much, even when they emerged from the mountains, that it took a startled exclamation from one of her scholars to make her turn her towards the sea.

It had been raining heavily during the Sunday night and there had been claps of thunder from time to time, so they had all been relieved when the morning showed fine and sunny. But the sea that stretched between them and the Aran Islands was tumultuous, boiling over with white-capped waves, and the sky was full of seabirds, squawking with noisy elation. For a moment Mara enjoyed the sight, the contrast between the deep blue of the sea, the foam on the immense breakers that rolled, one by one, into the shore, the long level shining black slabs that stretched out to meet the water, the scarlet legs of a large flock of oystercatchers overhead, their call like the drumming of the waves themselves, and the plumes of water smoke rising high above the coastal fields, but then the dismayed words of sixteen-year-old Domhnall, her eldest scholar, penetrated her brain.

'The boats will never put out in a sea like that,' was what he said.

'Of course they will,' contradicted Cormac, Mara's eleven-year-old son.

'Of course they will,' loudly asserted the MacMahon twins, Cael and Cian, but no one else said anything, just looked out to sea. Art, Cormac's foster-brother, almost his twin as they had been babies together, usually agreed with him, but Art was the son of a fisherman and knew more about the sea than any of the others. Fifteen-year-old Slevin took his opinions from his great friend, Domhnall, and fourteen-year-old Finbar was so depressed about his examination results that he had not opened his mouth for the whole morning.

'We'll see,' said Mara as they turned their horses off the road and went down the sandy path towards the beach, Mara carefully picking her way in and out of the clumps of wiry-stemmed sea-pinks, and the scholars riding at top speed towards a tall figure that had just climbed up the thick wedges of rock and was coming to meet them.

'Fernandez, Fernandez,' screamed Cormac. 'We'll be able to go out in the boats today, won't we?'

Even from a distance Mara could see Fernandez shake his head and she relaxed. She had been feeling tense. During the last few weeks, long before the sight of those turbulent seas, she had been a little worried about the eleven- and twelve-year-old children going out in the boats, though she knew that Setanta, Art's father, and Cormac's foster-father, would take good care of them. Fernandez, she thought, was a young man who enjoyed taking risks, but even he had decided against the expedition today and that gave her confidence in him.

'We'll have to give it a couple of days to settle down,' he said and then held up his hands in mock-surrender as he was assailed with complaints.

'Peace, peace!' he exclaimed. 'We'll go as soon as possible. But the midsummer's eve party on the beach will go ahead, unless it rains again. And if it does, then we'll all eat at the castle, and if it's too windy for the tents, then you lot can sleep in the castle until the weather settles down a bit. In fact, that will probably be the best thing for all of you. Come and sleep in the castle and help to guard me against invaders from the sea. After all, you wouldn't be much good to me if you were down in the sand dunes, would you?' He looked with understanding at the disappointed faces.

'Yes, yes, I know,' he said. 'You want to sleep out of doors, but you know that wind will blow canvas tents away if it keeps on gusting like this. Still, it might die down by evening, and if it doesn't,' his eyes met Mara's with a twinkle of reassurance, 'if it doesn't you will be snug and warm in my castle at Cathair Róis – there'll be no beds, I'm afraid, just mattresses in front of the fire. How about that? But you won't go hungry, any of you. Etain has promised a great feast to celebrate midsummer's eve. Everyone is helping. Everyone is bringing food and stuff to drink. What about you, Brehon, would you like to come also? We can provide only one extra bed, I'm afraid, but that one bed shall be for you.'

Mara shook her head. 'No thank you, Fernandez, but if they wouldn't be a trouble to you, I'm sure that the scholars would love to stay here at Fanore and be ready as soon as you think it's safe to go. They've been looking forward to the midsummer feast.' It was, she knew, a big event at Fanore year after year and already there was a large bonfire all set to be ignited piled under the shelter of heavy tarpaulins on the dry sand of the beach, well above the summer high-tide mark. Her scholars were beginning to cheer up. They had been worrying about having to go home, which would have been a terrible anticlimax, but now their eyes brightened as they looked away from the sea and surveyed the castle. Mara gave Fernandez a grateful smile.

'I'll take good care of them all,' he assured her.

Fernandez was earning golden opinions from all of the O'Connor Clan, she thought, and now he won her good opinion also. It was perceptive of him to see how disappointed the scholars were and generous to offer to put them up, when he had the more enticing prospect of Etain to keep him company. The midsummer bonfire and the feast to follow it would be a great event for the scholars, whose everyday life was full of almost relentlessly hard study – the continual translations, writing of essays and memorization of facts. It would be fun for them to stay in Fernandez's castle and have an exciting end-of-term celebration before returning to their homes for the summer holidays.

And of course Fernandez's castle was a magnificent new structure. It had been built within an ancient enclosure, named Cathair Róis after the linseed with which it supplied all the linen growers of the Kingdoms of Burren and of Corcomroe. The old enclosure had consisted of the usual circular wall protecting three or four small houses within, but the new dwelling that replaced the houses stood high above that ancient wall, in fact four storeys high, overlooking the sea. Mara did not care for the castle greatly, finding that its rounded, pepper-pot shape and white-plastered exterior did not fit into the landscape as well as the traditional tall, square, grey, crenellated tower houses and small oblong stone cottages. Nevertheless, she had to admit that the new castle was furnished in great style and with an eye towards beauty as well as comfort. Fernandez had brought back from Spain some fine tables, beds, bed hangings and wall carpets and as they had been unloaded, one by one, from his ship the news had spread through the hinterland of the wealth of this new member of the O'Connor clan.

A year previously there had been great excitement when the young man, Fernandez MacFelim O'Connor, purporting to be the son of the long-lost brother of Finn, the O'Connor of Ballyganner, *taoiseach* (chieftain) of the O'Connor clan in the Burren, had arrived in that kingdom on a ship that came from Spain. He bore the exotic name of Fernandez, and spoke his few words of Gaelic with a strong Spanish accent, but he appeared, according to those who had known Felim O'Connor at that age, to be the living image of his father. Moreover, he bore with him a precious cloak brooch, an enamelled deer head on an oval of pure gold, and the hilt of the sword which he wore at his side incorporated a piece of deer antler, of great symbolic importance to the O'Connor clan. Both these articles were readily identified as belonging to Felim O'Connor and to his father before him. Faced with the evidence of the family likeness and the probability that Felim himself had bestowed articles of value on this boy, and thereby recognized him as a son, Mara had not hesitated to declare Fernandez as the nephew of the present *taoiseach*. The clan welcomed him and were happy that he proposed to take up residence in an ancient enclosure which had belonged to members of his part of the clan.

But the matter had not stopped there. The *taoiseach*'s only son, Tomás, the present *tánaiste* (heir), had an unfortunate weakness for strong drink and was a spoilt, lazy, idle young man. Fernandez, on the other hand, possessed a huge store of energy, quickly mastered the language of his father and was full of ideas to better the lot of the O'Connor clan, who were mainly fishermen. And the clan had begun to talk, in ones and twos and threes, to Mara about the possibility of replacing young Tomás with Fernandez. It was felt, said some cautiously, that Fernandez might have more interest, more involvement in the position and in the affairs of the clan.

He did seem, she thought, to be an able man and certainly one who had the interests of his people at heart. And if he had brought back plenty of Spanish gold, well he spent it recklessly. He had employed labour during the winter months to construct his new round castle, still called by the old name of the enclosure, Cathair Róis, overlooking the beach at Fanore and when that was done he had retained the men and set them to work on weaving huge nets that would stretch from boat to boat. This summer, he planned, there was to be a giant fishing expedition with all of the O'Connor boats, rather than competing with each other, working together to catch the shoals of mackerel and herring. And not only that, he had devised the plan that the boats would land their catch on the sandy beach at Fanore and the women and younger children would immediately smoke it over fires of salt-impregnated driftwood and dried seaweed. And, moreover, there would be a great feast, supplied by him, and eaten on the beach to celebrate midsummer's eve. The excitement was intense; the seven young scholars in the law school had successfully begged to take part, and once their examinations were over had talked of little else. And now, of course, at the news of the postponement of the fishing expedition the disappointment was just as intense.

Still, the prospect of the midsummer's eve supper and of staying in the newly built castle inside the ancient wall of Cathair Róis – that was exciting even if the tents were impossible, and the prospect of being ready at the very first moment to set out to sea was wiping the gloom from their faces now.

'And you can all help us, you know, you can help us in putting up the supports for the tents. We'll have to wait in case the wind rises again before putting the canvas over them, but there's no reason why you can't make a start in putting in the poles; you can have three tents to share between you– that will do you, won't it?' asked Fernandez, pointing down to one of the sheltered hollows in the sand dunes. Already quite a few tripod structures had been erected in other hollows and there were neat fireplaces made from stones from the beach near each of them.

'Great! Is that place just for us!' shouted Cormac. 'Me and Art in one, the twins in the second one and Domhnall and Slevin in the other – and Finbar,' he added.

Mara reminded herself silently to ask Cliona, Cormac's foster-mother, to find another tent for Cael, the girl of the MacMahon twins, or better still keep the child with her. I really should try to discover another able girl to keep Cael company at the law school, she thought. Cael was an extremely clever youngster, brighter even than her brother, and it would be a shame for her not to qualify as a lawyer, but this insistence on being a boy and doing everything with the boys was quite a problem. There had been a huge fuss when Mara decreed that she had to live either by herself in the one-roomed girls' house, or else with the farm manager and his wife, and not share the boys' accommodation in the scholars' house. It was a shame that Cael could not be happy to be a girl, she thought and looked an appeal across at Fernandez.

'Well, I was hoping to get Cael to share with Etain's sister,' said Fernandez diplomatically. 'Síle is afraid of rats and she thought she saw something moving in the sand dunes. I told her that you were pretty handy with the knife,' he added to Cael.

Rabbits more likely than rats, thought Mara. There was no doubt that the dunes were full of rabbit burrows – and she had just seen one leap from inside an old discarded boat that had been abandoned upside down, high up between the cusps of two sand hills, but she applauded Fernandez for his quickness of wit. Even now he was shouting, 'Etain, Etain, I've got someone with a knife that will make sure that no rats come to Síle's tent at night. Here are Etain and Síle,' he said as a red-haired young woman, carrying a dripping basket and followed by a young girl, came up from the beach. Mara hastened to settle the question of the tents by firmly allocating Cian and Finbar to one of them and Art and Cormac to the second. Domhnall and Slevin could have the third tent and some peace from the younger boys and then she rapidly silenced all protests by telling them to greet Etain and her sister.

'Cael is afraid of nothing; you can trust to her; she's expert with the knife and would make nothing of killing a rat,' she said to Etain, laying her hand on the girl's shoulder so that Etain would know which one of the short-haired, identically dressed scholars, in knee-length cloak, *léine*, bare legs and sandals, was the girl.

'That's good! Síle, this is Síle, she's my younger sister, she'll be glad of someone who's handy with a knife, won't you, Síle?'

Mara liked her for the quick-witted and matter-of-fact reply. Etain, she thought, would make a good wife for Fernandez. So far they hadn't bothered with the marriage ceremony, but happily lived together in the newly built castle. No doubt at some stage there would be a wedding. And perhaps it might, she thought, looking around at the meticulous preparations for the great fishing expedition, at the giant net, at the boats lined up on the shore with their sails folded within them, at the orderly crowds moving around the beach, each one with a task to perform, perhaps it might well take place at the same time as the clan elected a new *tánaiste*. There seemed to be a great affection between Fernandez and Etain, though they had a joking, playful relationship; and the younger scholars were amused when she demanded that they hold Fernandez a prisoner while she robbed his purse of some silver to buy goods for tonight's midsummer's eve supper.

'I must go in and change into a fancy gown,' said Etain waving her piece of silver aloft triumphantly. 'I have to take this samphire to Galway City and I'll bring back some nice things for the midsummer's eve supper. Come in with me, Cael, and you and Síle can choose something for me to wear in the city streets. Cormac and Art, be angels, and take this basket down to the pier, won't you? I daren't ask Domhnall and Slevin to do anything these days, they are getting bigger than I am. Finbar and Cian, could you go and get nine poles from the heap by the wall in front of the castle. They'll do you for your tents and there's plenty of canvas stacked up in the hall. Just help yourself, all of you.'

And Etain, rapidly engaging Cael in an animated conversation about throwing-knife competitions, went off with long strides towards the castle, leaving all the boys in good humour and willing to do her bidding. Even Cormac and Art made no fuss about carrying the dripping basket down to the pier.

Etain O'Connor, and her brother Brendan, had set up an industry collecting and selling the samphire which grew prolifically along the coastline between Black Head and Poll Salach, but especially on the rocks in front of Cathair Róis, and Etain's basket was full of the plants, their fleshy leaves of palest green looking like transparent deer's antlers. Mara's mouth watered at the sight of it. Picked early in the morning before the sun got at it and boiled while still fresh, it had a crisp salty texture and went marvellously with a fried sole or plaice. She turned her eyes from it resolutely, though. She knew that if she offered to buy some, she would be pressed to take a present of it and that was something she did not want to do. Brendan, she had heard, ran a daily boat across the Galway Bay inlet, going from Black Head to Galway Docks, and did a very good business in supplying the many inns there with the ingredient that the wealthy merchants of the town enjoyed.

Two

Crích Gablach
(Ranks in Society)

There are three stages in the qualification of a lawyer.

The first stage is that of an aigne, *who can plead for a client in court for a client.*

The second stage is that of an ollamh, *who is qualified to own and manage a law school.*

The third stage is that of a Brehon. The Brehon has the power to judge all cases of law-breaking within the kingdom, to allocate fines and to keep the peace.

Each kingdom in the land must have its Brehon, or judge. The Brehon has an honour price, lóg n-enech *(literally the price of his or her face), of 16 séts.*

Three days after her first visit to Fanore, three days of peace without her scholars, three days when she had given herself a rest from school work and had visited friends and neighbours, Mara had woken late on the Thursday morning. The night before she had stayed up until after midnight going over and going over the examination papers of the scholars at her law school. Then she had slept badly for the early part of the night pondering over what to do about Finbar. He had now spent two years at her law school and she hated to think that she had failed with him.

Mara had two positions in the Burren. The first was to be judge and investigating magistrate of the one-hundred-square-mile territory of that stony kingdom, but the second was to be *ollamh* or professor of the law school that her father had established at Cahermacnaghten in the north-west of the kingdom. She taught her scholars, once they were past the basic stages of reading and writing, all that they needed to know about the ancient laws of Ireland, and also educated them in languages, such as Latin, French and even Greek, so that they could read the great works penned in the past. At the end of the Trinity term of each year, in June, her scholars sat the examinations laid down by the Brehons of Ireland at their annual congress.

Six of her seven scholars had a satisfactory result. Domhnall, the eldest, and Mara's grandson, had achieved an outstanding result – excelling in Greek, which he had only studied for four terms. Twelve-year-old Cael MacMahon, the only girl, had done excellently, also, with top marks in every subject and that gave Mara great satisfaction as she had been at the school for less than two years and had spent most of the first term arguing about everything from where she was to sleep to whether she needed to obey orders. Art and Slevin had both done well also, and Cian's result was better than she had expected. There was a slight disappointment in the very average score from her son, Cormac; although he had done well in French, he had forgotten quite a few of the Triads he had been supposed to have memorized. He was clever, but not interested, she told herself and knew that she would have to face the fact within the next few years that he might want to choose a different environment. Just now he was barely eleven years old and she would endeavour to keep him at school and by her side as long as possible.

But the big worry was Finbar, son of the Brehon of Cloyne, in the south of Ireland. Finbar had been sent to her two years ago by his despairing and angry father. Initially he had made progress in a more sympathetic atmosphere, but it had become increasingly clear that the boy's aptitude was insufficient for the arduous and demanding study that qualification for even the lowest grade of lawyer demanded. He had failed his examinations last year, and there was no getting away from the fact no matter how often she re-examined the papers that he had failed again. According to the rules of the Brehons of Ireland, he could not have a third chance even if his father was willing. And what was even more worrying was the news Domhnall, in confidence, had told her during the winter, that Finbar had been threatened with expulsion from the family home if there was another failure. There were younger brothers, the Brehon of Cloyne had said, and Finbar had already had every chance to make his way in the law. Now he had to choose a different path and go his own way without further help from his father. Mara sighed over the harsh decision. Finbar, she thought, was not yet fifteen years old. She looked back over her own life. At fourteen she had rushed into a disastrous marriage with a boy who degenerated into an idle, drunken sot, only too willing to live on his wife's patrimony. At Finbar's age she had been a mother, but her father had stuck by her, had believed in her. With that belief and love behind her, she had the brains and ambition to succeed and sailed through her law examinations with great ease, qualifying at the age of sixteen, then, after her father's death, conducting her own divorce, going on to get the further qualification of *ollamh* so that she could manage the law school and then reaching the height of her profession at the age of twenty-one when she was examined by two erudite men and given the rank of Brehon, with responsibility to solve and judge all crimes committed within the kingdom. Finbar, she thought, now needed to display similar courage and industry. He was shrewd, clever with his hands and could be hard-working. Cumhal, her farm manager, thought he might make a good farmer, but farming land was inherited – as she had inherited her farm, as well as the school, from her father. Something else had to be found for Finbar.

Mara got to her feet and walked out to the gate of her house and then down the road towards the law school and the farmyard. Everything seemed very quiet. Even the animals seemed quieter after three days of peace. The cows were all in the fields with their calves – only the house cow would be milked in this season – and most of the workers were up on the peat bog *footing the turf*, as the process was named: stacking the wet turves in little groups of three leaning slabs supporting a top slab, like a miniature flat roof over a tripod. Cumhal was the only worker in sight, carefully removing the surplus tiny green apples from the trees in the orchard outside the wall that enclosed the houses of the law school. He turned when he saw her, but was forestalled by his wife, Brigid, who popped out from the kitchen.

'There you are, Brehon. I was just coming over to see you. Cumhal was up on the bog this morning and he saw the ships and boats come in. Came in before the turn of the tide, that's what he said. He saw the sails from the mountain – and he heard the O'Connor victory song! So they're all safe and well. I was just about to come over and tell you when I heard your door close. So now you can relax and not worry any more. Give yourself a bit of a holiday. You're looking tired, so you are. I said the same to Cumhal, last night. She looks tired and worried, that's what I said.'

'That's good news,' said Mara, ignoring the bit about herself. Brigid had been her nurse, almost her mother, and she still fussed over her as though she was only five years old. Cumhal was a very sensible, experienced man and there was a good view of the ocean from the farm's bog, which lay in a dip between two mountain peaks. He would have been able to see whether all came in good order – and they would not have been singing unless all had gone well with this fishing trip.

Her scholars would be having a holiday of a lifetime, going out in boats, eating and sleeping on the beach of Fanore, helping to smoke the enormous catch of mackerel and herring that was brought in from the sea by the fishermen and themselves. Mara missed the sound of the eager voices from the law school, but revelled in the quiet that allowed every note of the larks' high song and the swallows' chirping to be heard clearly in the still air.

It was a beautiful late June morning, she thought as she walked on down the road, averting her mind from the problem of Finbar and just luxuriating in the calm and peace. The cows and their calves wandered in a leisurely way over the limestone that paved the fields and snatched morsels of succulent green grass from between the stones. It was interesting that they avoided the clusters of dark and light purple orchids which grew amongst the grasses. Instinct was a marvellous thing, she reflected, watching how the bees seemed to go straight towards a cluster of pale woodbine flowers that had just opened that morning – instinct was something that she never ignored in herself, though the long training of the law school had guided her towards overlaying it with reason, with probability and with a strong respect for the law.

Her thoughts had strayed to some past cases when she was roused by the sound of hoofs on the paved road that led from the law school to the coast. Immediately she was alert. The sound alarmed her. It was not a neighbour trotting along to see to cows in an outlying farm, nor yet a visitor – the hour was far too early. This was someone coming fast towards her – coming for an urgent reason. Mara stood very straight and waited until around the corner came, very quickly, on a powerful pony from the Connemara Mountains, the oldest pupil in her law school, and her grandson, Domhnall O'Davoren. Had something happened during the three days since she had left her scholars at Fanore?

Is all well? She almost said the words, but then checked herself. If all was well, Domhnall would not be here. He would be helping to beach the morning catch of fish, would be slotting them in line above the fires made from dried seaweed and pieces of sun-baked driftwood. No, something was wrong and she braced herself for the news. Cormac, she thought, and realized how vulnerable any woman with child would always be.

But Domhnall, when she pulled up his pony in front of her, said nothing about Cormac.

'Brehon,' he said with his usual calm air of respect, 'Brehon, we've found a body.'

'What happened?' she asked when they arrived at Fanore less than an hour later. She had already heard the story from Domhnall, but he was discreet beyond his years and said nothing when she asked this question of the small crowd assembled to meet her, and it was Fernandez, the natural leader, who came forward. His voice was quite loud, almost as though he deliberately pitched so that it would be heard by all who were on the beach.

'Well, it happened like this; we came in on the tide, Brehon,' he said. 'Just about an hour before full tide. We left the boats in the water while everyone got buckets and bags and emptied the nets and boats of the fish.' He told the story well, thought Mara, imagining how the beach would have been alive with

activity, the children, the women and the men running up to
the top of the beach, well outside the summer high-tide line,
depositing the piles of fish on the tarpaulins which she could
see spread out on the marram grass, anchored by heavy stones.
There would have been frantic activity, everyone engaged in
gutting the fish, hanging them from well-soaked alder rods,
stacking dried seaweed and pieces of driftwood onto the fires.

'And then we got the boats tied up or beached just before
the high tide,' he finished. 'We had everything unloaded by
then – all was as you see it.' He waved an arm, indicating the
numerous fires, the drifting smoke, the silver spear-shaped fish,
suspended above the fires, and the crowds of men, women and
children.

'And the boat with the corpse also came in on the tide?'

'That's what we think, Brehon. Probably before high tide,
because none of us spotted it on the sea. It landed at the spot
where you will see it to be, over on the far side of the beach,
away to the south of where we were working.' Was it her
imagination, or did his voice become a little cautious, as though
he was trying to distance himself from the event? He wouldn't
like this, she thought. The people were superstitious. So far
everything to do with Fernandez had borne the sheen of glittering success. This might do him harm.

'Let me see,' she said and Domhnall, silent at her elbow,
moved forward towards the spot that his fellow scholars guarded.
The fishermen, their families and the shore-dwellers, together
with Fernandez, followed at a respectful distance, straggling
across the sands in twos and threes, coming after the two of
them as they crossed the rocks and came into a sheltered,
hidden tiny bay of sand surrounded by boulders and rock pools.

The boat had come to rest on the sand and the body of a
man lay in it – hands outstretched and dangling over the sides
and the face, framed by shoulder-length hair, turned up towards
the sky. And the significant thing was that there were neither
oars nor sail.

Mara looked down at him. The sun had risen to its full
height; the light sparkled across the blue sea and it cast a warm
glow on the face, but there was no doubt the man was dead.
The worst thing about the corpse, she thought, was the way

the swollen tongue protruded as if seeking moisture and the eyes were fixed and staring – almost betraying the horror of the final moments. She stood there silently for a few minutes, noting everything.

'It's nothing to do with us, Brehon.' The slightly belligerent tone came from Brendan O'Connor, the samphire-gatherer, Etain's brother. His voice was loud and quite hoarse – a man who spent his life on the sea, ferrying the delectable fronds from an inlet on the northern side of Black Head rocks across the bay and into the docks of Galway City. He wouldn't have taken part in the fishing expedition; his own business was too valuable for him to take a few days away from supplying the cooks and innkeepers of Galway with the fresh samphire.

'Did you find the body, Brendan?' she asked.

'No, no, it wasn't Brendan. It was young Síle here.' Fernandez sounded almost alarmed as he contradicted her. He dragged Brendan and Etain's young sister forward, Cael's tent-mate, a child of about eight, thought Mara, noticing with an inward smile that Cael looked disdainfully at the girl and moved a step nearer to the law-school scholars, placing herself firmly between her brother Cian, and Art, the fisherman's son. The little girl gave her evidence in a frightened whisper. She had gone to collect some pretty shells and then seen something glinting from a rock and so had climbed out from over here . . . And she pointed back to where a line of rocks, still splashed by the retreating tide, ended in this small oval of sand, surrounded by pool-filled boulders.

'We thought it best to leave it until you came, but we should get it buried before the tide comes in again and sweeps it back out to sea,' explained Fernandez. 'In this weather the corpse will soon be in a bad way and the boat can be buried with it. It's useless, as a boat. You can see for yourself, Brehon, that the timbers are as thin as linen in some places.'

'Stands to reason that those who laid him on the tide wouldn't have wanted to waste a good boat,' said Setanta, Art's father, and there was a low murmur of agreement from all of the fishermen around him.

'Nothing to do with us, as Brendan says, Brehon,' said Michelóg, a local farmer whose land stretched down to the

beach. Brendan nodded his agreement, while the other fishermen, Mara noticed, glanced at each other. Michelóg was not
popular amongst them, and yet they were nodding when she
looked at them as if to say that they were all in agreement.

'You can see for yourself, Brehon,' said Brendan, taking over
the leadership while the fishermen turned gratefully from
Michelóg towards him. 'You can see for yourself that the boat
did not come from the Burren because there was a south-
westerly wind last night – you can still feel it on your left
cheek and it was a south-westerly gale three nights ago. That
boat would have been swept up here from west Corcomroe
or even from the Kingdom of Kerry during the storm – it's
nothing to do with us,' he repeated. 'It's an affair belonging to
another kingdom.'

'Your young lad, here, young Cormac, has been explaining
to me about the custom of putting a murderer in a boat with
no oars and pushing him out to sea. I had forgotten all about
it,' explained Fernandez. Mara said nothing. She felt furious
with Cormac. 'Say nothing except to me when there is a case
going on' was the rule that she had given to all her scholars,
but Cormac, obviously, had not been able to resist airing his
knowledge. It was, perhaps, a pity that Domhnall had felt
that he should be the one, as the eldest in the law school, to
bring her the news. If he had remained she was sure that he
would have managed to silence Cormac. Slevin did not have
the same easy authority, and may have been busy with safe-
guarding the boat and its terrible contents.

'This is nothing to do with any of us, Brehon.' Michelóg
was looking at her very intently and she suddenly found this
insistence, this slightly belligerent tone of voice to be strange,
and she found the respectful silence of his listeners even stranger.
She was surprised to find Michelóg on such good terms with
the fishing community. A couple of years ago she had judged
a case, brought by the fishermen of the area, that Michelóg
deliberately and continually allowed a very savage bull of his
to wander on the sands in order to alarm the fishermen and
prevent them from using the bay at Fanore. Mara had quickly
found a precedent among her law books and had told Michelóg
that he had to keep his bull under control, either locked in a

shed or in a field with no road access and near his house. Now, however, he seemed to be on the best of terms with Fernandez and Brendan.

There was, she thought, a certain impetus from the crowd that surrounded her to say that this sad event had nothing to do with the people of the Burren. So what was wrong?

'I've got a horse and cart ready here, Brehon,' put in Michelóg. 'We can take the body to Kiltonaghan Church. Someone has slipped up there to get the priest. We want to do everything in the right way according to the rules,' he ended sanctimoniously.

'We've all decided that we will bury the poor fellow in our own churchyard; he has made his peace with God and man,' put in Fernandez, looking around him. Heads were nodding, but there was a feeling of tension in the air which did not accord with Fernandez's pious words. Children were very silent, the younger ones clutched by mothers, the older ones wide-eyed and apprehensive. The whole of this maritime community acted as though they were under threat, and the threat, she realized, came in their eyes from her presence. If Domhnall had not gone to fetch her, would the man already be under the earth, in the same way as the stinking remains of a giant whale that came ashore after a storm last winter had been hastily buried until the earth had stripped the flesh from the valuable bones?

'Father O'Connor is waiting for him,' said Setanta and it was his voice, anxious and somehow slightly guilty, that aroused her suspicions even more. She had known Setanta for over twelve years and had entrusted him with the care of her beloved son, and would have been certain that he trusted her and was devoted to her interests, but he avoided her eye when she looked straight at him. All her instincts told her that something was wrong here, that this was not what it appeared to be – that it was not a body that had drifted up from the Kingdom of Kerry.

And then she looked up at the dunes. Something had just occurred to her. She remembered the old boat that had lain there where a rabbit had jumped out – was it there? Somehow, she thought, as she rode down, and looked across at the tents in the hollows, the boat was no longer there, though it had taken her eye three days ago.

And yes, it had been about the size and shape of the one which now held the dead body. She glanced at her eldest scholar and saw that he too seemed to be gazing at the body in a slightly surprised way. When he sensed her eyes upon him, he made up his mind and turned to her with an air of decision.

'Could I have a word with you, Brehon?' he asked quietly and immediately she moved away from the crowd and only halted when she knew that they were out of earshot of all.

'I think that I know this man,' he said, before she could ask him anything. 'I could be wrong, but I don't think so. It has been puzzling me ever since I saw the body, but looking at him there again, I suddenly remembered. I think that he is a gold-smith and dealer in gold from the city of Galway. I haven't seen him for a few years, but I'm fairly certain that is who he is.'

Mara nodded. This was enough for her. Domhnall's parents, her daughter and son-in-law, lived in Galway and he spent his holidays there. He was a careful boy, would be most unlikely to speak unless he was reasonably sure of the facts. This combined with her instinct that something was wrong was enough for her for the moment. Step by step she would check the facts, and if necessary unravel the mystery. She returned to her place beside the boat and allowed all eyes to fix upon her before she spoke.

'Domhnall,' she said quietly, 'would you ride to Rathborney and ask Nuala, the physician, to come here. Tell her that I want her opinion on the cause of death. Go now, the sooner she is back, the sooner we can discover the truth.'

The cause of death, in the opinion of all that surrounded her, was probably obvious. The man had committed the crime of *fingal*, had been judged, had been sentenced – somewhere along the south-western coast, probably, certainly well away from the Kingdom of the Burren – had been placed in a boat with no oars, had been set adrift upon the Atlantic Ocean, had been delivered over to the judgement of God Almighty, had died by exposure to the wind and the waves, by lack of pure water.

And yet some strong instinct made her wonder whether this

was the true story, and Domhnall's words had now confirmed this. If the man was from Galway City, then English law prevailed there. A man who committed a murder would not be left in the hands of God, but would be hung from the gallows that stood just outside the city walls.

And if this weather-worn boat came from the Fanore sand dunes, then the murderer might well be standing there in front of her.

'Art,' she said looking at her son's foster-brother, 'would you go and tell the priest that the Brehon is investigating the death of the unknown man and there may be no burial today.' Art was a polite, pious boy and would be tactful and careful of the priest's feelings.

He was, of course, also, the son of Setanta the fisherman and of his wife Cliona, the sheep farmer, both of whom were present among the uneasy, rather guilty-looking crowd who faced her at the moment. This errand would probably remove the boy from the sands until the preliminary details had been taken and there were still plenty of scholars to serve her purposes until Nuala the physician arrived and either confirmed her suspicions, or, which Mara hoped, dismissed them. Mara had great reliance on Nuala and felt that she would probably be able to tell without any lengthy examination whether the man had died out there on the Atlantic Ocean or whether there was some other reason for his death.

Three

There is a common right to all seaweed cast upon the beach. It may be taken and used to fertilize the land.

All edible plants, such as the seaweed duilsc *which grows upon the rocks of the foreshore, may be taken freely by those who wish to gather them.*

Mara, with one last look at the body in the boat, deputed Slevin to stay on guard and to keep the seabirds from molesting it, and then walked out of the small inlet and back across to the main area of the beach. The crowd of fishermen and their families followed her in unusual silence.

The sands at Fanore were scored diagonally with a long level line of black limestone, rather as though some long-gone race of people had built a road to run from where the River Caher entered the beach, between the sand dunes, right down to the low-tide mark on the other side. Here and there on this smooth flat surface a rock had been left and had been sculpted by the sea into a square shape, as if a giant had deposited a shining black stone box there in the centre of the roadway. Mara took up her position on one of these, seating herself on the smooth surface, warm from the sun, and sending Finbar to get her satchel from the pony's side. She always kept it ready packed with slips of vellum, a travelling inkhorn and a case of well-trimmed pens. For the moment, though, she thought, her words would go unrecorded. She looked up at the still silent people.

'Does anyone know who this man is?' she asked and as she expected, heads were shaken.

'Or how he was washed up on the sands?' she continued and again there was this silent shaking of heads. Men looked at each other uneasily, though, and the women's eyes were shielded or fixed on their children.

'I don't wish to hold up your work,' she said to them all. 'I shall just sit here and perhaps anyone who suddenly remembers the man, or knows anything about the boat, could come and tell me if anything occurs to their mind. But in the meantime, I know that you need to tend to your fish and my scholars here can tell me what happened this morning. Síle,' she said to the eight-year-old, 'perhaps you will stay, too, since you were the one that first saw the boat.'

It was very interesting, she thought, to see how glances were exchanged at that and how the women grabbed the hands of young children as though to prevent any chatter and how the older boys and girls sidled away with quick looks at their parents' faces. There was definitely something quite wrong here. No one is at ease with a dead body, but fishermen and their wives had often seen the dead, killed by Atlantic storms. Etain was the last to go. She watched her young sister for a moment with a troubled look on her face but eventually went away with many backward glances.

'Come and sit down,' Mara invited her younger scholars. The MacMahon twins, Cian and his sister Cael, sat side by side at her feet and Cormac perched on a smaller box-like rock at a slight distance. After a slight hesitation, Síle went and squeezed herself onto the rock beside Cormac. He half got up, caught his mother's eye and sat down again. Cael sniggered and Síle gave a proud smile. Mara decided to get rid of the child as quickly as possible. It wasn't fair to embarrass Cormac to that degree in front of his friends.

'Just tell me again, Síle, how you found the boat,' she said. Looking across the sands she realized that the boat, on its narrow spit of sand, even from this position in the middle of the beach, was completely hidden by surrounding rocks. She stood up, but still could not see it, so sat down again.

'I didn't know it was there,' said Síle, seeming to be slightly alarmed. She repeated the words and her voice rose to a shrill pitch. Mara noticed that Síle's brother and sister, Etain and Brendan, had not gone back to their hunt for samphire, nor had they joined the groups tending to the fires and gutting fish but stood together halfway up the sands.

'You didn't see it until you had climbed over the big rock; that's right, isn't it, Síle?' Cormac's voice was unusually indulgent and had a soothing note in it. Mara gave him a grateful nod.

'That's right,' repeated Síle. She smiled adoringly at Cormac and snuggled a little nearer to him. Etain and Brendan turned back from the sea and went slowly up towards the fires.

Mara briefly considered cross-questioning Síle about the boat, but then abandoned the idea as unworthy. The girl was obviously very young for her age and not too bright. She should really have kept Etain if she had wanted to do any interrogation. The parents, she remembered, were dead so Etain was probably mother as well as sister to Síle. She thanked the child effusively and sent her up to join the sister and brother, noticing with amusement the sigh of relief from Cormac when he got his rock back to himself.

'Did any of you see her go across the rocks to discover the body?' she asked in a low tone.

'I did,' said Cormac instantly. 'And she was alone; no one went with her; they were all up at the top of the beach by the fires with the fish, Brehon,' he added and his quick-witted understanding of what Mara would need to know made her sorry that he would not study a little harder and show more interest in the law. 'She climbed over the rocks and then she screamed at the top of her voice – we didn't take any notice of her, but then she kept on screaming until everyone came running.'

'She's just so stupid,' said Cian with scorn. He turned to Mara with a businesslike air. 'Where do you think the body came from, Brehon?'

'And could you tell us about the procedure Brehons follow when a body floats in from another kingdom?' enquired Cael with a thoughtful air. The girl was a natural scholar, always thirsting for new knowledge and with a memory that retained facts and figures in the same way as those sponges that floated in on the Atlantic tides retained water.

'Do you know, Cian and Cael, I'm not certain of the answer

to either of those questions,' confessed Mara. 'Of course, I will be able to send a message to the Brehons of north and south Corcomroe if it does turn out to be a case of *"fingal"*; though further south as far as Kerry might be a bit more difficult with the countryside down there in a state of unrest, but we'll see what the physician says first.'

She wished that Nuala's husband, her law-school assistant, Fachtnan, was here, but it was the end of term and he had gone on a journey to the north of Ireland to see his father and mother. It might be, she told herself, that there was no case here for her to deal with, that it would be just a matter of burying the body, but somehow she didn't think so. Reason and instinct told her that this was unlikely to be a case of *fingal*. She was quite certain that no such case had been judged recently in Corcomroe. Only two days ago she had met Brehon Fergus MacClancy, her near neighbour from north Corcomroe, who lived near the giant cliffs of Moher, visible from where they stood, and he had said nothing about such an unusual case – and moreover, she suddenly recollected, Fergus had talked of a visit from his lawyer cousin, another MacClancy, from the south of the kingdom and surely a matter like this would have been discussed.

'If the dead man is the result of a sentence of *fingal*, and I'm not sure of that,' she said in answer to Cael, 'then I suppose our only duty is to see that he gets a decent burial. It seems to me that if it is, then the body must have been swept up from beyond the River Shannon, from the Kingdom of Kerry. Brehon MacClancy, the cousin of the Brehon that you knew, Cael and Cian, the one that died at Bunratty, well, he said nothing to me about judging such a case and his cousin, Brehon MacClancy from the south of the kingdom, has recently visited him, therefore this body must have come from further down the coastline.' The MacClancy dynasty of legal families stretched over the entire south-west of Ireland.

'So, it must be Kerry. Cian and me have been to Kerry, went across on a boat when we were living with that old man, Brehon MacClancy, the old goat,' she added with her usual downrightness.

'*De mortuis nihil nisi bonum,*' said Cormac with a lofty air and then spoiled it by saying, 'Mind you, he deserved to be killed.'

Mara allowed them to chat on about the events surrounding the death of the former Brehon MacClancy for a few minutes, though she was surprised that their attention was so easily diverted from the present to the past. It was not like any one of the three. They were still discussing the death of the elderly Brehon as she walked up to meet Finbar and take from him her satchel and to give him an errand to take his mind off his troubles. He looked, she thought in a concerned fashion, very white-faced and worried.

'Finbar,' she said, 'could you move all over the beach, top, bottom, sand dunes, and let me know any places from which the boat with the body can be seen. Be very thorough about it, won't you.'

That she thought would keep him busy until Nuala arrived and also keep him away from the rather awkward and excessive pity that the other scholars still showed towards him ever since the end-of-year results had been announced. She would have to make up her mind what could be done with him if he was sure that his own father, the Brehon of Cloyne, would not welcome him home. He wrote a neat hand and perhaps it might be possible to get him a job as a clerk to a man of affairs – even perhaps someone in Galway, she thought, and resolved to have a word with a lawyer friend of hers in that city.

'How many fishing families are there at this camp?' she asked when she returned to the other three. They seemed to have exhausted the subject of Brehon MacClancy and were sitting silently gazing out to sea. She took from her satchel a sheet of vellum, her horn and a well-mended pen. The flat rock made a good surface and she handed the pen to Cian and Cormac began to recite the names – he had known them all since babyhood:

'Fernandez MacFelim; Brendan and Etain, the samphire-gatherers; Setanta and Cliona . . .'

One by one the names were mentioned and checked by frequent glances to the top of the beach and when they had finished Cian had written a neat column of ten families, including Brendan and Etain. To her relief her scholars did not then do what she had expected them to do, which was to speculate on this death, but began questioning her about the lands ruled over by McCarthy Mór, who still styled himself King of Desmond – although the majority of the lands in his one-time kingdom were now owned by the Earl of Desmond. They all, she thought, fancied a jaunt down into the southern part of the country and were rather more stimulated than made anxious by the news that most of the Kingdom of Kerry was in enemy hands.

'Brehon MacEgan,' she said now in answer to their questions about the household of McCarthy Mór. 'He is a relative of the MacEgan who runs the law school of Duniry in east Galway.'

'We could go down there, all of us, if you're too busy,' offered Cormac. 'I could borrow a few of the King's new guns. We know how to fire them.'

'It's too far,' said Mara. She had been thinking hard while replying mechanically to the questions. 'If Nuala thinks that the man died of exposure, of thirst, or of any cause of death that would result from spending days or even weeks on the face of the ocean, then we will just have to bury him in the churchyard here.'

'There's no mark on him,' said Cormac.

'His tongue is sticking out; he was probably trying to catch raindrops,' said Cian.

'His eyes look like he died in agonies of thirst,' said Cael and that was an unusually imaginative thought from a girl who was usually very keen on facts and logic. Obviously this death had impressed the young people.

'The first duty of a lawyer is to gather evidence,' said Mara, rising to her feet. 'Let's go across to Slevin and see whether there are any particulars that we can observe from the body before Nuala arrives and can tell us how he died.' As she went along she could see how the discovery of the body would not have been made except for the accident of the child climbing over the rocks looking for shells. If this had been on land, by now the birds would have discovered it, but here on the beach today fish were being gutted at great speed and buckets of innards thrown into the sea, giving enough tasty morsels for the grey and white kittiwakes and larger fulmars which were continuously swooping down and picking them up. The dead body had not been spotted by any of them.

Slevin was glad to see them – he had amassed a small pile of smooth black limestone pebbles just in case he was visited by some large seabird, but now he was just sitting on a rock and staring out to sea. He jumped to his feet when they arrived and greeted them warmly.

'I was wondering about his clothes, Brehon,' he said speaking in a discreetly lowered tone of voice when they were near enough to hear him. 'Have a look at him.'

Mara bent over the body and nodded slowly. 'I see what you mean. What do you think, the rest of you?' And then, when they made no answer but just looked blankly at the body, she said slightly impatiently, 'Come on, think, all of you, look at him; what's he wearing? No cloak, you'll observe . . .'

And then when they still did not answer she said in exasperated tones: 'Tell them, Slevin.'

'It's linen, but it's not a *léine*,' said Slevin triumphantly and she nodded to him approvingly. 'I must say, Slevin, that I didn't notice that when I looked at him first. I suppose it was all that dried seaweed heaped on top of him.'

Slevin had not disturbed the dark brown strands of crinkled seaweed, but with the sun shining down on the body Mara could now see quite clearly that the front of the garment was fastened together with small knotted woollen buttons inserted into slits of buttonholes.

'He's dressed in a linen shirt, not a Gaelic *léine*,' said Slevin eventually to the younger scholars. 'Can't you see the buttons? We don't have buttons – we just pull it over our heads. And the linen seems different, doesn't it? May I touch, Brehon?'

He had already done so, she guessed, but she nodded permission. It was part of her method of teaching that the older should instruct the younger. Slevin, she thought, had not wasted his time. While he had been gathering stones he must have been thinking hard. She listened to him telling the others how superfine the linen was, and pointing out that most men in the Burren and other Gaelic kingdoms, unlike this corpse, did not usually wear hose during the summer months.

'They must have taken his sandals off?' said Cian eventually.

'Perhaps he wore boots,' said Slevin and this fitted so well that she half-wondered whether Domhnall had said anything to him. She didn't think so, however. Domhnall was a boy of the utmost truthfulness and discretion and he had spoken as though the memory had just come to him.

So, yes, of course, thought Mara, the man had come from Galway City, he had worn English dress: a shirt, a doublet, breeches and nether hose, summer as well as winter, and doubtless a pair of leather boots. But someone had deliberately removed those very defining articles of clothes and just left the man in his shirt and under hose as though he was a fisherman or farmer, dressed only in the *léine*, or what could have looked like a *léine*, as though, she told herself, he could be a victim of the Brehon law punishment of *fingal*.

'Here comes Art,' said Cormac joyfully. He was very friendly with Cian and Cael, but his foster-brother Art and he were like twins, seldom happy out of each other's company. 'May I tell him, Brehon?'

'Yes, but quietly.' Mara had no thought of sharing her findings with the whole beach and she explained that to them all when Art and Cormac came back. Art looked pale, sallow beneath the summer tan, she thought, and resolved to keep an eye on him. He was a very sensitive boy, a good scholar, a hard worker, but one who always needed plenty of encouragement and praise. Things that other scholars shrugged off could upset him for days.

'What do you think about the boat, Art?' she asked. It was a question that she might put later on to the fishermen, but this fisherman's son must surely have an opinion on it. He felt it carefully, and to her surprise was quite assertive in his belief that it could have stood up to an Atlantic storm.

'Something light like this would ride the waves, Brehon,' he said earnestly. 'It's the heavier boat that would be more likely to overturn and sink.'

Mara nodded, but she was sceptical that this boat, as thin as a cockleshell, could have been swept all the way up from the coast of Kerry without sinking.

And if the man was from Galway then the south-westerly

wind would have brought him up north to the coast of Spiddal or somewhere like that, certainly in the opposite direction to the Burren. And this was not the kind of boat that they used in Galway City. Theirs were bigger and more substantial.

In fact, this boat, she was beginning to be sure, was the one that she had seen the rabbit jump from a few days earlier, the one that had been abandoned on the sand dunes of Fanore.

And not only the fishermen, but her scholars, also, were aware of that fact and the uneasiness stemmed from that.

Now she had to wait until Nuala arrived to see what she thought about this man's cause of death. She walked forward to meet Finbar and to listen gravely to his report that the boat could not be seen from anywhere on the beach until the rocks which surrounded it were scaled. She worried again about how pale and hollow-eyed he looked. She had hoped that the holiday and the excitement about the midsummer's eve feast, the sleeping in tents and the fishing expeditions would have taken his mind off his father's edict.

'Let's walk back to where your shelters are pitched,' she suggested to the others and encouraged them to talk about sleeping out of doors for the last couple of nights and about how warm and comfortable they were. Cael related, rather drolly, an exaggerated account of Síle's fears during the night while Cormac and Cian vied with each other about how many hours they had stayed awake. They were all very anxious to show her the tents and to display how well the tar-soaked canvas kept out rain, but she did not allow too much time to be wasted on that.

'There's something missing here,' she said looking all around innocently, though she had immediately noticed the absence of the boat.

The others looked around, also, with blank faces. Cael had a slight frown between her brows, but she said nothing.

'Don't you remember that old boat that was wedged in over there?' She pointed to the spot between two pointed grass-covered sand dunes. She waited for them to look at each other, but they didn't – they looked straight at her with innocent and uncomprehending faces. Mara almost wished that Brigid was here with her. She could just hear her housekeeper, who had been her father's housekeeper before and had almost forty years of coping with scholars. '*He had that puss on him like butter wouldn't melt in his mouth*,' she would say.

'It's strange that you don't remember the boat,' she remarked. 'Finbar, would you go back and wait by the body and send Slevin up to me. In the meantime,' she said to the four remaining scholars, 'let's just cross over and have a look around.'

The sand was held firm by the coarse green blades of marram grass and it was easy to walk on. She went down the hill to the small hollow where the three tents for the boys were grouped around one large fireplace. They were anxious to show her their sleeping places, but she put them aside. She was beginning to feel a little annoyed at their efforts to divert her from thoughts of the boat that held the corpse. Cormac, she guessed, was at the back of this. His loyalty to his foster-father and to the fishing community was great, she knew, but his first loyalty, if he was ever to make a lawyer, should be to establishing the truth about a crime as serious as murder – and she was beginning to think that this body in the boat was going to be a case of murder.

There were no marks in the sand to show whether a boat had been dragged out towards the pathway, or even to show its resting place when she had noticed a rabbit leap from it, but now at midday there was a breeze coming in from the ocean and the fine, very dry sand of the dunes was continually in motion, little flurries stirring and rippling. It had been blowing hard the night before; she remembered noticing from her window, just before she had blown out her candle, how the ash tree across the road from her house was bending and swaying.

'Slevin, come over here, will you?' she said over her shoulder as she saw his tall form appear on the roadway beside the dunes.

'Someone's taken away the old boat, then,' he said instantly the moment he joined her, and then before she could say a word he blew a whistle through his pursed lips.

'Of course,' he said immediately. 'That's the boat that has the corpse in it – I bet that's what it is.' Slevin's voice was breaking and it rose quite high as he spoke. Mara, looking back at the younger boys, saw that they had heard, but at that instant Cormac shouted, 'Rabbit!' and the attention of all was distracted as the grass was parted by the long-legged and agile leaps. They chased exuberantly after it only giving up when it dived into a burrow.

'Saw it a minute too late; otherwise we'd have had rabbit stew tonight instead of more fish,' said Cormac, twisting his hands to show how he would wring the animal's neck. He and Cael began to argue with each other as to which had killed the most rabbits during their short lifespan and eventually Mara tired of them and suggested they return to their work on the beach.

'After all,' she said, 'Fernandez is probably relying on you and it's not fair to deprive him of seven pairs of hands. Tell him that I'll just keep Slevin until Domhnall comes back with the physician.'

They went readily and she sensed that they were glad to have something to do. At the moment, until and unless it was confirmed by Nuala that a crime had taken place, there was little to do and certainly not enough for them all. Now it was more a matter of quiet speculation and the summing up of possibilities.

When they had gone she turned back to Slevin. 'If the boat that was here last night . . .' she began and then he interrupted her. 'No it wasn't,' he said immediately. 'The boat wasn't here last night. I remember now. It was here when we saw the place first, before we went to stay in the castle before the wind blew itself out, but I don't think I saw it when we were actually camping. You could ask Domhnall when he comes back with Nuala, but that is my memory.'

'I see,' said Mara. But surely, she thought, that body could not possibly have lain in the boat on the beach for three days and three nights. Even after the fishing boats had set out to trawl for mackerel and herring, the women and younger children had stayed behind to build up the fires. The beach would have been scoured for every trace of driftwood and dried seaweed. There was no possibility that they could have missed something so startling and so obvious. According to Cormac, little Síle began to scream as soon as she was on the rocks above the small strip of sand.

Nevertheless, Slevin had a good, clear mind and a very accurate memory so she had no doubt that he was right. She looked back at the rounded shape of the castle with its magnificent view of the ocean, the far islands of Aran and the dark orange sweep of the sandy bay of Fanore. 'Where did you all sleep?' she asked idly.

'Domhnall and I slept in the main guard hall, Cael with Síle in one of the wall chambers and the others,' his grin broadened, 'the rest of the boys, Cormac, Art, Cian and Finbar, they decided to spend the night in the dungeons and Fernandez allowed them, but made them promise that when they got tired of it they would come up and join us.'

'And they were all right?' Mara was glad that she had not known, but she supposed that there was no harm in it.

'Well, I must say that I slept like a top that night – and Domhnall, too. We had really comfortable mattresses stuffed with heather and it was nice and warm by the fire. Anyway, when we woke in the morning, there were the other four, lying down on their mattresses with their eyes tightly shut. Strange being in a castle with no men-of-arms there – in fact, most of the time there's nobody there but Fernandez and Etain, themselves – no servants, nothing. They have the whole big place to themselves – never even lock the front door, either.'

This could change if the young man was elected by the clan to be their *tánaiste*, thought Mara. In the meantime, the young couple probably enjoyed the peace and seclusion – she rather envied them as she and her husband, King Turlough, always seemed to be surrounded by large numbers of people, whether they were at the law school, Ballinalacken Castle in the Burren, or in Turlough's main castle, Bunratty Castle, by the River Shannon. Still, it would have been unlikely that either Domhnall or Slevin would have noticed any movements in the sand dunes – after a day in the wind and sun, hauling boats around and building fireplaces, they would have slept soundly all night. The other four might have seen something when they left the dungeons in order to lie in front of the fire, but they would have had the trouble of hauling their mattresses up the narrow spiral staircase and probably would not have bothered to glance out of the windows at the beach below.

'Let's go up to the spot where we both remember the boat was lying,' she suggested and led the way up to the gap between the sand-dune hills.

'It would have been here,' said Slevin with a quick glance around him before pointing to one spot. 'Look, Brehon, you can see there's very little grass growing in this spot, just between the sand peaks.'

'I wonder how it was taken away. It was very worn and thin in the timbers, but it still would have needed two men to carry it, I would have thought,' said Mara.

Slevin bent down low and then straightened himself. 'I'd say it was dragged, look at those broken bits of grass, Brehon, but not dragged onto the path. I'd say that it was dragged in the opposite direction, down towards the Caher River. Look at this, and this.' Slevin pointed towards the dunes leading to the north of the beach and went excitedly ahead of her, following the trail.

Mara obediently bent down and examined the narrow, brittle shafts of blue-green grass. It was a marvellous grass for knitting the sand into a bank – its roots spread and entangled each plant with the others around it, but its very brittleness made it vulnerable and the narrow keel of the small boat had sliced the stems and leaves, leaving the broken edges to mark the path between the top of the sand dune and the channel of the Caher River which wound its way through the mountains and discharged its fresh water into the ocean. The puzzle of how the body got to the sea was now solved.

Four

Uraicecht Becc
(Small Primer)

The physician has an honour price of seven séts and this does not increase for any reason so a master of the profession has the same honour price as an ordinary physician.

Before a physician is allowed to practise in a kingdom, he (she) has to have public recognition. This is bestowed by an examination of the candidate's training and proficiency by two recognized physicians.

A fine is exacted if the physician does not cure a curable illness, either through lack of knowledge or because of malice.

Nuala was with them half an hour later. She had brought her apprentice Liam and a man who worked on her farm with her and all three had panniers suspended on either side of their horses. Domhnall conducted the horses across the firm sand and courteously helped her to dismount before organizing the others into various tasks which allowed Mara to speak to Nuala in private. She was glad to see the physician, glad to have her professional advice in this case, which had started off as a sad occurrence, and now, in her mind, had changed into a puzzling case of murder.

'I thought that I could probably do an autopsy here on the beach rather than bring him all those miles through the mountain back to Rathborney,' Nuala said in an undertone to Mara as she surveyed the dead man in the boat. 'I can put up a screen, we've brought a tarpaulin and there will be plenty of sea water to wash away the marks afterwards. We've brought a bucket, but I thought we could probably get some more from the fishermen, if necessary, and I've got my tools here. The boat will do as well as a table, or we can use one of the flat rocks. In any case,' Nuala took a quick look at the damp, firm sand beneath her feet and nodded, 'yes, it's certainly tidal up to here. By the next low tide all marks will have been washed away. An ideal place for an autopsy; I must tell some of my colleagues about this.' She gazed thoughtfully at the body, bending over and examining the tongue and then straightening up.

'What is it that you want to know, Mara?' she asked.

'The cause of death, certainly; and I suppose,' continued Mara, 'I am wondering whether this is a death from exposure – a man who was judged in some place south-west of here and who was set upon the tide as a murderer of close kin and was abandoned to the wind and the ocean waves, or whether,' and here she could hear her own voice hardening, becoming direct and focused, 'or whether,' she continued, 'this man was killed somewhere near here, and that the appearance of a death by the sentence of *fingal* has been faked and the corpse should be investigated as a secret and unlawful murder.'

'Last meal – time of death, you'll need to know all that sort of thing.' Nuala, as always, was brisk and professional. Even when she was twelve years old she was so accomplished in medical matters that it was whispered in the Burren that the child was a better physician than her father, Malachy, and was, in fact, a reincarnation of her grandfather. Many people sought the advice of the daughter rather than the father and this made tensions and divisions grow between them. Now, twelve years later, after long years of study under the supervision of the physician at Thomond and travel to Italy to learn the latest methods and knowledge of the human body, she was the envy of many kingdoms. Mara was her godmother and trusted absolutely the young woman's skill and knowledge.

'I think that once I know how he died I may want further information, but at the moment, I think I just want to know the cause and the time of death,' she said now and Nuala gave a brief nod.

'I'll send Liam for you, then, as soon as I have anything to tell you,' she said and began to take some fearsome-looking implements, saws, knives and pincers, from her leather pannier. Domhnall and Slevin, at her command, had led the three horses back up the sands towards the fresh water of the River Caher and after tethering them to a couple of stakes were standing there. Mara retreated from the curtained-off space, walking first up towards the smoking fish and then changing her mind and turning aside to walk towards the northern end of the beach, to the place where her two eldest scholars stood, still by the horses, but obviously, even from a distance, deep in earnest conversation with each other.

The River Caher ran on stony ground, down from the mountain, through the sand dunes and then across the open beach. Not deep, thought Mara, looking down at it and wishing that the beach was empty and that she could shed shoes and stockings and paddle through the rippling water. She bent down and put her hand and arm in until her fingers touched the bottom – not much more than a foot deep in places, she thought, but, of course, it was now dead tide. She took out her hand and licked the tops of her fingers – still quite fresh, she thought, but no doubt at high tide the river would be flooded with salt water and a boat could easily be slid down this waterway and into the sea.

She looked affectionately at Domhnall and Slevin still deep in talk. They were a nice pair, she thought, Slevin, tall and leggy, Domhnall, though a year older, not quite as tall as his friend, a dark-haired, dark-eyed, olive-skinned serious boy, contrasting with Slevin's fair hair and skin and lively, fun-loving temperament. They had entered her law school at the same time, at the beginning of the Michaelmas term when one was eight and the other seven years old, and they had immediately been best of friends – Domhnall, quiet, studious, her grandson by her first marriage, son of her daughter Sorcha and of Oisín a merchant from Galway, and his best friend, Slevin from Mayo, more extrovert, a very good musician and a talented dancer. She walked down to meet them and could see that they were glad to see her. They cherished their privileges of being the leaders of the law school and now they probably guessed that she wanted to talk about this puzzling affair before the presence of the younger scholars brought irrelevancies and silly jokes into the proceedings.

'Advise me,' she said to them seriously. 'I'm wondering what

to do when Nuala has finished with the body. Domhnall, how
sure are you that this is a gold merchant from Galway?'

She was interested to see from Slevin's startled glance that
Domhnall had said nothing about this to his friend. Very
discreet, she thought with a flicker of amusement, but better
to be too discreet than someone who tells before being given
permission to do so.

'Yes,' she said to Slevin now, 'Domhnall thinks that he might
have recognized him, that he could be a gold merchant from
Galway, and, of course, that would fit in with your conclusions
that the man wore English dress – Slevin thought,' now she
addressed Domhnall, 'that the man was wearing an English
shirt, linen, but made in the English style with buttons down
the front, and hose, and could well have had the doublet, cloak,
boots and nether hose stripped from him as part of attempt to
make a case of murder appear like a judicial sentence of *fingal*.'

'*Iontach!*' exclaimed Domhnall. 'It's all beginning to come
together, isn't it, Brehon. I had another look at the man's face
while you and Nuala were talking and I'm sure that he is a
goldsmith from Galway. I was used to seeing him all dressed
up – he was a fancy dresser, and seeing him there, all bedrag-
gled – just dressed in a *léine* or a shirt and covered with seaweed,
he looked so different, but the more I looked at him, the more
I thought that he was, indeed, the goldsmith from Galway City.'

'Do you know his name?'

'Niall Martin,' said Domhnall without hesitation. 'Niall
Martin. I'm sure that was his name. Mind you, my father
would know more about him than I would.'

'And was he married?'

'Not that I remember.' Domhnall sounded a little unsure,
thought for a moment and then resolutely nodded his head.
'No, he wasn't,' he said. 'I remember my father talking to him,
well, Brehon, you know my father – he was giving him advice,
telling him that he could expand his business, get a bigger
shop, take on some workmen, or an apprentice, make his business more profitable. My father had all sorts of good ideas to
give to him, and Niall Martin listened to them all, but in the
end he just shook his head. And he said that he had neither
wife nor child and no near relations and that he preferred to

his voice. 'After all, Brendan, the samphire-gatherer, goes to
Galway every day and comes back every evening.'

Mara met his eyes. 'That's an interesting point,' she said
slowly. 'It does, does it not, provide a link between Galway
and this place.'

'Though there appears to be no link between samphire and
gold,' said Slevin.

'I wonder,' said Mara pensively. She looked at the long line
of rocks at the far side of the river. The sun had moved a little
into the south-west and she could see the prominent vein of
silver-white quartz which seemed to bisect one large flat boulder
of black limestone. There had been a lot of excitement, she
remembered hearing from Ardal O'Lochlainn when gold had
been found on the west coast of Galway in a seam of this soft
quartz. Men had laboured night and day but there had been
only a small amount of gold found, and the interest had soon
faded. She told the two boys about it and Domhnall nodded
his head wisely.

'Of course, if ever there was a man who knew the rocks of
Fanore well, then it must be Brendan. He's been scouring the
rocks here for samphire ever since he was the height of a rabbit
– or so he keeps telling me,' he added and Mara smiled her
appreciation of the dry humour and shrewdness of her grandson.

'You're right, of course. That makes a double link.' She
thought about the matter. This case, if Nuala confirmed what
she suspected, could turn out to be unexpectedly complicated.
She looked out to sea, turning over the various possibilities in
her mind.

'Dinner!' shouted Cormac. 'Dinner, everyone!' He stuck his
two fingers into his mouth and shrilled out a whistle in the
direction of his mother and she smiled, raised a hand in
acknowledgement and, with her two oldest scholars, made her
way to the top of the beach where the cooking fires burned.

There was plenty of deliciously fresh fish for lunch and
Brendan had generously added some of his morning's gathering
of samphire, though he had not stayed for the meal but had
set off for Galway.

'The tide is coming in and there's a nice fresh, south-westerly
breeze so he will be in time for the evening meals in the inns

manage everything himself. I'd say myself that he was cont
with what he had – that he didn't want anyone else to ha
a nose in his affairs. He had a little shop at the bottom of R⟨
Earl's Lane; you know the place, Brehon, don't you, and, we
it didn't look anything great, but he did his business there.'

'I see,' said Mara. She was thinking hard. Domhnall was only
sixteen years old, but he was astute and reliable, and above all,
because of his father's connections with the merchants of Galway,
he knew all there, spoke perfect English as well as fluent Gaelic,
and would be able to make his enquiries acceptable to all. And
Slevin, as usual, would make an excellent second-in-command
to his admired friend. Should she go herself to Galway to make
enquiries, or send these two as her deputies? The key to the
mystery of this death, she felt quite strongly, would lie in
the Burren rather than in the English city of Galway.

But in the meantime . . .

'But in the meantime,' she said aloud, 'I have to decide what
to do about the body. If it turns out, as I suspect, that this is
not a case of *fingal* but is a murder of a man from the city of
Galway, then should he be sent back to Galway, or buried
here?'

'It depends on how long he has been dead,' said Slevin in
a practical fashion of the son of a farmer who would have had
many dead bodies to dispose of in his time. 'If he has been
dead for only a day, then it wouldn't be too bad to take the
body to Galway City, but if he has already been dead for longer,
and myself I would guess that he has been – well, given the
heat of the sun, and the length of the journey and then finding
a priest and a graveyard . . .'

'Better to bury him here,' put in Domhnall. 'There are plenty
of men to dig the grave and if any relatives turn up, they can
always come and pray there. After all, if he died at sea, he
would be buried at sea.'

'You're right,' said Mara, cheered by the matter-of-fact philos-
ophy. 'We'll bury him here at Fanore, that's settled. So what
do you think that this man, Niall Martin, if it were he, was
doing here on Fanore Beach? It is, after all, a long way from
Galway City.'

'Not that long,' said Domhnall with a cool deliberation in

and pie shops in Galway,' Etain explained to Mara. 'They like to have the samphire as fresh as possible and, of course, it only takes minutes to cook – you put it straight into boiling seawater if possible, if not ordinary salt water, boil and then taste.'

Mara ate it with relish. If it were not for the dead body only a hundred yards away, she would be enjoying this out-of-doors meal, the fresh mackerel, the chunks of buttered soda bread and the delicious salty taste of the samphire.

'You and Brendan have a good trade with the City of Galway, haven't you?' she asked.

'Brendan has been very clever,' said Etain enthusiastically. 'My parents used to gather samphire, but they just bartered it for fish from the fishermen and the people around here were not that interested – they could easily gather their own seaweed. Brendan was the one that thought of getting a boat and taking some to Galway City where all of those rich merchants live – people who like to have their food tasty, who like to try different flavours, different dishes.'

And, yes, it had been clever, Mara thought. Surprisingly there was no provision for the worth of a merchant in the list of honour prices that Brehon laws provided, but yet, here in the sixteenth century, this buying and selling was a new livelihood, something which was as paying, as lucrative as the age-old trades of fisherman or farmer, of weaver or carpenter. An urban society such as Galway City was dependent on traders and merchants to supply its table. Traditionally the wines came from France and from Spain, the exotic fruits and spices from far-flung places, but the simple pleasures of oysters, fresh fish and samphire could come from the nearby Gaelic communities. Doubtless, this was a flaw in her beloved Brehon laws. There should be an honour price fixed for a merchant, something that echoed his or her status in the community, and there should be laws that regulated the trading of goods for profit and for a livelihood rather than a mere bartering of produce produced on the farm or lands. Brendan's venture into the world of trade had been profitable to him. She could see the boat that he used these days, moored to the short new makeshift pier made from a line of rocks, well padded with narrow tree trunks, that jutted out into the sea, no fishing boat, but a

Galway hooker or *bád mór*, a gaff-rigged boat about thirty feet in length, ideal for carrying goods swiftly and easily with its three brown sails. By sea, the journey to Galway City was less than half the length of the journey by land. And in a boat like that one, it would be accomplished quickly and easily and there would be no deterioration in the samphire, unlike if it was carried by cart along the dusty roads.

'Here comes Liam,' said Domhnall in her ear and she nodded her appreciation at his judgement at not calling the attention of the others to the appearance of the physician's apprentice. She raised a hand of acknowledgement, said quietly to Domhnall, 'I'll leave you in charge,' and then strolled down towards the hidden stretch of sand within the rocks.

The tide had turned, she thought, as she climbed the rocks. It would be urgent to move the body as soon as possible. Certainly there were enough strong arms to carry it to the churchyard and that would be best solution. Many of the men lived close to the shore and spades and pickaxes could be quickly produced to make a grave for the stranger. When she had got to the sand she saw that Nuala had covered the body with the sheet of tarpaulin and he could be buried in that, buried within the boat which was surely worthless, if, as she felt sure, it had been abandoned in the sand dunes.

'Take a seat,' said Nuala, nodding towards one of the flat-topped rocks and Mara seated herself, waiting until Nuala had finished her instructions to the man who was emptying seawater over the rocks. All was almost as it had been and the fresh breeze from the sea had blown the smell away.

'Perhaps I should move my hospital down here,' said Nuala as she came across and sat beside her. 'The air would be good for my patients and salt water is a great cleanser.' And then, almost in the same breath, 'The man you are interested in was middle-aged to elderly – over fifty, I'd say. He ate a substantial meal a few hours before he was killed.'

'Killed,' queried Mara.

Nuala nodded. 'And not by exposure, nor by thirst, nor by starvation; he was killed by a sharp blow to the head about eight hours after his last meal. In fact,' she said in a matter-of-fact tone, 'he certainly didn't die of starvation. He had enough food in his stomach when he was killed to last him for almost a week, I'd say. Wine also, or some form of alcohol.'

'I see,' said Mara. She wasn't surprised. All her instincts had told her that she was witnessing something that had been arranged like a picture, arranged to deceive. The boat with no oars, the seaside location, that body stretched out with eyes wide open to the sky, and that tongue, artistically arranged as though dying of thirst.

'Something interesting about the meal,' said Nuala. 'Among other fragments there was an almost whole apricot in the stomach. I've eaten one of those in Italy but never here on the Burren, or at Bunratty Castle.'

'I've eaten apricots, but it was in Galway City,' said Mara. The pieces of puzzle were beginning to knit themselves together, just as a carpenter puts together the carefully sawn timbers to make a jointed stool.

Nuala absorbed this without comment. 'And I would say that the man has been dead for about three days,' she said.

'Three days. That's a surprise!' Mara looked all around the tiny bay. The sand was soaking wet and every dip and declivity in the rocks around them was filled with seawater and most of them held tiny shrimps or other sea creatures. It was obvious that the tide would cover this spot and extend far up to the high-tide level where the smoke from the fires drifted back towards the sand-dune cliffs.

Nuala had followed her thoughts. 'Came in on the tide, Liam thinks. He's had a look at the boat. Says the bottom timbers are more soaked than they would be if it were just resting here. He knows about boats; he's the son of a fisherman.'

'That's what everyone here has been telling me – that the boat came in on the high tide in the early morning.' Mara stared meditatively at the boat. And yet, she thought, she was fairly certain that the boat had been there on the dunes when she had noticed the rabbit jump from it. And Slevin remembered it also.

So, he could have been killed three days ago, launched out to sea and then drifted in on the tide, thought Mara. The south-westerly wind had just got up this very morning, she remembered. Perhaps that had made a difference. Or perhaps it was just fate. Perhaps one boat looked like another to someone like herself, or even Slevin. She got up and walked all around but there was nothing to make it look different – no name, no marks, just a boat whose timbers were worn out, were fragile with the passage of time.

'There was something else strange about the body.' Nuala had been watching her, waiting until Mara's thoughts had unravelled themselves.

'Yes.' Mara turned to her with relief. Gathering evidence, she often reminded her scholars, should come before speculation.

'The man's tongue was pulled out after death – I don't mean that it was torn out, but a certain force was used before the body stiffened. It was pulled out and then the upper teeth were closed over it and probably held in position – this probably happened about an hour after death. You see, the body starts to stiffen from the head down, so the eyes and the mouth stiffen before the neck and shoulders. Someone did this when the jaw had begun to stiffen. It would not have taken long.'

She made no further comment, but Mara nodded. 'I can understand the reason for this,' she said. 'I think that it was all part of painting a picture, of giving an appearance of a man who was put out on the ocean in a boat with no oars. My own scholars are always fascinated by that – by the fact that a man would be launched out to sea and that his fate would be in the hands of God. In fact, it probably condemned him to die of thirst. The murderer wanted the corpse to present the appearance of a man who died of thirst.'

'Whereas, in reality, the man had died from a blow to the head,' said Nuala drily.

'Can I see?' asked Mara, nerving herself to stand up.

'There's nothing to see,' said Nuala without moving from her seat. 'You can look if you like, but no mark has been left. The damage is internal. The instrument that hit the skull must have been well padded. And, as well as that, he wore a wig so that also protected the skull.'

'I'd better have a look anyway,' said Mara. She didn't want to, but she felt a responsibility to this man who had drifted up onto the shores of the territory where she was Brehon.

She was embarrassed that she had not noticed that he wore a wig. She had focused on the face, the open mouth, the widely opened eyes. Now she needed to find out more about him. He was not a man from her jurisdiction and he had, if Domhnall was correct, no relations to be compensated for his death, but for the sake of law and order and of justice within the kingdom, the truth had to be established. Resolutely she walked towards where the dead man lay within the boat.

The body had been washed, the incisions neatly sewn up, the linen shirt laid over it, under the tarpaulin. Most of the seaweed that had draped it when she had first seen the corpse had now been picked off and left at the side of the boat. She bent down and looked at it: reddish-brown leaves of dillisk, white carrageen, sea cabbage, long brown broad strands of kelp and flat purple slices of laver – there were even a few strands of samphire.

'Nothing unfamiliar here,' she said. 'All of this could be found on Fanore beach. When I was a child I used to come here with Brigid. She used to pick carrageen to make cough syrup to give to my father's scholars. I used to bring back these long brown kelp streamers – Cumhal told me that they could be used to forecast the weather – if they were stiff, then we were in for a dry spell and when they went limp we could expect rain.'

She looked resolutely at the mouth of the corpse and saw what Nuala meant. Someone had deliberately closed the upper jaw so that it held the tongue between both sets of the yellow teeth.

'Wait here,' she said to Nuala. Her indignation at this treatment of a dead body, at this deliberate attempt to mimic a judicial procedure, was so great that she hardly noticed the difficulty of climbing back across the rocks and onto the orange sands of Fanore beach.

The meal was over as she came back up the sands. No one had resumed work, though. The fishermen, their wives and their children stood in a group and she noticed that Michelóg the farmer stood amongst them. Fernandez, Etain and Brendan were a little apart. They were deep in conversation but moved away from each other as Mara came up the sands.

'We were thinking, Brehon, that since the tide is on the turn, we should bury the body,' said Fernandez. There was a hint of diffidence, of unsureness in his voice and she ignored his suggestion.

'Call everyone to come down and inspect this boat,' she said abruptly. She waited until he beckoned and until there was a line of about thirty people in front of her. 'I want every man, woman and child to look at this boat, and at the man in it, of course. I want you to tell me whether you have ever seen either before.'

It would be, she thought, noticing the closed-in faces, a waste of time. Even the children had been warned to say nothing.

Nevertheless, it had to be done so she stood beside it patiently as all filed past, efficiently managed by Domhnall and Slevin. Her other five scholars, were, she thought, not showing them-selves to be much help. Their loyalty, for the moment, appeared to be with their fishermen friends, although she did see Cael shoot an enquiring look at her brother, as though asking a question, which was silently answered, Mara reckoned, as after a glance from Cian, his sister's face became as hooded and expressionless as the others. Still this could not be helped for the moment. Mara watched the faces as they filed past the body in the boat and sorted out the words that she would use when the procedure was over. To each one she asked her questions – asking for information about the boat and the man. Nothing but head-shakes answered. She waited until all the family groups stood uncertainly before her and then she signalled to Liam to cover the body again.

'I am not satisfied about this death,' she said, raising her voice to contend with the roar of the wind and the waves, and the high melancholy calls of the white and grey seabirds. 'The matter will have to be investigated, but in the meantime, the body will have to be moved; the tide threatens it. I would like it if someone,' here she looked directly at Fernandez, 'could bring a cart to the top of the path through the dunes, and then we'll take the body to the church. It can lie there in the church and within the boat as its coffin until I can establish the identity of the dead man.'

No one dared ask her how she was going to do that, so she waited until they had gone back up to their fires again, Fernandez stopping to assure her that a cart would be with them in ten minutes and then when they were out of earshot she turned to Domhnall. 'Do you think that we could possibly ask your father to come here to Fanore,' she asked. 'I have to be sure of the identity of this man before I investigate what did, in fact, happen to him.'

'I'm sure that he will, Brehon,' said Domhnall readily. 'Shall I ride over to Galway and ask him to come back.'

'If you wouldn't mind, Domhnall, and do tell him that I am very sorry to disturb him – and give my love, and my apologies, and to your mother, also.' Sorcha, her daughter, she knew was so pleased about how well her eldest son was getting on in the law school that she would not grudge the absence of her husband and Oisín would feel the same. It would not be a busy time for him – his major business was the importation of wine from western France and that would mostly occur in the autumn. 'Take Slevin with you,' she ended, 'and bring your father straight to Cahermacnaghten, not to Fanore.'

It would be best, she thought, to talk with the merchant from Galway before taking him over to Fanore.

Five

Do Breithemhnas for Gellaib
(On Judgement about Pledges)

*The creditor who holds your brooch, your necklet or your earrings as a
pledge against your loan must return them so you may wear them at the
great assembly. Otherwise he will be fined for your humiliation.*

Oisín O'Davoren was Mara's second cousin, as well as
being her son-in-law. He came from an obscure branch
of the O'Davorens. His father, his grandfather and his uncles
had all been coopers, and had been content to live out their
lives in the useful trade of barrel-making. Oisín, though, had
been ambitious. In his teens, he had visited Galway to sell
some barrels and had decided that the life of a merchant was
the one for him. He began to buy and sell wine as well as
barrels. By the time he was a young man of just thirty, he had
done so well that he now had a fine stone house as well as a
shop in the city. He also had three children and had been very
pleased and proud that his mother-in-law had accepted his
eldest son, Domhnall, then aged eight years old, as a scholar
in her renowned law school.

And the placement had worked out. Domhnall, to Mara's
mind, had inherited the brains and the integrity of her own
father, Domhnall's great-grandfather. The immense toil of the
law school, the hundreds of legal decrees, triads, heptads and
other lore that had to be memorized, the languages, English,
Latin, Spanish and even Greek, were easily absorbed by the
boy. What was almost more important, though, was that from
the start he showed signs of a mature judgement which made
Mara hope that he might, in his time, take over the law school
of Cahermacnaghten from her.

To Oisín, however, she contented herself with praising
Domhnall's prowess and his sense of responsibility towards the

younger pupils. She knew her son-in-law well enough to know that ever since Cormac, her son by her second marriage, had joined the law school, he had been on tenterhooks to know how that would affect his son who was, of course, oddly, Cormac's nephew. In her own mind, Mara was by now fairly sure that Cormac would not want to be a Brehon and that even the amount of work involved in studying for the further qualification of *ollamh* was going to be a great deterrent to him, if he did indeed have any ambition to inherit the law school from his mother. No, she thought, Cormac was like his kingly father and would prefer to be engaged in warfare and in the affairs of the three kingdoms.

However, these were early days and so Mara plied Oisín with some of his own imported wine, thanked him very sincerely for coming to see her immediately and not waiting until the morning and then led the conversation around to the question of the dead man.

'If it is indeed Niall Martin, then he has neither wife nor child,' he declared with decisiveness that she expected from him. 'I've known him for a long time; have had some dealings with him when he has given me gold articles for sale in France. An honest man, though very keen on money. His shop was tiny and he never expanded it, though I think he did very well for himself. He lived above it. An old woman came in and out and cleaned the place. She had her own key. I've seen her climb the steps at the side of the shop with it in her hand. As for meals, well, I think that he ate breakfast, dinner and supper in the various pie shops around, and you'd often find him, of an evening, in one of the inns. Not a very strong man; he could have dropped dead of a heart attack. He'd be sixty, I'd say. Could be more, could be less. He looked an old man when I came first to Galway, and that's some time ago. He loaned me money for my first shop.'

'What would have brought him to the Burren?' queried Mara and Oisín hoisted his shoulders and pursed out his mouth. Mara did not press him. Oisín was a man who always liked to know everything – and to be known as the man who knew everything – and she didn't want him inventing knowledge.

'How would a man get from Galway City to Fanore?' she

asked. Of course, she thought, a search must be made for a stray horse, and it was possible that one was now quietly feeding from the sparse grass on the rocky fields that overlooked the sea.

'Not by horse, anyway,' said Oisín unexpectedly. 'He didn't ride. He told me once that horses frightened the life out of him. No need for a horse if you stick to the city streets; that's what he used to say.'

That was true; thought Mara. Galway was a small city. She thought about it for a moment. This goldsmith hated horses; so how had he got to the Burren?

'So it has to be by boat,' said Mara thoughtfully.

'Someone must have brought him.' Oisín sounded quite sure of that. 'He didn't have a boat of his own. I can't imagine him managing one. He was quite a feeble old man. It will have been one of the fishermen from around here.'

It was, of course, a possibility. It could have been anyone. All of the O'Connors had been involved in this great new enterprise of selling these carefully smoked fish to Galway inns and pie houses. Fernandez had explained to her that the brine-impregnated wood and the seaweed gave the fish a delicate flavour that was relished in a city famous for its places to eat.

But there was one man from Fanore who was not involved in this enterprise, but this one man crossed and re-crossed Galway Bay almost every single day.

'You've never traded in samphire, have you?' She put the question idly to Oisín and was not surprised to see him shake his head.

'No,' he said decisively. 'I trade in almost anything. In fact, I make money by combining loads, by sending heavy flagstones and light leather cloaks to Bordeaux and bringing back barrels of wine and parcels of French lace. Or it could be that I send hunting dogs and salted meat to Spain and bring back oranges, apricots and gold and silver bullion. I might do something with these smoked fish if they taste good, but I'd never touch anything like samphire – too short-lived – they say that it should be in the boiling water as soon as it's taken from the sea. Now Brendan O'Connor knows that. He carries it in barrels filled with seawater right over to the quay in Galway.

He tells me that for a special customer he sometimes even chips off pieces of the rock and brings it, still growing, into the kitchen. But in any case he's got woven baskets to put it in when he fishes it out and he just carries it dripping down the street. The cooks like that; it shows the people in the street that they are using fresh ingredients,' said Oisín with a nod of admiration towards another successful merchant.

Mara listened with amusement. Her son-in-law had forgotten about the murder in his interest in how another man made money. She was not surprised when after a minute he burst out with: 'I've just got such a good idea. I could sell him some of my worn-out half-barrels. I know a sign-writer – does some great pictures for the inns – he could paint a picture of the samphire on the barrels and Brendan's name. It would look good and he's getting more business as he goes along the streets. The inns and pie shops would like it, too. Regular customers could have their names painted on them as well. I must have a word with Brendan, see what he thinks. It could be the making of him.'

'Well, you'll see him tomorrow morning,' said Mara rising to her feet. 'I hope Brigid makes you comfortable. She was getting ready your room in the guest house when I was over there a couple of hours ago – and you will want to have a word with Domhnall before you go to bed so I will say good-night, now.'

She ushered him to the front door, but did not go to bed. Her mind was very active and now, in the privacy of her own thoughts, she could indulge in some speculation. She waited until she heard the gate to the law-school enclosure slam closed and then went out into the summer's night, crossing the road and walking across the limestone paved field, keeping close to the wall to avoid disturbing the cows with their young calves.

The wind had died down and hardly a breath of air came through the wall, though it was one of those gossamer walls, constructed of stone leaning against stone, looking in half-darkness like a white pattern drawn on a darker background. The pink and purple orchids and the ragged robin that grew in the crevices were almost invisible now, but the tall moon daisies shone silver and gold through the twilight, and tiny luminous blossoms of bright yellow star grass flowered here and there at her feet. There was a strong perfume from the pale cream woodbine in the hedgerow and somewhere in the distance the churning sound of the nightjar's evening song sounded like the noise of the waves on the beach.

What did happen to that man? She sat down upon a boulder and shut her eyes for a moment, seeing the beach at Fanore.

It would have been evening. Nuala had said that he had eaten a meal a couple of hours previously. Oisín had confirmed that the man, Niall Martin, ate in pie shops and inns – the presence of the half-digested apricot in the stomach corroborated that. So one evening, three or four days ago, Niall Martin, a prosperous gold merchant, a single man who lived alone, did not, on that evening, return to his rooms above his shop, but had perhaps walked down to Quay Street, found a boat there – perhaps by prior arrangement, or perhaps it was just an impulse – whatever it was, Oisín had made it clear that the gold merchant was not a person to manage a boat by himself. Therefore another man was there in the boat, had taken the passenger on board, had untied the rope from the quayside – cast off – and sailed – surely sailed – rowing would be too slow – sailed back across Galway Bay and perhaps moored at the little pier built by the fishermen of Fanore well over fifty years ago. Niall Martin had got out of the boat, her thoughts went on; he had got out of the boat, but the owner of the boat, the faceless one – what had he done? Stayed there, probably, she thought. If another journey had to be made across the bay, then, despite the long summer nights, it could not have been delayed too long. But why did Niall Martin come to Fanore? And who dealt that fatal blow? And what was the weapon? Something hard, smooth, and well-padded according to Nuala – not a club, she had thought – perhaps an axe, but it would have been padded, otherwise it would have broken the skin and bone. It was the impact of the blow that had killed the man.

But why did he come? That was the main question now. Oisín had made it clear that Niall Martin had only one interest, one commercial involvement, and that was in gold. He bought gold and he sold gold. There was a possibility that he had heard a rumour that there was a gold seam in one of the strips of quartz that ran like white veins here and there through the black limestone of the coast, but somehow Mara intuitively felt that from what she had heard of Niall Martin, he would not have wanted to engage in a huge industry of breaking up the stone and mining the gold from it. She took a sudden decision and turned aside until she was opposite to one of the neat gaps which Cumhal had built into the wall where one of the giant leaning slabs had been replaced with a small, almost square stone, which still kept the herringbone framework of the wall intact, but allowed a human, turning sideways, to slip out onto the roadway, without permitting the escape of the cows.

The tower house of Lissylisheen, the home of Ardal O'Lochlainn, *taoiseach* of the powerful O'Lochlainn clan on the Burren, was the nearest residence to the law school at Cahermacnaghten. Thirty years ago Mór O'Lochlainn, sister of Ardal, had been Mara's dearest friend and, after she married Malachy O'Davoren, the mother of Mara's goddaughter, Nuala. They had remained friends until her early and tragic death from a lump in her breast. Mara had mourned her bitterly, but her relationship with Mór's brother, Ardal, had endured and she relied on his common sense and his loyalty.

Ardal was a man of wide knowledge, a man whose judgement Mara trusted and, above all, he was a man who had extensive commercial interests taking him to Galway City and beyond. If anyone could advise her, then he was the man.

It was late, she knew, but lights still shone from all three storeys of the tower house. Ardal was a hard-working man and as she came through the gates and into the courtyard, he emerged from his barn in conversation with his steward.

'Brehon,' he said with what sounded like a genuine pleasure. 'Come in and have a cup of wine.'

'It's late for a call,' said Mara, allowing herself to be ushered up the stairs, 'but I've come to pick your brains.'

It was, she thought, typical of Ardal that he made no queries, just busied himself with getting her a comfortable chair by the window, pouring wine from a flagon, and then joining her peacefully relaxed on a low bench.

'You heard about the body at Fanore,' she said and he nodded. She knew that he would have heard. He made it his business to hear everything and to say little unless his opinion was asked for.

'It came in from the sea in a boat with no oars, but I believe that it was a murder that was made to look like a case of *fingal*,' said Mara. 'It's a strange case,' she went on, finding that as usual she talked freely with Ardal and the less he said, the more that she said. 'I had three queries in the beginning' she continued. 'Who was this man? Why had he come to the beach of Fanore? And, of course, who had killed him? I think I might have found the answer to one of the queries. It does look as though he was a merchant from Galway City, a man called Niall Martin.'

'Niall Martin, the gold merchant.' Ardal's response bore a note of interest and Mara looked at him hopefully.

'You know him, knew him?' she asked and he nodded.

'I'm not sure that I can help you very much,' he said, 'but I am not altogether surprised that the man came to Fanore.'

'Had he links there? Contacts? People that he knew in Fanore?'

'All I can tell you is that he had an interest in the place,' said Ardal. 'I went in there, into his shop, fairly recently. I was going up to Connemara to visit the mother of my son. I went in to buy a present – I wanted a gold bracelet.' Mara nodded in a matter-of-fact way, but it was a long time since he had spoken of his son and of the woman who had lived with him for a short while at Lissylisheen tower house, before returning to her family and friends in her native Connemara, north of Galway. The boy, she realized with a feeling of shock at the passing of time, was older than Cormac. If anything happened to Ardal, then this boy, as his acknowledged son, would inherit his personal fortune. It was time, perhaps, that he came to live with his father although, no doubt, this would cause trouble with the O'Lochlainns' present *tánaiste*, Ardal's brother, Donogh O'Lochlainn.

Ardal flicked a glance at her as though he could read what was going on in her mind, but went back to his story.

'When I went into the shop, Niall Martin was there – he may have been a little deaf, because I don't think that he heard me, but he had a map open, a large sheet of vellum, and it was, I would swear, a map of the beach at Fanore – I recognized the curve of it, and the river, the Caher, was clearly marked. He was completely absorbed in it until my shadow fell across the sheet and then he gave a little jump and he rolled up the map and put it away. I did my business with him, but before I left, he said something strange . . .' Ardal paused and Mara knew that, meticulous as the *taoiseach* of the O'Lochlainn clan was, he was making absolutely sure that he recalled the exact words.

'Yes,' he continued, 'he said to me: "You come from the Kingdom of the Burren, don't you? Could you tell me why Fanore has that name?" Well, I must say, Brehon, I was puzzled. I told him that it was two words in the Gaelic; that *fán* meant "slope" in English and that *ór* meant "gold". And when I said that to him, Brehon, well he just nodded his head at me, and said: "Yes, but the sand is not golden there, is it? It's the colour of a dirty orange, that's what it is." And, you know, Brehon, when I came to think of other beaches along the coastline, An Leacht in Corcomroe, for instance, well they are golden, but Niall Martin is right. The sand at Fanore is not really the colour of gold.' Ardal paused and looked at Mara expectedly and she nodded.

'So that means that he had visited Fanore and had looked at it carefully – and, of course, he is right. The sand at Fanore is mixed with that streak of black limestone that goes through the middle of it – it is not gold, but a dirty shade of orange.'

'So, you think that his question was a good one?'

Mara nodded again. 'The question is a very good one and I don't know the answer to it. As far back as I can remember it has always been called that, and no one, in my hearing, has wondered why it got that name. It has taken a gold merchant from Galway to bring up the question.'

'There is another thing, also, Brehon,' said Ardal. 'As I said, he rolled up the map when he saw that he was not alone, but just before he did so, I noticed something on it. As I was telling you, the beach was drawn, and the sea was marked at what looked like low-water mark, just little wavy lines, and the rocks were marked, and so was the river – clearly labelled

"The River Caher", but that was not all. On either side of
the river, on the sand, looking as though they had been cast
out by the river when it was in flood after a rainstorm, were
some shapes. They were beautifully drawn,' said Ardal, drawing
out his tale with the skill of a professional storyteller, 'I could
recognize what they were immediately. They were old ornaments, gold, I'd say, there were bracelets, rings, torcs – you
know, Brehon, those ancient necklets.'

Mara drew in a deep breath. Despite the seriousness of the
matter she could not help smiling.

'Well, Ardal,' she said. 'I think this will be of huge interest
to my scholars. Can you imagine any better treasure-hunters
than the seven of them? They won't leave a stone unturned,
will they? How many pieces were marked on the map, can
you recollect?'

Ardal thought seriously about the question, half-closing his
blue eyes and running his fingers through the greying red-gold
of his hair, then he opened his eyes and said with his usual
decisiveness: 'I would have thought that there could be as many
as ten.'

'Ten! Well, it's no wonder that he came over to Fanore to
see for himself, is it?'

'Fishermen would have brought in those things, one by one,
perhaps over a period of years. The price of one of them
would be worth a month's fishing out on the ocean.' Ardal
stated the fact with the indifference of a man who is so rich
that he probably did not know on what to spend his own gold,
but Mara thought about the huge pleasure that must have given
to the man or his wife who found the precious object. There
must have been knowledge of the gold merchant from Galway
City. Of course, these fishermen would often sell their catch
at the fish market and would soon be able to find their way
to the shop in Red Earl's Lane.

'Ten,' she said aloud, 'well, Ardal, unless one man, or one
family, was extremely lucky, this means that a considerable
number of the fishermen must have known who Niall Martin
was, and would have known what brought him to Fanore.'

She got to her feet, thanking him very sincerely for his
help. Ardal did not urge her to stay. He knew her well, and

would know that now she wanted to be alone with her thoughts.

As she walked back along the familiar road Mara's mind was very busy. Now she could understand what had happened. The gold merchant had become greedy. He was no longer willing to pay the fishermen for the pieces of treasure which they picked up on the beach. He had decided to come to see for himself. And was there any significance in the fact that the evening he chose was probably the evening after the storm? She brought her mind back to the towering strength of the waves on that Monday morning when she had come out from the mountain pass and had first seen the sea. But there was something else, other than the thunder of the Atlantic breakers, there had also been the roar of the small Caher River in full flood sweeping down its stony passageway on its way to the sea.

Before she went to bed that night Mara busied herself with pen, inks and a piece of vellum and from memory she sketched out a map of area, the mountains, the beach and the river that ran down the northern side of the steeply sloping beach.

Of course, she said to herself as she worked on the drawing, of course, Ardal was right. The name Fanore did not refer to the dark, almost dirty orange colour of its sand, but to the rumours and occasional finds of gold ornaments. *Fán Or* meant 'the slope of the gold' – the slope where the golden ornaments were discovered.

Six

Bretha Comaithchesa
(Laws of the Neighbourhood)

Grazing rights of the shore for cattle belong to the owner of the land adjacent to the shore. The owner of any other cattle found on the shore will be deemed guilty of 'shore trespass'.

All seaweed found on the shore is the property of the finder but a whale washed onto the beach is the property of the whole clan whose lands adjoin the shoreline.

'Brigid, I want to set off early and get to Fanore before the boats set out. Will it be a nuisance for you to serve breakfast to Oisín and to the boys quite soon?' Mara was not surprised to find Brigid, though now in her late sixties and with several girls to assist her, up and bustling around the kitchen at half past six in the morning. Already the porridge oats were bubbling in the cauldron slung from the iron crane above the fire, and Cumhal and one of the lads had just brought in the milk.

'Not a trouble in the world,' said Brigid, as she tilted more milk onto the oats. 'You'll be in plenty of time, the boats will be going out on the tide, so Cumhal says – and he says that will give you another couple of hours. You'll be busy there all the day, I suppose.' It was a hint, but only a hint, for information. Gossip was Brigid's lifeblood, though when asked to remain silent she would faithfully do so. However, the news had spread far and wide by now, Mara reckoned, so there could be no harm in talking it over with her housekeeper and farm manager.

'You heard about a body being found, washed in from the sea,' she said and was surprised that even the voluble Brigid said nothing in reply to this. She even looked slightly uneasy.

Of course both Cumhal and Brigid were of the O'Connor clan and clannishness was a very strong instinct in the people of the Burren.

'It looks like it's a man from Galway,' continued Mara and was amused when Brigid snapped out, 'Nothing to do with us, then.' It was exactly what the other members of the clan, the fishermen of Fanore, had been saying yesterday. 'Still,' she went on, 'you enjoy yourself, Brehon, it's a lovely day for the sea.'

'Why don't you come with me,' said Mara on impulse. There had been a hint of envy, a shade of longing in Brigid's voice – a woman who always loved to be in the thick of affairs. And, thought Mara, looking back into the past, Brigid was a fisherman's daughter. Perhaps someone reared by the sea had the sea in their veins and always wished to be back with the sand between the toes, the smell of the seaweed, the noise of the waves and the high, lonely sound of the sea birds overhead. The older you got, she thought, the more you wished to be back with the scenes of your childhood. She would take Brigid for a few days by the sea.

She owed so much to this elderly woman who had been her mother after her own mother died and who had given her such love and loyalty – had, indeed, also, been a mother to the numerous scholars who had passed through the gates of Cahermacnaghten.

'Yes, do come,' she urged. 'The scholars would be pleased to see you.'

Brigid's face brightened at the mention of the scholars. 'God help us, they'll be tired of fish,' she exclaimed. 'I'll get young Séanín to put panniers on the cob and bring enough to cook them a good meal.' And then she was off to her storeroom and calling shrill instructions to her helpers.

Mara drank some milk and chewed a piece of newly baked soda bread while she meditated on the morning's work. Of course, the first thing to do was to confirm the identity of the dead man, then to get him buried and after that, with the help of her scholars, she would test the validity of her first guess about the effect of storm water flooding down from the mountain and channelled within the narrow pathway of the Caher

River. She left Brigid to her preparations and went off to
where Cumhal was checking the house-sized haycocks that
had been built against the inner edge of the massive twenty-
foot stone wall that encircled the law school.

'There's a good reason for building them in the same place
every year,' he was saying reprovingly to a bright-faced lad
who, from the height of the wall, was adjusting the small square
tarpaulin that acted as a sloping roof to shed the worst of the
rain from the hay. 'It's been done from time immemorial and
there's a reason to it. Hay needs shelter from the wind and the
rain, but it needs air. Now the air comes through the wall
stones, but the wind is blocked. You stick to the ways of doing
things that your great-grandfathers used and you won't go far
wrong, Séanín.'

Séanín made a comic face behind Cumhal's back and Mara
was conscious of a certain sympathy for him. The world would
be a boring place if the young felt that they had no chance
of improving on their elders. However, the strength of tradi-
tion was certainly upheld in Brehon laws, and she, like Cumhal,
was busy inculcating a sense of respect and even reverence into
her schools for the laws of their ancestors.

'I always remember the haystacks here, even when I was
younger than you, Séanín,' she said with a smile up at the boy,
'but I never knew the reason for it. It's good to question
everything, isn't it, Cumhal? That's the way that you learn the
reasons for doing things.'

Cumhal gave a grunt that probably meant that young
Séanín had no reason to query any of his commands, but his
respect for the Brehon did not allow him to say anything. He
listened courteously while Mara told him that Brigid would
be coming with her, gave his opinion about the time of high
tide when the boats would go from the beach, if they were
going out today, and then she managed to slip in a question,
putting it casually as she turned to go away.

'I wonder why the place is called Fanore, Cumhal, have you
ever heard?'

He considered the question but shook his head. Cumhal
never speculated and spoke only when he was sure of his
ground. Séanín, from the top of the wall, informed her that

it was because of the golden sand and Cumhal told him to make sure that the tarpaulin was in the exact centre of the top of the haystack in a voice which warned him to mind his business and to speak when he was spoken to.

So there was no general knowledge, among either young or old, of why Fanore might have got its name, thought Mara as she went to greet Domhnall and Slevin, but that, of course, did not mean the guess was wrong. Names are accepted and seldom questioned, remnants of people and events long forgotten. She allowed her two scholars to eat their breakfast and then while Oisín was being fed she called the boys into the school house and told them Ardal's story of the gold merchant of Galway and his map of Fanore.

'And I've drawn one here,' she said. 'You see, if my theory is right, then from time to time, a gold object, probably an ancient piece of jewellery according to the little drawings that Ardal saw on the map, is swept onto the beach at Fanore. And it can't be happening all of the time, or we would have heard of it, so what do you reckon?'

'At the time of a storm,' said Slevin quickly. 'A high tide comes up and washes out something – perhaps a treasure hidden in one of the caves.'

'That's possible,' admitted Mara. 'What do you think, Domhnall?'

'I was wondering about the river,' he said slowly. 'You see,' he went on, looking now at Slevin and not at her, 'you see, if it is the sea that washes things out of a cave you would expect something like gold to go to the bottom; it certainly wouldn't float. Of course, it might be found, but it's quite unlikely if it is on the ocean floor. But if the river, in full flood, washed something out of a cave on the mountainside, then it would be swept down, tumbling over the stones and could easily hit one of the rocks and stones on the riverbed and be spilled onto the beach. A fisherman coming out early would see it and immediately pick it up. Also the sea would have to drag it back and since the gold would not float, that's less likely – the chances are that something in a cave would never end up on the beach. But the Caher River, coming down from the mountains, could just sweep one thing, say a

necklet, out and tumble it downstream and then leave it stranded
on the beach.'

'You're right,' said Slevin enthusiastically. 'I'd say he's right,
wouldn't you, Brehon. Old brainbox,' he added affectionately,
clouting Domhnall on the side of the head.

'Well, let's see what Domhnall's father says when he sees the
body,' said Mara. 'We mustn't rush ahead until we are sure of
our facts.' Nevertheless, she packed her little map carefully in
her satchel and felt sure that it would be of use on the beach
of Fanore, once Oisín had confirmed that the body was, indeed,
that of Niall Martin, the gold merchant from the city of Galway.

Cumhal had been right when he told Mara about the likely
time for the boats to embark. The beach was busy when
they arrived, but everyone was still there. The boats were
already loaded with nets and dragging hooks, but all of the
fishermen and also the five younger scholars were still on
the beach .waiting for the high tide. Fernandez was in his
big ship, but came off it and ran lightly up the pier and then
across the sand once he saw her arrive.

'I'm sorry to delay your departure, Fernandez,' said Mara
briskly after she had introduced Oisín to him, 'but the body
will need to be buried soon and many hands will make light
work. Could you ask the men to bring spades to the churchyard and once Oisín has identified him, then the corpse should
be buried as soon as possible.'

'There's plenty of odd pieces of timber lying around,
Fernandez,' said Etain in a businesslike way. 'We could get them
carried up and they can be nailed to that boat – that boat is
useless anyway – and then the man will have a perfect coffin.'

'That's a good suggestion,' said Mara appreciatively. She noted
Etain's use of the words 'that boat' and wondered whether
there was any significance in them. She said nothing, however,
and watched Etain organize her younger scholars, putting them
into pairs – Cormac with Cael and Art with Cian to carry
the boards – and giving Finbar a large hammer and some nails.

'How are you, Finbar?' asked Mara, going to walk beside
him up the road to the church.

He started at her words and looked taken aback and she

guessed that he did not want to talk about his future at the moment, so she chatted about Brigid who was on the beach already with young Séanín to assist her in getting a good fire going in order to cook some of her splendid sausages. The younger children had been grouped around her when they left, but most of the older ones climbed the hill silently beside their parents. The words, '*Say nothing!*' seemed to Mara to hang in the air and even her scholars, apart from Domhnall and Slevin, said little. Most waited outside in the churchyard or by the gate when they came to the little church on the hillside.

It was one of the smallest churches that Mara had ever seen – not much bigger than an average kitchen. It had small plain altar made from a slab of the stone that lay outside. A candle was burning on it and the priest stood beside it, looking grim and unwelcoming. Already a faint smell of decomposing flesh made the warm air unpleasant and Mara hoped devoutly that there would be no further delay in getting this poor man underground. She walked steadily to the top of the church and stood for a moment gazing down at the elderly man. Already his features had changed subtly – the skin was almost translucent. She glanced at Oisín and he nodded.

'Yes,' he said loudly enough for all within the church to hear him, 'yes, Brehon, that is the body of Niall Martin, the gold merchant from Galway City.'

'In that case, Father,' said Mara thankfully to the priest, 'I think we should bury him here. My son-in-law, Oisín O'Davoren, is also a merchant from the city and he knows this man well and knows that he has no relatives in Galway.'

'He was originally from Bristol in England, I seem to remember,' said Oisín looking at the priest. 'He told me once that he had no kin living that he knew of.'

'I'll say the prayers out by the graveside,' said the priest hurriedly and he went off to allocate a space. He was quickly followed by everyone else and Mara was left alone with the dead man. '*Their silver and their gold shall not be able to deliver them in the day of the wrath of the Lord,*' she quoted, saying the words from the Bible aloud within the empty echoing walls of the small church. Why had an elderly man without wife, child, or family of any sort bothered to leave his city home and to come over here to Fanore on the Burren? Surely he had enough silver and gold for his modest needs. *Nevertheless, she told the silent corpse, I shall see you buried with dignity and then I shall find who hit the fatal blow and I promise you that I will not rest until I have avenged you.* When she was a child she had a fanciful notion that a murdered person would not find their proper place in heaven until the facts of death were established by her father, the Brehon, and until the culprit had made open acknowledgement of the crime in front of the people of the kingdom.

That, she swore a silent oath, she would endeavour to accomplish, even for a stranger.

And then she left the church and walked towards the grave-yard deep in thought.

There were a large amount of men with spades available, and they were driven by the urgency in placing this unwanted corpse below ground and the soil of the graveyard was light and sandy – all of these must have contributed to the fact that the grave was ready by the time that she came out. Two men, with averted faces, were placing the boards across the top of the fragile boat while a third hastily hammered in nails attaching them to the gunwale. Once that was done, the makeshift coffin was soon lowered down with ropes into the grave, the priest rushing through the prayers and within five minutes the exca-vated earth was heaped up on top of the mortal remains of Niall Martin, the goldsmith from Galway who had come to an obscure beach on the north-western corner of the Gaelic Kingdom of the Burren, and who had been killed at that spot.

Seven

Muirbretha
(Sea Judgements)

Any goods found on the seashore belong to the owner of that shore unless it can be proved that they have come from beyond nine waves from the shore – in which case they will belong to the finder.

'Brigid! Sausages! You're an angel!'

'*Iontach!*'

'And how's the old place getting on without us?' queried Cormac with the air of a traveller newly returned from a long sea journey.

'Terrible, terrible, the whole place is going to rack and ruin! You won't know it when you see it again.' Brigid entered into the game.

'Cumhal got drunk and ploughed up the home meadow again?'

'The pig's lost weight!'

'Rats in the storeroom!' Cael gave Brigid a sly look at that. She and Brigid had many a tussle over how a young lady should behave.

'Haycocks have fallen down!'

'And built up again in the wrong place! At least one foot from the place they've been put in for the last five hundred years,' Séanín adroitly turned a sausage while putting in this piece of exquisite humour.

It was good to see them all in such good spirits, thought Mara. Even Cael had got over her annoyance at having to share a tent with Síle and was bandying jokes and sarcasms with the other scholars. Mara munched absent-mindedly at a sausage and gazed out to sea. Everyone was enjoying the change from fish. Brigid kept a supply of willow twigs which she always used when cooking sausages for the boys, so no plates were needed and they all enjoyed the informality. The fishing community, whose normal diet was almost entirely taken from their sea-catches, was praising Brigid's cooking loudly and enthusiastically and the housekeeper's cheeks were flushed with pleasure.

'Brehon, who owns the shore grazing here at Fanore?' asked Domhnall. He spoke in low tone and did not cease to eat, but his brown eyes were alert and thoughtful.

Mara was taken aback. It was a very good question, and a question, she acknowledged to herself, that she should have asked herself before now.

'To be honest, I'm not sure, Domhnall,' she said immediately. Her mind went to Michelóg, and yet there was that case of the bull. Had Michelóg owned the shore grazing then the community would have been on more unsure ground when they objected to the animal grazing there. Her mind went back to the case, sifting through the thousands of other cases with which she had dealt during her time as Brehon. It had not been a very noticeable, nor a very complicated case, she seemed to remember. The chances were small that it was Michelóg that traditionally owned the grazing. It had not been Fernandez; she was almost certain of that. And yet he above all men was one that would know the answer to this question. She half-rose to her feet, but then decided to leave her query until later on. She relaxed her back against one of the squared-off rocks and listened with amusement to the bantering between Brigid and her scholars.

They had been glad to see the housekeeper; Mara had been pleased to observe that. There was a relationship between Cormac, Art, the MacMahon twins and her housekeeper which was a sort of mother/grandmother tie that made them feel at ease with her, made them accept her frequent scolding and her right to see after their food, their welfare, their donning of clean clothes, and their moods of depression or anxiety. Brigid, she noticed, was paying particular attention to young Finbar, teasing him, making sure that he ate his sausages and his slices of newly baked soda bread spread with newly salted butter and that he finished his portion of strawberry pie and telling him that young Eileen in the farm had been asking after him. Finbar moved from one-syllable answers to giggles and seemed to make a good meal and join Cormac and Cian in their teasing of Brigid.

'That's an interesting question that Domhnall asked, isn't it?' said Mara meditatively to Cael. After Domhnall the girl was probably the most promising of her scholars and so she was not surprised when Cael wrinkled her brow and said thoughtfully, 'You're thinking that the gold merchant came here for some reason, something to do with his trade, perhaps, aren't you?' She looked around her carefully, but the law-school crowd were seated at some distance from the fishermen and their families. Nevertheless, Mara noted with appreciation how Cael lowered her voice before saying: 'Perhaps there's a possibility that he heard that someone had found some gold and that's why he came here; that's what you and Domhnall are thinking, aren't you? And I know that if something is swept in from the sea, from beyond the seventh wave, then it's *finders, keepers* but if it's not, then it's the property of whoever owns the shore-grazing rights – so that's why Domhnall asked you who owned the shore-grazing rights.'

Mara gave her an approving nod. 'It's interesting that the Romans also had that as one of their laws – whether they took it from us, or we took it from them, I don't know, or perhaps it just makes sense that there should be a law about that,' she remarked, but she said no more as she saw Setanta, Art's father, approach, walking down the beach towards her.

'Is it all right if we go off now to catch an afternoon's fishing, Brehon?' he asked. 'There should be a good moon tonight – I think that the weather is set to remain fair for a few days now.'

'That should be all right, Setanta,' said Mara. It would probably be at least midnight before the tide would be right for them to moor their boats against the pier. 'I and my scholars will be busy here for the afternoon,' she went on, ignoring the disappointed and dismayed looks from her pupils. They had been hoping to go out in the boats again, but by now they should know that law-school business had to come first. If ever they were to become Brehons, this lesson could not be learned early enough. 'I will return tomorrow morning and then I may have some questions to ask. Hopefully this matter will soon be unravelled,' she finished to Setanta and saw a tightening of his mouth and a flash of concern from his eyes.

Mara waited until the fishermen departed and then called her scholars to her and walked across to where the Caher River entered the beach. Brigid had set Séanín to work in gathering various kinds of seaweed from the rocks and piling them onto one of the flat table-like stones so that the sea water could drip from the fronds. The housekeeper was a great believer in carrageen moss for sore throats and cough syrup and kelp was used in soups and in stewed mutton. The wives and children left behind were busy with their smoking fires, so that this corner of the beach was as private as the school house at Cahermacnaghten could be.

'Domhnall and I were discussing this matter,' she began and then stopped, momentarily disconcerted by a flash of irritation from the very green eyes of her son Cormac. Could he be jealous of Domhnall, she wondered – there had been no sign of it previously. Cormac had always accepted Domhnall as the head scholar of the school and had shown no signs of resenting a boy five years older than himself. However, the immediate concern now was to solve this murder so she hastily put the matter aside, telling them of the map of Fanore which Ardal O'Lochlainn had seen in the possession of the gold merchant and of how he had noticed that small pieces of jewellery, necklets, bracelets, brooches and rings were marked on various parts of the strand, on either side of the River Caher.

'It may be that there has been a history of finding these objects on Fanore beach and that might be why it is named the as "the slope of the gold" – because, as you can see, the sand is not as golden as on other beaches along the coastline – that it is, in fact, rather more a dark orange colour than golden,' she concluded.

'A treasure hunt! *Iontach!*' exclaimed Cael.

'I was wondering whether some gold objects might have been washed in from the sea,' said Slevin, 'but Domhnall came up with the idea that it was more likely that they had tumbled down the hill when the river was in flood – and I must say that I think he is right. The gold would be too heavy to float.

A cask might have been picked up the waves but the necklets and rings would have been more likely to be swept further out to sea, or to remain on the seabed.'

'And it has to be just one or two every few years,' put in Domhnall. 'Otherwise, we'd have heard about it. Just something that a fisherman saw, picked up, took to the gold merchant in Galway, sold, and said nothing about. It makes sense that the gold merchant became suspicious and started to question the fishermen as to the exact spot where they had picked up the pieces of jewellery.'

'Yes, and then he put two and two together.' Cael was bubbling over with enthusiasm.

'He would have had no right to it,' said Finbar in a low voice and Mara gave him an encouraging smile.

'But who does own the rights?' said Domhnall coming back to the point with his usual pertinacity.

'I should have asked Setanta.' Mara felt annoyed with herself, though in the face of the hesitation shown by all of the fishermen, she had been very wary of disclosing anything.

'I think I know.' Art spoke out so seldom that all heads turned towards him immediately.

'Not Fernandez,' said Cormac.

Art shook his head. 'No, not Fernandez,' he said. 'He just bought that land. That Cathair Róis is just new. He comes from south of the Burren, not from around here.' He looked across at Mara. 'I believe that it is Brendan,' he said, his voice steady and confident, though the words were tentative. He would be right, thought Mara. Art did not speak until he was sure of a matter, unlike her volatile son who chattered continuously and gave vent to a thousand theories every day.

'Of course!' she said. The fact that Brendan did not have a herd of cows had prevented her from thinking of his name. But, of course, Brendan and Etain's father before them did have cattle. It was Etain, she thought, who had started the business of gathering samphire for sale in the nearby Galway City and this had proved so lucrative that Brendan had given up keeping the cows and had turned his attention towards getting a better boat and becoming a full-time trader. It suited his personality better, she thought. Both he and Etain were sociable, talkative people. The life of a cattle farmer was restrictive and solitary.

'There's Etain now; shall I run down and ask her,' volunteered Cael.

'Are you calling Art a liar?' Cormac's tone was angry and aggressive.

'That's a little unnecessary, Cormac,' said Mara coldly. 'Art himself said that he was not sure. But I think we won't say anything about rights to things found on the shoreline, yet, Cael. It's just as well to keep our thoughts to ourselves at the moment, don't you all agree? We don't want to start people talking and speculating about this matter before we can solve it. A secret and unlawful death in the community always makes people feel deeply uneasy and the last thing we want is to set tongues wagging.'

She had talked on at length in order to get over that awkward patch. She felt a little sorry for Cael. As the only girl, she had felt somewhat excluded from the others when she had been refused permission to camp with them and she had expressed her fury and, boy-like, the others, including her brother, had perhaps banded against her. It was the first sign of awkwardness that Mara had seen between Cael and her fellow scholars and she hoped that it would soon pass.

'You see,' Mara said earnestly, lowering her voice so that they had to lean a little towards her, 'it looks as though we have a few mysteries to solve here. Niall Martin, the elderly gold merchant, would be most unlikely to visit this spot unless something attracted him. I wondered about a rumour of gold in the mountains here, but a long-buried treasure is a much more likely reason. But then we have the problem of who took him here, to search for gold. And, did he find the gold?' She paused for a moment and Domhnall said seriously:

'The chances are strong that he did so, Brehon. Otherwise his death is hard to explain.'

Mara agreed with him, but said nothing, allowing the others to have their say. After a few minutes she produced from her satchel the rough sketch map that she had made the night before, handing it to Cormac, as the youngest scholar, and telling him to take it round to the others.

'Say nothing until everyone has had a good chance to look at it,' she told them. 'And then, I think, we should be able to discuss where I went wrong but also where it is likely that something could have been washed out by the river when it was in flood after the storm of the other night.' She could see herself that she had exaggerated one curve of the river and had omitted another.

'I think you did very well,' said Art politely.

'It's difficult to remember everything,' said Slevin, 'but . . .'

'Yes, go on,' said Mara and listened with an appearance of gratitude as one by one they pointed out her mistakes. Some she had not seen herself and she thanked and praised them, taking care that her voice bore no trace of condescension.

'There's one place that I think it might be,' said Domhnall, pointing up the hill to where there was a flash of yellow. 'Just up by those flowers there's a group of rocks.'

'Couldn't be there,' said Cormac immediately. 'The river doesn't go near it.'

'It did the other night; the flood has completely gone down now. Shall we go up there, Brehon?' Slevin was eager to start and Mara thought that the place Domhnall had picked was a good one. They climbed up alongside the river, now tamed to its channel and flowing demurely downhill on its bed of stones.

The rocks themselves were a disappointment, though. The sheltered side, away from the sea, was covered in flowers as intricately woven as a wall carpet, with scarlet pimpernel, mauve storksbill, and large clumps of yellow wall pepper. Could these fragile blossoms have withstood the onslaught of the mountain stream only five nights ago? Mara was inclined to agree with Cormac when he said scornfully, 'See; I told you it couldn't come over as far as that.'

Slevin searched around in a half-hearted way, more out of loyalty to his friend than with any real conviction. Mara set the others to look afterwards but was not surprised when they all returned to her shortly with downcast expressions. The trouble with the young, she thought, was that they expected results instantly. It was one of her hardest tasks as a teacher to keep their spirits up and break down the work into manageable parts. It was no good handing a seven-year-old a book filled with over three hundred triads and telling him that he had three months to memorize them. On the other hand, three of these three-line aphorisms a night were an easy task and with the mixed ages in her school, the triads were being continuously chanted by someone or other during the education of a scholar.

'What we're looking for, I suppose,' she said cheerfully, 'is a sort of cave that might have been blocked at one stage by a slab of stone, but in recent years, perhaps the slab has been swept away, and now, whenever there is a rainstorm, or perhaps only sometimes when there is a rainstorm, the water enters the cave. I think,' she went on, 'we should split up. Cormac and Cael and Cian, cross over the river up there where there are some big stepping stones, and then go straight up towards the mountain. Finbar and Art, will you go down from here. Slevin and Domhnall, go over to the other side of the river and go back down to the beach, and I will go upwards from here.'

They did as she told them and she waited where she was for a minute, listening to their eager voices, and wondering, trying to edge her way into the mind of that elderly goldsmith from Galway City who had taken the venture, had asked a fisherman to take him across the bay and towards those sands where treasures had turned up from time to time. She tried to imagine what he had done. He had, perhaps, left one of the fishermen with the boat moored against the makeshift pier, had gone out onto the sands, had looked upwards, just as she had done today, had wondered about the occurrence of various treasures, whether they were necklets, bracelets, brooches or rings, but all of them swept down onto the sands and brought to him by a fisherman who was abroad early and whose eye had been caught by the glint of gold on sands that were not gold, but were coloured a dark orange by the ridge of black limestone which bisected them.

And so he had come ashore, had looked upwards; perhaps, like herself, he had already worked out that the Caher River, rather than the ocean, had been the source of the treasure which had spilled onto the beach after nights of wind, thunder, lightning and above all rainstorms, nights of flooding when the mountain streams turned into cascades.

But where was the source of the treasure hoard? Where had those people long past, the people, who, like herself, lived by the Brehon law, and had worshipped, not the God of the Nazarene, but the sun god, people who had robbed the mountain streams of their gold and had fashioned tributes to their god, necklets to be worn around the throats of great warriors, bracelets for their wrists, rings for their fingers, and brooches to pin their cloaks back against their mighty shoulders.

But the mountains, she thought as he looked upwards, were full of rocks, of boulders, and here and there the rain-filled streams had hollowed out caves from the soft limestone. She began to climb up. The eager voices of her seven law scholars reached her and she wished that, like them, she could hope for the best.

But there was an immensity of stone above here. Mountains of limestone that seemed to reach up to the blue sky; and beneath the mountains there were cliffs of rocks and the limestone everywhere could be dissolved by rainwater and caves hollowed out beneath and between the outcrops of rock. It would be, she thought, like searching for a needle in a haystack. If they ever found it – well, that would just be a matter of chance.

And then, as she was thinking this, her attention was caught by the patch of sea bindweed, just a few feet above where she stood. She had never seen it elsewhere but it was a common plant around the sand dunes, the pink flowers forming a pretty contrast to the bright green spade-shaped leaves. However, there was something about this particular clump, where the faint, translucent green of the centre was almost turned into gold by the glare of the sun overhead, and the five white lines that striped the pale pink, horn-shaped flower seemed to be directing attention to that centre point. Mara climbed up and bent down to examine the blooms. Yes, the white lines were indeed directing her attention and as she bent over one of the flowers she saw that the sun had drawn sparks from its centre. In a moment her hand went down and it touched not the cool, pollen-dusted centre of the plant, but something that was warm with the sun and hard and smooth. She picked it out and held it up where it gleamed with the colour that only comes from the true and precious metal. It was made from gold and had its warmth and its colour.

Mara held the object to the bright light that came from sun and sea. There was no mistaking it. She held in her hand a small gold ring. In a moment, and instinctively, her fingers went to her mouth and she summoned her scholars with a shrill whistle, which would have appalled Brigid if she heard it and realized that it came from the Brehon of the Burren.

Domhnall and Slevin were the first to reach her and they immediately realized the significance of the object that she held. It was, she thought, the purity of the shape and the lack of any other ornamentation which marked it out as a possession of one of the ancient ancestors of the Celts. They had worshipped gold and had distained to add trumpery ornaments to dilute its purity.

'It must have come from somewhere near here.' This was Domhnall's first reaction. Before the other scholars arrived, he and Slevin began the search, methodically turning over stones and using their young muscles to move slabs aside.

Cormac, impatient of this slow work, climbed swiftly up the steep bed of the stream, accompanied by Art and Finbar.

'We've found something!' His voice floated back after about five minutes and Slevin scowled. 'He should keep his voice down,' he said crossly. 'Doesn't he know that this is law-school business?' Nevertheless both he and Domhnall began to climb swiftly up to where the others were standing. Mara followed, thinking wryly that she was beginning to get a little old for this climbing up rocky, boulder bestrewn paths.

Cormac's face was shining with triumph and Mara was touched to see how Domhnall expressed admiration of the find, interrupting Slevin's homily about secrecy with enthusiastic appreciation of the small, slab-covered cavity. It did, indeed, look like the sort of place where a hoard of gold could have been concealed.

'Found anything inside it?' gasped Cael. Cormac shook his head.

'Not yet,' he said briefly, bending down to pluck some moss from the stones beneath the slab, while Finbar industriously combed through the sand with his fingers. Art did not seem too hopeful, but stared out to sea as though he wished that he were out there with his father and the other fishermen.

There was no doubt that Cormac's find would have been a good hiding place, far away enough from the stream to give an illusion of safety to whoever buried the treasure, and yet not so far as to make it impossible that an unusual flood could, perhaps, have penetrated the hiding place. However, hopes soon began to fade.

'It's no good,' said Domhnall, eventually after they had spent about twenty minutes minutely exploring inside and outside the small cavern. 'Either the murderer found the gold and removed all of it, or else we are in the wrong place. I think we should go on searching.'

'Let's search until the shadow from that tall rock moves over to that clump of pansies,' said Mara pointing over to where the yellow flowers, with their distinctive violet markings, were profusely growing beside a rabbit track, leading to one of the innumerable burrows in the soft sand between the boulders. She sat down for a short rest, speculating about the last hours of the goldsmith and about that map which Ardal O'Lochlainn had seen him handle.

She would allow them to go on searching, but she was beginning to lose hope of finding anything more. No doubt it made sense to think that the murderer removed the hoard of gold; that formed a good motive for the crime. Tomorrow, she thought, she would have to begin a systematic questioning of the fishermen and their wives. She and Brigid would bring over the satchels belonging to the scholars so that each was equipped with pens, penknives, ink and small sheets of vellum and would be able to take down the details.

'Art, could you name me the ten families who are here at the moment,' she said when the time was up and they straggled back looking disappointed. She waited until all were seated on various rocks or clumps of marram grass around her. 'There will be twelve all together, of course,' she said before he could gather his thoughts. 'There is Brendan the samphire-gatherer, and his two sisters. And then, of course, there is Fernandez – perhaps I should say Fernandez and Etain.'

'Well, there's Muiris the Bridge, and then there's Roderic of the Rocks and Séan the Shark Slayer . . .' began Art and Mara smiled. The clan custom of bestowing nicknames to distinguish individual members made the fishermen and their families easy to remember. She remembered Séan the Shark Slayer, a large, powerfully built man, with a wide grin and enormous hands. He had wielded a pickaxe very effectively when finishing off the grave for the goldsmith from Galway.

It would be a small matter for someone of his stature to inflict a fatal blow on the skull of an elderly man.

Eight

Muirbrecho
(Sea Judgements)

Any judge who hears matters to do with the sea has to be well-versed in sea judgements, has to have knowledge of great depths, and be learned in three topics: in the ownership of flotsam, the ownership of jetsam and the ownership of goods carried off by the stream and either deposited downstream or carried out to sea.

Brigid was delighted to be invited to visit Fanore again. Cormac had announced the decision, not just to her, but to the women and children who were tending the fire and they set up a great cheer, which pleased the housekeeper immensely. While she, Séanín and Mara were riding home through the mountain pass, she was pondering over various dishes that they could bring and was delighted to hear that the cart was to be brought the following day. Séanín won her approval by suggesting a shoulder of pork and that, she thought, with some roasted onions, carrots and parsnips would make a fine meal for those unfortunate enough to be confined to fish for most of their lives.

'Put some meat on the bones of those poor children,' she said, approving of her own plans. Mara had thought the children all looked very well, lean, brown-faced and agile, but she did not contradict Brigid.

'You ride ahead, Séanín, and tell Eileen to have the bread on the griddle so that it's ready when we come,' commanded Brigid and waited until the boy was well ahead of them both before saying to Mara: 'Finbar doesn't look well, not well at all.'

'I know,' said Mara with a sigh. 'I suppose you've heard.'

Brigid didn't bother replying to that. Of course she had heard. She knew everything that was to be known about the business of the law school; she had been employed there at Cahermacnaghten since she was fourteen years old.

'You couldn't give him another chance,' she said tentatively.

'I can't, Brigid, it's against the rules. In any case, it's going to get harder and harder for him as he grows older. The work will get far too difficult.'

'He's got beautiful handwriting and draws wonderful pictures,' said Brigid wistfully.

'That's true,' said Mara with a sigh.

'Cormac says that his father won't have him back in his own household so he is going to ask the King for money to set Finbar up as a fisherman,' said Brigid with approval.

'I'm not sure that it's so easy to become a fisherman,' said Mara wryly. Her son had an optimistic temperament, but it was hard enough for the existing fishermen to make a living without having an untrained boy suddenly entering the business. However, Brigid was right about Finbar's nice handwriting and his ability to draw little sketches was admired by all of the scholars. There was, after all, a wider world out there than one of farmers and fishermen, with a few professionals such as lawyers, physicians, and craftsmen such as blacksmiths and carpenters. All of these professions and crafts required that a boy should start to learn them at a young age, but then there were people like her son-in-law who had started something completely new when he was already a grown man and who had made a wonderful success of buying goods made by others and selling them into different markets, both at home and abroad in France and Spain. She wished now that she had discussed the matter with Oisín and then an idea suddenly came to her and she nodded with satisfaction.

Mara was a busy woman with a school to run, the laws and justice of a kingdom to administer, two households and a farm with numerous servants – it was always satisfying to her when two different problems might be solved with one expedition. She thought back to the time when she had gone to Galway City, in the time of the notorious Mayor Lynch – it must have been in the February of 1512, more than nine years previously, she thought.

And now the long-buried Mayor Lynch's brother-in-law,

Valentine Blake, held the position of mayor in that city. For old times' sake, she was sure that he could help her in the two matters which now troubled her. A visit to Galway was an essential. She would go there on Monday morning.

Early on Sunday the cart was loaded with all of Brigid's belongings, the half cooked shoulder of pork in its cauldron with its tasty vegetables grouped around it and pots containing Brigid's famous sauces, a small casket of wine and a larger one of ale, some firewood in case all the driftwood had been used up, and a basket filled with the scholars' favourite honey cakes. Séanín was to accompany them, on condition, according to Brigid, that he did not get above himself, and he loaded the cart with great goodwill and then came back to carry out the satchels from the school house and place them carefully into a box at the back of the cart. He harnessed the big carthorse in a competent way and Mara thought approvingly that he was a bright boy who could well be an understudy for Cumhal as a farm manager, if Cumhal ever consented to think of retirement.

The fishing boats were all moored by the pier when they arrived. Some of the fishermen were dozing on the warm sand of the upper beach, while others were busy packing the smoked fish into wooden barrels. The air was full of the complicated smells and scents of driftwood, seaweed and the crisp aromatic smoke from hazel shells collected the autumn before from the thousands of hazel bushes that grew everywhere on the Burren.

'Brings me back, that does,' said Brigid, sniffing the air hungrily. 'We used to do that when I was a girl, save all the hazel shells from the nuts that we ate during the winter and then use them to smoke the mackerel in the summer. My mother used to leave a small barrel by the fireplace and into it would go every single hazel shell – or else there would be trouble.'

'Taste one, Brehon,' said Setanta, listening to the reminiscence with a smile. 'Cliona swears that it's the best of all, better even than smoked with seaweed.'

Mara took the mackerel, proffered on an enormous scallop shell, and shared it with Brigid. It did taste delicious, she thought, and the hazelnut shells lent a sweet nuttiness to the fish.

'Mind you, nowadays, I'd think that they would be better using apple wood – that's what I use to smoke our ham,' said Brigid in an undertone to Mara. Her tone was slightly sad and Mara understood that, like lots of things, the memory of the past was more potent for Brigid than the taste of the present.

'Wait until they taste your pork,' returned Mara and this had the double effect of allowing her not to take sides on the issue of what was the best method of smoking mackerel, and also of getting Brigid away from herself and the scholars and on to her preparations.

It was time that they all began work on the affair of the dead man in the boat.

'There are two main questions,' she told her scholars. 'First of all, when you are interviewing the fishermen and shore-dwellers, I think that you should ask whether they had ever heard of, or had ever encountered, antique pieces of gold on the beach. And the second question – just as important, in fact, perhaps more important, you must ask whether any of them had ever ferried Niall Martin, the goldsmith from Galway City, to these shores.' And then, having briefed them, she dismissed them to their tasks, walking back up to the fishermen and addressing them for a brief moment, explaining the scholars' role and beseeching their help in tracing the dead man and finding out what had happened to him during his last hours of life.

Domhnall and Slevin soon had the scholars scattered over the beach at their makeshift stone tables. Domhnall had taken Art's list and had distributed the ten fishermen among the scholars. Many of the wives had come too, amused and interested and already fond of the young people from the law school. There now seemed, it appeared to Mara, to be an atmosphere of not caring much, almost as though the accident of the boat – whether or not it had come from Fanore – had been wiped away once it had been buried in the sandy soil of the graveyard outside the little church.

'Yes, I met him a couple of times.' To her startled amazement the voice was that of Setanta, Cormac's foster-father. He was being interviewed by Slevin and Finbar and his voice was loud, clear and unconcerned. Mara had known Setanta for most of his life. Long before he had married Cliona and become stepfather to Art, and subsequently foster-father to Cormac, he had been known to Brigid and to the household at Cahermacnaghten as a reliable purveyor of fresh fish and shellfish on Fridays and on the eves of saints' days. Cormac, her son, was devoted to Setanta and his wife and, to Mara's secret jealousy and chagrin, Cliona was far more Cormac's mother than Mara had ever been. 'Brehon', he invariably called his birth mother, but Cliona was known by the softer, more intimate term '*Muimme*'. He respected the 'Brehon', but he went for comfort and for love to Cliona. If there was any involvement of either Setanta or of Cliona in this matter of the death of the gold merchant from Galway, that would, she knew, be a serious blow to Cormac. She was conscious of a feeling of fear in her heart at the thought of any possibility of guilt attaching to those two people who were of such vital importance to her son. Despite trusting Slevin, she felt compelled to listen to what was being said and walked towards the slab of rock where he had perched himself with Finbar at his side.

Slevin was a good interviewer and he kept his head well, despite an inevitable moment of surprise, thought Mara as, unobtrusively, she moved closer to where the two boys sat. Unless Setanta looked around, he would not notice her and the line of rocks here partially screened her from his view.

'So you knew him well, did he employ you?' came Slevin's calm, relaxed voice.

'He did, indeed,' said Setanta. Mara listened closely, trying to decide whether or not she heard a slight note of strain in his voice.

'So what did he want you to do for him?'

Finbar had said nothing and that, thought Mara, was probably his decision. Her older scholars were well trained to give a chance to the younger ones to ask questions if they wished.

'Oh, he just wanted to have a bit of fresh air on a Sunday. He was stuck in a stuffy little shop from Monday to Friday, so on summer evenings at weekends, he liked to get away and get out on the sea, and walk on sands. That's what he told me, anyway.' Setanta's tone was quite unconcerned.

Slevin made a note and Mara admired the way that he

allowed a long pause to intervene – a pause that asked its own question.

'I didn't recognize him when I saw him lying in that boat and that's God's honest truth,' said Setanta defensively, after a moment, 'but then when Oisín O'Davoren was so sure, well then I recognized him. It's a matter of eight months or so since I've seen him,' he explained. 'And so the Brehon thinks that he came here for some purpose, is that right?'

'That's right.' Slevin threw an air of confidentiality into his voice. 'We think that he might have come here to meet someone.' He beamed at Setanta and Mara suppressed a grin at his inventiveness. 'So you weren't the only one to bring him over here?' Slevin had a very relaxed manner of questioning.

'Lord bless you, no,' said Setanta. His voice rose up to a pitch that carried well across the water. 'That's right, isn't it, lads? That gold merchant was always coming over here?'

There were a few subdued murmurs though most of the fisherfolk looked taken aback and rather appalled at Setanta's outspokenness.

'But why did he come?' Mara decided that it was time she took a hand in the questioning so she came forward and looked around, appealing to everyone. 'After all,' she said, 'if the gold merchant wanted just fresh air and a rest from the city there were other places much nearer for him to go to. What about Salt Hill? What about Spiddal?'

Her intervention, she thought afterwards, was ill-advised. Slevin had been doing well by himself. She should have said nothing, not all the fishermen had the same open relationship with her as had Setanta. In truth, the very fact of his relationship to her, through the fostering of her son Cormac, might make him slightly suspect. Others around had heard Setanta's words and had listened to her rejoinder. The effect had been to make them clam up instantly. Only Brendan was willing to admit that he had ferried the goldsmith over from Galway on a few occasions – didn't know why the man came; took no interest in his doings; remembered the first time that he came; was tired out when he arrived; had gone up to their house at Morroughtuohy, just north of Fanore beach; he had breakfast and then had gone to help Etain who was collecting samphire on the rocks, and when they had filled all of the baskets in the hold the man suddenly appeared and climbed on board very quickly, 'almost as though,' said Brendan, with an air of wonder which Mara found to be rather false, 'almost as though he did not want to be seen.' His eyes went around the group and found those of the farmer, Michelóg. Mara could swear that a look was passed between them, even that a question had been asked and replied to in the negative.

By the time that all the twelve families had been interviewed Mara had begun to get irritated. Standing aloof from them all and wearing a stern expression, she requested Domhnall to gather them all together, men, women and children. She waited until all stood before her and then addressed them.

'I must confess,' she said evenly, 'that I am feeling rather puzzled. When the dead man, Niall Martin, the goldsmith from Galway City, was first discovered on the strand by little Síle, Brendan and Etain's younger sister, you were all asked whether you recognized him and none, if I remember rightly, expressed any recognition of him.'

Glances were being exchanged, though heads remained immoveable, each looking straight at her. They reminded her slightly of a flock of sheep, standing very close to each other, eyeing a strange dog and wondering whether ill boded for the flock. Despite herself she softened. Apart from Fernandez, and perhaps Brendan and his sister Etain, these fisherfolk were possibly among the poorest of the kingdom. The O'Connor clan had originated in Corcomroe and then a split in leadership, and a fortunate inheritance, several hundreds of years ago had led to land being acquired in the Kingdom of the Burren and a new clan established there. However, the lands that they held were small and families large. The majority of the O'Connor clan on the Burren had taken to fishing as a way of life and the three other clans, the O'Lochlainns, the MacNamaras and the O'Briens, had been glad to barter goods and silver for a steady supply of fish to satisfy their taste and the religious observation of no meat on Fridays and fast days which the Church endeavoured to enforce.

'It was the wig, Brehon,' said Setanta eventually and his voice sounded defensive. 'He was bald when we saw him in the past. I haven't seen him myself for months.'

'Bald as a coot,' said Muiris with emphasis.

'Looked quite different, didn't he? Didn't recognize him at all,' said Séan the Shark Slayer.

'Funny the difference that hair makes to a man's face,' said one of the women.

'Changes the shape of it entirely,' agreed another.

'I see,' said Mara, glad to accept this excuse. Privately she considered that they had all come to an agreement, whether voiced or unvoiced, that this was none of their business and that considering the man was found in a local, though abandoned, boat, all knowledge of him should be denied.

And, of course, it made sense that Niall Martin had made several visits to Fanore beach. Looking for a buried hoard would have been very difficult. Had he succeeded? She feared that he had and that he had been murdered for gold.

'And the boat, the boat with no oars, was that known to you?' she queried and then added swiftly, 'I myself thought that I had recognized it as an old boat that had been beached over there between two sand-dune hillocks. Did anyone else recognize it?'

After a moment Setanta spoke. 'It could be that it was that one, Brehon,' he admitted. 'It's been there for so long that I, for one, had forgotten about its existence.'

There was a murmur of agreement and faces brightened a little, most of them glancing longingly back towards the top of the beach where the fires still smouldered and the neat, flat, triangular-tailed shapes of the mackerel, hanging from the well-soaked twigs, showed faintly through the grey-blue haze of the smoke. She would have to let them go soon – she had no wish to allow their catch to spoil from lack of attention.

'Now that we have established that this mysterious stranger was known to you all,' she said mildly, 'perhaps you would tell my scholars when you took him here from Galway, how long he stayed at the beach here in Fanore, any conversation that you can remember, anything that he took back with him that he had not brought with him. In fact,' she finished, looking around keenly, 'any detail which may help me in the search for anyone who murdered a man here only days ago. Fernandez, could I have a word with you?'

She waited until all were occupied, some going back up to tend to the fires, others clustering around one or other of the scholars seated on the rocks with ink pots beside them and leather satchels on their knees. And then she strolled aside with him a little.

'And you?' she queried. 'Were you, too, deceived by the wig?'

'Never saw him in my life before, wig, or no wig,' Fernandez said, lifting his hands in mock-surrender. 'I think you're scaring the life out of them, poor things,' he said with a warmth which she found rather endearing. 'They have a hard life; they don't want any complications, and, you know, every single one of these people here have lost a relation to the sea. A dead body doesn't mean that much to them.'

Mara nodded. She wondered whether if her scholars had not been present the man would have been hastily buried and no one the wiser. A close-knit community like this would keep its secrets. And Fernandez? Well, she reckoned he would have gone along with their decision. This matter was hindering his great money-making design, and, also, it might affect his relationship with the merchants, innkeepers and shopkeepers of Galway City. The sooner that it was forgotten, the better he would be pleased.

'Do you think the murderer should be found?' she challenged him directly and was interested to see the look of annoyance on his face.

'If it does any good to anyone,' he said shortly.

'The law of the land must be upheld,' said Mara, still watching him. 'The law is the King's law, it flows from him to his chieftains and is administered by the Brehon of the Kingdom. I think that the King would consider any man who did not uphold the law to be unsuitable for the position of *taoiseach*.' There was a mild threat behind her words and she did not regret it. Who was he to play God and to say whether death of a man against the law of the kingdom did not matter?

She left him to think about this and went to collect the results from her scholars. There was still remarkably little information. Five of the ten fishermen had admitted to taking a strange man with a bald head from Galway to Fanore beach about a year or so, ago, and to taking him back again within a space of a couple of hours. None had admitted a more recent visit. They had been paid well – a silver penny for the journey. The man had brought a leather bag with him each time and no one had noticed whether there was something in it or not. None had seen a map in his hands, but then he had quickly disappeared behind rocks as soon as he had got out of the boat.

'And none of them speculated on what he was doing, is that right?' Mara asked Domhnall.

'None related their thoughts to us on that subject, Brehon,' he corrected her gently and she had to smile at his precision and his acute mind. She turned and began to walk down towards the sea and he accompanied her, knowing instinctively that she needed a sounding board for her thoughts.

'You see, all of this may have nothing to do with the murder, Domhnall,' she said after a minute. 'It could well be as Fernandez says . . .' And then she related to him her conversation. 'On the other hand,' she continued, 'it seems to me to be very unlikely that they didn't keep an eye on him, didn't wonder what he was up to. After all, these children here have been scrambling over rocks as soon as they are able to stand – didn't anyone ask them to keep an eye on the stranger, to check whether he was gathering seaweed or shellfish or looking for rare seashells, or something like that – something that they could have understood? It just doesn't make sense to me, Domhnall.'

'And if he came to look for gold and went back, time after time, empty-handed,' put in Domhnall.

'But, on one occasion, a week ago, he perhaps found something,' said Mara. Her conscience began to trouble her about her other six scholars left by themselves in the middle of the beach, grouped around one of the squared-off black limestone table-like rocks. It was against her principles to favour one above the others. They must all feel that they were part of her investigations. Without saying any more, she turned and went back to them, seating herself on a dry spot and signalling to them to sit down. They perched on spots very near to her and she was pleased with their discretion. Her voice, she knew, was a carrying one. She had trained it from an early age, standing in an empty field at Poulnabrone where the ancient dolmen made a focal point for the administration of justice in the kingdom. Hour after hour, during her girlhood, she had aimed fragments of the law at the tall cliffs on the eastern edge of the field, waiting, as her father had taught her, for the echoes to die down before embarking on the next sentence. Here on the beach with the shrill, childlike cries of the trim, sea-grey kittiwakes calling overhead, the temptation was to raise her voice to compete with the sounds around her.

Instead she lowered it and forced them to lean close to her in order to catch her words.

'Did anyone admit to bringing the goldsmith over here from Galway four days ago?' she asked and waited for every head to be shaken before asking the next question. She kept her face turned down towards her scholars at her feet, but from the corner of her eye she could see that all the faces from the top of the beach were not turned towards their fires, or towards their barrels, but were angled down to where she sat.

'And did anyone catch sight of him before they saw the dead body?' She wished now that she had mentioned the matter of the wig to Oisín before he returned. At the time, she had thought it of little importance, many middle-aged to elderly men wore wigs in the City of Galway; she knew that and in this case it was only of interest because the false hair was made from springy horsehair and was so thickly woven onto a heavy woollen base that it had served to protect his skin from the force of the blow, even though the brain itself had been split.

As she had expected, no one had admitted to seeing the gold merchant on the fatal days before his murder.

'High tide was at about ten o'clock in the evening,' put in Cael. 'I asked Etain and she told me. I'd say that means he arrived some time between eight and twelve.'

'It seems impossible that no one saw him get out of a boat, even if the man who carried him is not willing to admit the truth,' said Mara. She hoped that her voice remained calm and judicial, but she was beginning to hate this case. It was a most

uncomfortable feeling to think that a whole community might
be pitting its wits against her. Was it just because the boat, in
which the dead man had lain, had belonged to Fanore, or was
there a more sinister reason?

'I was thinking that he might not have been put down at
Fanore at all,' said Cael. She looked impatiently at her friends
who were staring at her with mouths open. 'Birdbrains!' she
said with scorn. 'These small boats could land anywhere along
the coast – the men would know where it was shallow enough
to stick an oar into the sand and hold it steady while someone
scrambled out and onto the rocks.'

'That's good thinking, Cael,' said Mara. She had waited a
few seconds to see whether the others, Cian, Cormac, Art and
Finbar, would say something. Usually they were generous in
their praise when it was deserved, but now nothing was said.
Perhaps Cael, in her anger at being excluded from the boys'
camp on the sand dunes, had said something that they regarded
as unforgiveable. She would ignore the situation – Cael herself
didn't seem upset, just slightly puzzled – everything would be
forgotten within a few days. She sat and thought for a few
minutes and knew that the decision she had taken earlier was
the right one at this stage.

'I think,' said Mara eventually, 'that I shall go to Galway in
the morning. It is of the utmost importance that we do our
best to find if there are any more remains of an ancient hoard
of gold, but that is something you can do as well, if not better
than I can. So I will go to Galway and you scholars can go
on searching. I shall leave Domhnall in charge of you all. I
really do feel that it would be good to have the map that Ardal
O'Lochlainn saw with the goldsmith – after all, he just had
one short glance at it. Who knows, it may have more to reveal
that we can tell just now.'

She looked around at her scholars and said in a cursory way,
'I'll take one of you with me.' She looked them over, pretending
to endeavour to make up her mind and then said decisively,
'I think that I will take you, Finbar. You will be useful to me.'

Nine

Bretha Nemeð
(Laws dealing with Professional People)

Except when on military attacks, or when going on pilgrimage, or attending a fair, all inhabitants of a kingdom should stay within its boundaries. Only professional groups, such as poets, lawyers, physicians, and such like these, are permitted to travel to other kingdoms or states.

Mara and Finbar set off soon after dawn on the next morning. Her scholars had been surprised and a little scornful that she had not taken advantage of one of the boats going to Galway to sell the delicately smoked fish, or with Brendan and the streaming baskets of samphire in his magnificent new hooker, but Mara decided that she would prefer to ride and took Finbar back with her, leaving Cumhal's assistant, Séanín, in his place to assist with the gutting and smoking of the fish and the preparing of a midday meal.

'We'll probably have found the buried treasure by the time you get back,' said Cormac optimistically and then looked apologetically at Finbar who seemed to have winced slightly. 'Or we'll probably wait until you get back until we do it,' he said quickly.

'It's not going to be shared out amongst you all, you know,' said Mara. 'This is not a treasure hunt, Cormac. What we are looking for is to unravel the mystery of this goldsmith's death, to find out where the death occurred and then who was responsible for it.'

Cormac nodded in an off-hand way but Mara had the feeling that, as usual, he was only half-listening to her. He was young, she thought, and tried to remember what other lively scholars of hers had been like at that age. It was no good comparing her son with Domhnall; he had been logical

and sensible at even five years old and Slevin had come to
the school at the same time as Domhnall, though a year
younger, and had fallen tremendously under Domhnall's
influence, admiring and copying him in every respect. Still,
she thought, Cormac was a different character completely and
she would make no decisions about his future until a few
more years elapsed.

Mara and Finbar set off early, but it was almost noon when
they arrived at the gates of the city. Mara had often visited
Galway – her married daughter, Sorcha, son-in-law, Oisín, and
Domhnall's younger sister and brother lived there – but for
Finbar it was his first visit. He had been very silent on the
journey and she had given up trying to get him to talk and
had eventually allowed him to ride behind her and occupied
her mind with thinking about the Galway connection to this
murder.

But at the first sight of the great stone city surrounded by
a high wall and packed with tall houses, built side by side,
Finbar's depression seemed to slip from him. Mara had
mentioned the name of Mayor Valentine Blake to the soldier
on guard at the gates and they were ushered in and told that
the Mayor was in his castle and Finbar was very impressed by
the salutes of the military and the shouts of '*Make way for the
lady!*' Used to the open spaces, the scattered cottages and the
widely separated enclosures of the Burren, he was astounded,
Mara could see, by the sheer volume of buildings pressing in
on them and he rode down the middle of the street, with his
head continually turning from one side to the other and staring
upwards with a stunned expression. In fact, a very large amount
of the buildings in the city were tower houses or even small
castles and they reared high up above their heads, their castel-
lated roofs outlined against the sky. The streets were well paved
with limestone cobbles – a drain running down the centre of
each street and a narrow pavement for pedestrians on either
side. It was a city built around a western seaport on the Atlantic
Ocean, and despite the crowds of people and numerous houses
it was fresh and airy even on this hot day in late June. They
rode through it, Mara directing their steps towards the northern
wall, just where the River Corrib entered the sea.

'Amazing, the amount of people, isn't it?' said Mara after a while. She wondered whether Finbar was overwhelmed by the noise and by the sheer numbers of people and buildings that pressed upon them.

'It would be a good place to get lost,' said Finbar. A rather surprising sentiment, she thought, and wondered whether perhaps he felt that he would be glad to get away from the pity of his fellow scholars and the concern of his teachers. She could understand this and decided that she would have a word with the others and try to get them to treat Finbar in a more normal way. She did not bother him with any more questions, just allowed him to look his fill at all the wonders around him.

Finbar exclaimed with excitement when he saw their destination. Blake's castle was very splendid. In fact, Mara thought that it was the most splendid and the largest building in the city of Galway. It had been newly built when she first saw it, ten years ago, and even now the white surface of the limestone walls, the towers and the battlements shone and glittered – almost as white as quartz. It was in a wonderful position, with the restless blue and white inlet of the Atlantic Ocean as a backdrop and surrounded by neat gardens, well walled and guarded from any marauders. Above its gates was a stone shield, with the figure of a cat standing out in bold relief and painted black. Beneath it were the words '*Virtus sola Nobilitat*' pricked out in gold and black, and Mara drew Finbar's attention to this.

He did not question whether it was true that virtue alone ennobled the merchant princes of Galway, or whether successful trading played its part. Others of her scholars, like Cormac and the two MacMahon twins, would have done so, she knew. And she began to think that it was just as well that a decision was now forced upon her about his future. To be a Brehon, logic, reasoning, memory – all of these things had to be present but, above all, the mind itself had to be a lively one, not willing to take anything on trust until it was proved to be true. A Brehon had to be, above all, someone who questioned and who probed. That, she thought, was not Finbar.

Servants came forward to take their horses as soon as they

came through the gate, and Mara guessed from their excessive courtesy that she had been spotted from a window. A moment later the door was thrown open and a handsome dark-eyed man, whose hair was just beginning to turn grey, came to the door and called out exuberantly:

'Welcome! Welcome, Brehon! Welcome to Galway! Come in, come in.'

The interior matched the glamour of the exciting exterior. As Finbar walked through the front door, held open by her host, he gasped and stood very still, gazing around him, his eyes wide with amazement. Mara was not surprised – she had felt like that, the first time she had seen Valentine Blake's place. It did show, though, that Brigid was right. Finbar, as she had said, did not just have the most beautiful handwriting, but he was also very artistic.

And, of course, the hall was magnificent. Finbar's eyes wandered from wall to wall and then fixed themselves on the spectacular floor that, as Mara remembered from her last visit, appeared to mirror the colour of the ocean outside the windows. The whole expanse was tiled in grey-green marble, flecked here and there with subtle pinpoints of cream, just as the foam of the ocean highlighted its emerald depths.

'That's Connemara marble,' she said to Finbar and he nodded and then sank to his knees, while Valentine looked at him with amusement. Finbar was touching the glossily smooth surface, so unlike the rough flagstone slabs that formed the floors of the school and the Brehon's house at Cahermacnaghten. Here and there mirrors with gilded frames were placed on the walls, tilted at an angle so that they reflected the green of the marble. Heavy oak court cupboards, dark with polish, were placed against the white walls, but the room was dominated by that magnificent floor and Finbar's glowing eyes went back to it again and again.

The boy certainly is an artist, thought Mara and so, of course, in his own way, is Valentine Blake. However, she would allow time for the Mayor of Galway to assess the boy so merely said:

'I'm here to beg your help, Valentine, and to report to you

the sad fate of one of your citizens, one goldsmith. Niall Martin was his name.'

'*Was!*' Valentine was as quick as ever and had seized upon the word which she had used unthinkingly.

'Was . . .' she agreed.

'Let's go upstairs,' said Valentine. 'We can be private there.' He half-glanced at Finbar, but Mara said immediately, 'This is Finbar, one of my law-school scholars. Finbar, the mayor has just as beautiful a floor upstairs, come and see it. And a very beautiful room, if I remember it correctly.'

Once again the long floor of the room above was of the cream-flecked grey-green marble, but here the tiles were overlaid in places with colourful woven rugs in rich shades of raspberry-red and sea-blue. The walls of the room were panelled in dark gold wood that smelled of lavender polish. Small, precious tapestries hung on the walls, and sconces of sweet-smelling beeswax candles were placed in front of more gilt-framed mirrors. It was all as she had remembered it – a masterpiece produced by an artist with plenty of silver.

'Sit down, Brehon,' said Valentine heartily, 'and we'll have a glass of wine, first. I know how much you like a good burgundy and I have one that I think you will appreciate. And then you can tell me your business. Come and help me, Finbar.' Finbar crossed the room with him happily, his face flushed with colour, his head turning from side to side and his eyes full of wonder. Mara thought that she had never seen him look like this before. He held up a beautifully engraved glass as though it were the Holy Grail and only came to with a start when he realized that Valentine was waiting, decanter in hand, and a smile on his lips.

'You'll stay the night, both of you, won't you? It will be a kindness to me as I am on my own. My wife and son – would you believe it, he is quite a young man now, almost ten years old – well, they are both away visiting her parents, so you will stay, won't you?' queried Valentine.

Mara shook her head. 'I need to get back,' she said. 'I have some urgent business and the days are long at the moment. It's an easy ride. We will certainly be back in the Burren before it's dark.'

'At least have a midday meal with me,' he urged.

'I will, then, since you are so kind,' she said graciously. 'Could I ask one more favour of you? The last time that I was here I took my scholars to Blake's Pie Shop on Bridge Gate Street and I promised Finbar to take him there.' She told the lie unblushingly, before adding, carelessly, 'I remember we had a pie there with apricots in it. I wonder do they still make such pies?'

'Indeed they do; it's a speciality of the house,' exclaimed Valentine. 'Old Mr Blake is dead now, but his daughter runs the place. Apricots are her great love. We supply her with plates bearing a pattern of apricot leaves – well, when I say "we" I have to confess that I don't have much to do with the pottery these days – much too busy – it's no easy task being lord mayor of a city that is growing as fast as Galway and the trade links are increasing every day with all of this going and coming to the new world. Galway makes a good place to stop off. My nephew is running the pottery and making a great success of it. Yes, of course we'll have a meal at the pie shop. I'll send a servant down to tell Joan that we will be with her in an hour or so.' He was off in a moment and Mara sat there, gathering her thoughts and wondering the best way to handle the two affairs which had brought her to Galway.

When Valentine came back, Finbar, his ale untouched, was examining a tapestry of a unicorn, a small smile curving his lips. Mara had decided on a plan of action and immediately said: 'Finbar would love to see your pottery. Would it be possible? Would your nephew mind?'

'I think,' said Valentine, 'that any visitor from Mara, Brehon of the Burren, would be welcomed by him. Drink your ale, Finbar and I'll find a boy to guide you.'

When he came back, he wore a grin. 'So, how is that lad working out as a law student?' he asked bluntly, lifting an eyebrow at her.

Mara smiled back. This was the easiest part of her visit. She didn't think that he would say no to her, especially if it was made plain that the arrangement was to be a temporary one unless both sides were happy with it.

'His father has threatened to throw him out because he has twice failed his examinations,' she said, knowing that would engage his sympathies. 'He is well educated, writes a beautiful hand, draws well, and I have a feeling that he is very artistic – and that perhaps a trade such as pottery or engraving might suit him better than the law,' she said, mentally excusing herself to Brigid, who after all, was the one who had first voiced this observation.

'I could use a boy like that, and he might do very well at the pottery, but initially I could take him on as a sort of secretary and messenger and we could see how it goes.'

'Don't say anything to him yet, will you? I'd have to speak to his father first. The decision has to be his. The boy is well under the age of seventeen. In any case, I would suggest that you take him on just for the summer months to start with, and then you could review it and it gives his father a chance to reverse any decision made in anger,' said Mara firmly. Her husband, King Turlough, would be back quite soon from his visit to O'Donnell in the north of the Ireland, so if Finbar and Valentine did not suit, then something else could be arranged for the boy. Whatever happened he was not going to be turned loose on the world at the age of fourteen. Fourteen-year-olds should be protected from themselves as well as from a harsh world, she thought, looking back at her first marriage when she was no older than Finbar and how disastrous that had been. Her father had warned her against Dualta, had told her that the boy was idle, too fond of drink, too fond of girls, but she had not taken his advice and he, out of weakness, or out of his deep affection for his daughter, had allowed her to go her own way.

'Finbar is in a state of despair at the moment,' she said aloud. 'He worries me; he hardly said a word to me on the way over here.'

'Leave him here with me, now, if you wish.' He sounded eager to help.

'No,' she said. 'I'll take him back with me. He's not mine to dispose of so don't say anything to the boy until we find out whether the father will agree. It would be cruel to raise his hopes only to have them disappointed again. Have a look at him today, though, and ask Walter, your nephew, what he thinks. It won't do any harm for Finbar to see that there are different ways of making a living other than the very difficult route to qualifying as a lawyer. It will do him good to talk with Walter and see how happy he is. Oisín, my son-in-law, the merchant, tells me that Walter is universally liked and esteemed in the business world here in Galway, and that the plates and bowls that he makes sell very well in France and in England.'

'And he never forgets how much he owes to you,' said Valentine, adding hastily, 'But it shall be as you please; you know that you can ask any favour of me, as well as of Walter. We both owe you much. Now, tell me what else brings you here. You spoke of Niall Martin. I know – knew the man. What happened to him?'

Mara paused for a moment, gathering her thoughts. 'Niall Martin came, apparently on many occasions during the last few years, to the seashore on the north-western side of the Burren, to a place called Fanore – a name which is made up of two Gaelic words, the one meaning "slope" and the other meaning "gold", so the golden slope.'

'Referring to the sand?'

'Perhaps,' she said, not committing herself. 'There are reports that Niall Martin engaged various fishermen from our kingdom – people who sometimes sold fish in Galway – to take him over, leave him for a few hours to explore the area, and then to return with him.'

'Odd!' He brooded over this for a few minutes. 'Not a man that I would have expected to be interested in exploring the countryside, or venturing into enemy territory. If he wanted sea air, well, why not go to Salt Hill?'

'My own thoughts exactly,' said Mara and waited to see what conclusion he would come to.

'In fact,' he went on, without acknowledging her words, 'there is only one thing that I would think that he was interested in and that was his trade. He spent all his days in that dark little shop of his in Red Earl's Lane – not far from here – near to the fish market – you'll probably remember the place – and never employed even a boy to help him.'

'How did he dress?' asked Mara.

'Very fine,' said Valentine immediately. 'He was very careful
of his appearance. I'd say myself that he wore a wig – the
hair looked too thick and too much of a good colour for a
man of his age – didn't go with his skin – but if he did, it
was a very good one. They say that you can get ones that
you glue to the scalp and no one is the wiser – or so my
wife tells me.' He swept a hand over his thinning grey hairs
and grinned at her ruefully. He was still, she thought, as she
smiled back at him, an extremely handsome man.

'Yes, he was wearing a wig when he was killed,' she said.
'He was killed by a blow to the head with some heavy but
padded object, and, of course, the thickness of the wig, with
the horsehair and the woollen cap that the hair was attached
to, well, according to the physician who examined the body,
both of these helped to absorb the blow. But when he came
to the Burren on other occasions, by evidence of the fishermen
who took him, he was not wearing a wig; "*bald as a coot*" as
someone described him.'

'Trying to disguise himself,' suggested Valentine. 'He would
look different with a bald head. I mightn't even recognize him
myself. It was the first thing that you noticed about him – he
wore his hair very fine, right down to his shoulders. Do you
know why he was killed?'

'Not yet,' said Mara, 'and, of course, you will understand if
I don't discuss any half-formed theories, any guesses with you.'

'Of course,' he echoed, though he looked slightly disappointed. 'And, so, tell me what I can do for you. I'm sure that
you didn't come all the way just to announce the death of
Niall Martin to me, though of course I will proclaim it in the
court and discuss what is to be done about it and about tracing
any relations.'

'I'd like to look at his shop, at his residence and at his papers,
if that is possible, and I will need your authority for that,' she
said. She smiled at him. 'You see, I remember from my visit
here all those years ago, that the Mayor of Galway acts as a
judge, in the same way as the Duke of Venice.'

'Have you his keys?'

Mara shook her head. 'He was dressed just in a shirt and

hose when I saw him,' she said, deciding not to give any further details.

'I see,' he said. 'We'll have to break in, won't we?' He gave a sudden, rather boyish grin. 'It shouldn't be too difficult. Would you like to wait here, or to come with me?'

'I'll come with you; I'd like to see the streets of Galway again.'

And, indeed, she thought, it was quite a contrast to her homeland on the Burren with its wide sweeping landscape of white limestone slabs lying flat on the uplands, or piled unevenly on the mountain slopes. Here in this tiny space, probably less than the distance between the law school and her nearest neighbour, Ardal O'Lochlainn at Lissylisheen Castle, a whole city was crammed. Instead of a single meadow paved with clints and boulders and grazed by cattle, there were hundreds of houses almost touching each other, and between them narrow streets – all, she thought, the product of the same limestone that covered the fields and formed the mountains of her homeland.

Valentine led the way rapidly until they reached the court-house. The court official bowed to them both with great respect. He remembered her, he said, and she remembered him and his kindness in finding a hot brick for her feet when she sat in the chilly courtroom, for which she thanked him, but he said nothing, just ushered Valentine into his office and went off in search of a locksmith.

'Are you returning the body to us?' asked Valentine, care-lessly scribbling a note and then signing it with a flourish.

'No, the body was beginning to decompose; we buried it.'

'So much the better,' said Valentine, touching a bell on his desk. 'Take this to Lawyer Skerrett to get it countersigned,' he said briefly. 'Just an order to break into the shop and dwelling place of Niall Martin,' he said when the man had departed. 'We'll have to seal it up afterwards, of course. There will be a treasure in gold lying around. I wonder who is the heir to it all? I've never known him to have a family, or even a visitor, I'd say.'

'My son-in-law, Oisín O'Davoren, the merchant, reported Niall Martin saying that he had neither kith nor kin and that he came originally from Bristol,' said Mara. 'That was one of the reasons why I took the decision to bury the body in the churchyard at Fanore.'

'Come now,' said Valentine looking cheerful, 'if that's the case, if he really has neither kith nor kin, then we can probably use the gold for a worthy purpose. The grammar school could do with an endowment. It will have to be decided by the Mayor and the bailiffs – you remember our system of government here – the mayor and the bailiffs have the power to dictate the use of all taxes and money collected – this, I think, if we make an honest effort to trace relations and then fail, this can be counted as a legacy to the City of Galway.'

Mara let him plan while she thought over the matter. Her concern was not with the gold, but with the loss of life. Murder must not be ignored or it can lead to further loss of life. The culprit had to be identified and the community notified of his guilt. The scales of retribution had to be balanced. In this case the fine would perhaps end up in the hands of the authorities of the City of Galway, but so be it. The law could not be bent or twisted in any way. '*No Brehon is able to abrogate anything that is written in the* Seanchas Mór. *In it are established laws for king and vassal; queen and subject; for taoiseach and liegeman; for the man of wealth and the poor man.*' It was one of the first things that her father had taught her when she was five years old and beginning work in the law school at Cahermacnaghten.

'Ah, here he comes,' said Valentine as a heavy step sounded on the stairs outside the room. 'Good day to you, Master Locksmith.' The court official slid the piece of vellum across to him with a scrawled countersignature of Anthony Skerrett, a law student in London when Mara had last visited Galway, but now, apparently, back working in his native Galway. Mara wondered briefly what had happened to the glamorous Catalina, and whether Anthony had married her. But then she decided that this visit was going to be too short a one to look up all of the people whom she had known during that visit in February of 1512.

'Let's go,' said Valentine, barely glancing at the signature. His authority was enough for any tradesman in the city, Mara reckoned as the locksmith nodded to her respectfully and preceded them down the stairs and along the narrow lane.

The gold merchant's shop was certainly a mean, small building. The only thing impressive or even new-looking about it was the huge oaken door with an iron lock. The mullioned window was tiny, and although it did have two sheets of glass on either side of the stone bar in the centre, the space was too tiny even for a two-year-old child to fit through.

The lock was massive, and secured to the wood with enormous nails. The locksmith grinned at the Mayor, produced several small instruments made of iron, fiddled around with them for a while and then there was a sudden click and the sound of something falling and he pushed the door gently open.

'Good that you are an honest man,' said Valentine, looking slightly taken aback at the ease with which the door had been opened.

'He keeps a lamp there on the counter,' volunteered the locksmith, not replying to Valentine's remark, but addressing himself to Mara. Quickly he found a tinderbox by the dim light that came through the opened door into the small, dark shop and lit the lamp for her.

'I'll have to put another lock onto it, your worship, unless he keeps a spare key hidden somewhere here,' he said to Valentine while Mara held the lamp aloft, examined the shelves that held little but dusty instruments of his trade, and then, remembering Ardal's words, she went behind the counter, lowered it and examined the shelves concealed from the public. There was a large safe, secured by another enormous lock, and above it were open boxes containing many bills of sale, neatly stored in wooden boxes, but one large scroll caught her eye. She did not move or touch it, though, until Valentine and the locksmith had gone back outside the street and were arguing over the security of the door.

'Three locks, that's what I would advise,' the locksmith was saying. 'Put one lock and a man can work on it quickly while the nightwatchman is in another place. Even two is a possibility if he knows his business, but I defy anyone to get three of my locks open without attracting attention.'

While they were arguing, Mara opened the scroll and had a moment's thankfulness that some instinct had led her to call in on Ardal O'Lochlainn. This was, indeed, a map of Fanore, done more carefully and much more accurately than her own, she thought with a quick glance. Resolutely she rolled it up again and thrust it into her satchel and then went to the door to join the other two.

'Finished your business?' enquired Valentine.

'Yes, indeed,' she said briskly. 'I found the document that I was looking for.' Quickly she took it from her satchel, showed it to him and then said: 'Let me give you a receipt. It shall be returned when I have solved the mystery of the man's death in the kingdom of my legal jurisdiction.'

He protested that this was unnecessary, but she made out a receipt, signed it and gave it to him, describing the document as a map of the seafront and surrounds of the bay of Fanore in the Kingdom of the Burren. He gave it a cursory glance and tucked it away and turned his attention to looking around the shop and her eyes followed his.

It would, she thought, be difficult to steal anything from this place. The back wall of the shop, behind the counter, was lined with shelves and heavy iron safes were placed on these and were, as additional safeguard, bolted to the stone wall. Valentine wandered along, looking up at them with interest, and calling her attention to the huge locks on every one of them.

'Where is your pottery, Valentine?' she said after a minute, seeing that locksmith was waiting for his attention. 'Shall I walk down and wait for you there? I'd like to meet your nephew again.'

Valentine, she guessed, now that he had thought of a worthy use for the goldsmith's treasure, was eager to make sure that the place was thoroughly sealed up and kept safe. Even as she walked down towards the docks she could hear the blows of a hammer on the tough wood of the door. Probably a couple of soldiers would be left there on duty, until the gold was safely in the hands of the city's banker, she thought as she made her way down towards the docks and the splendidly impressive pottery building, where Walter greeted her with great warmth and insisted on showing her over the whole premises.

'The last time I was here it was in February,' Mara told Finbar as they walked with Valentine towards the Pie Shop in Bridge Street. 'I remember that we all ate out of doors, though the frost was on the ground and there was a fire going within the yard and boys brought heated blocks of limestone for us to put our feet on.'

Finbar nodded and smiled a little, but he wasn't really listening. He seemed to be immersed in all he had seen and touched and there was a dazed expression on his face. He had had a wonderful time at the pottery, had been allowed to sketch a design of pansies onto one of the jugs and had the fun of painting it in clear yellow and violet. He was eager and responsive to the men working on the moulding of bowls, plates and pots and when Mara came in he hardly noticed her as he was watching everything so carefully, and she could see that young Walter Lynch, Valentine's nephew, looked impressed by the few timid suggestions that he made. And then Valentine asked him to copy out a bill of sale, scrutinized it carefully and appeared so impressed by the excellence of the neat script that Finbar glowed with pride. If only his father agreed then he could spend the summer months in Galway. He could stay with Walter in Lynch's Castle – they seemed to get on well, but Mara thought she would have a word with her daughter, when Sorcha came to spend her usual summer holiday – if necessary Oisín and Sorcha would have him to stay in her fine big house. He could occupy Domhnall's empty room and would have the companionship of her two remaining children until he found his feet and hired lodgings of his own. However, nothing could be said until Finbar's father had been consulted. He had placed his son in Mara's care so that she could instruct him in the law and the next step would have to be his.

By the time that they arrived at Blake's Pie Shop, Finbar was chattering eagerly about the pottery and Mara could see that his depression had lifted. Joan Blake, primed by the message from Valentine, recognized them instantly and ushered them to an outdoor table already set out with plates and large, colourful ceramic goblets.

'As good as any of your Venetian glassware,' boasted Valentine, pointing out how the white interiors set off the deep ruby red of the wine.

'Where on earth did you find such wonderful goblets, Joan?' enquired Mara and Joan giggled appreciatively and related that they came from the local pottery run by the Mayor and his nephew.

'Lord have mercy on us, the way that the years have passed,' she said in a nostalgic way to Mara. 'It seems only yesterday that you were here with all of your scholars. What has become of them all?'

'Well, Fachtnan, the oldest of them, now works as a teacher for me,' said Mara. 'Moylan has gone to work for the Brehon of Waterford, Aidan, the chap with all the jokes, he's employed in the north of Ireland . . .'

'And what about the little red-headed fellow, the one that spoke out so well in court?' asked Joan with a maternal sigh.

'Hugh, well, he decided that the law was not for him, so now he is working for his father the silversmith; better to find that out young than to go on with something that is not quite right for a person,' said Mara in a matter-of-fact way, though she had an eye on Finbar, 'and Shane, the youngest, the dark-haired boy,' she continued, 'is now working for his father up in Tyrone.' She did not add that Shane, even though just twenty-one years of age, had passed with great ease the last and most difficult of the law examinations and was now a fully-fledged Brehon. That would not be a tactful thing to say in front of Finbar.

'I remembered your pies,' she said aloud. 'I've often told my scholars about them and I promised my scholar Finbar that we would not leave Galway until he had tasted one. In fact,' she went on, seizing the opportunity while Valentine went over to have a word with a friend, 'I was reminded of that wonderful pie with apricots by a visit to our area from the goldsmith of this city, one Niall Martin. He had a taste for your pies, did he not?'

Finbar, she noticed from the corner of her eye, had become

very still, but he had the sense to say nothing. Joan nodded easily.

'I'd say that he had every one of my pies,' she said. 'He'd work his way through them – sometimes he'd pop out of his shop, give a lad a farthing to bring a message to me about what he wanted for his dinner and if I could, well I'd do my best – it wouldn't be every time that I could, mark you, because I'm dependent on what the ships bring in and what is in season. Funny you should mention *apricots*,' she went on, 'because the last time that he came in here, it must have been this day week, yes, it was a Monday – well, he sent a message to ask if he could have a chardquince pie, but when he came I told him straight to his face that he had to give me notice of a few days if he wanted quince – because at this time of the year I only have the dried stuff and I have to soak it, you see, so he had to make do with the apricot, after all. He complained a bit but I didn't pay him much heed. I was busy talking to a girl about samphire.'

'A girl, was it someone from Galway? Was she with Niall Martin?' asked Mara, casually adding, 'Do tell me about chardquince pie – I've never had that before.'

'I can do better than tell you, you can have a slice and see how you like it. Fresh is best, of course, but they store well and even the dried stuff keeps its flavour. You come back in September and I'll make chardquince pie for you then from fruit just plucked. I grow the quinces myself on the garden wall at the back here and I tell you I have to fight the birds for them. I've even tried putting bags made from pieces of netting over them, and would you believe it, a bold thief of a grey crow just swooped down and broke the stem and carried one off, bag and all.'

Mara had begun to think that she had been too clever in hiding the question as Joan turned to go back into the kitchen, but then she came back.

'And I'm getting fresh samphire from the girl and her brother every few days now. I've been using it as a side dish, but I want to make a speciality out of it now that the summer fruits are nearly over and we have a gap before the fresh apples and the quinces. I've been thinking over my mind what would go with samphire best. What do you think?'

'I'm not sure,' said Mara doubtfully. 'I'm not much of a
cook.' She was dying to revert to Niall Martin and to the question whether he had been with or seen to speak to the
samphire girl when he ate his apricot pie on his last day in
Galway, but Joan's mind was now completely occupied with
a culinary question and her face showed that she was deep
in thought.

'Salmon,' she said triumphantly, just as Valentine came back
to the table. 'Salmon – I've just thought of that. It would
taste good and would look good. Nice fresh pink salmon with
a butter sauce and the samphire arranged in a trellis pattern
over it.'

'That sounds great,' said Valentine eagerly.

'Walter could make plates that would show the pie up properly,' said Finbar thoughtfully and Mara smiled to herself at the
intervention. Finbar had already begun to identify with the
pottery business.

'We could do you one divided into eight wedges – I've seen
one like that in Spain. It was coloured yellow and the decor-
ations were in pale blue,' suggested Valentine and Joan pursed
her lips, unwilling to disagree, but obviously not too impressed.

'Black,' said Finbar suddenly. His eyes had gone to a large
round pie that was carried in by one of Joan's assistants. 'Plain
black, with a good glaze to make it shine; that would be best;
you will have enough colour with the piecrust, the salmon
and the samphire.'

'That's the boy that has the good eye,' said Joan beaming as
she went back out into the kitchen. A moment later she re-
appeared with another steaming orange pie on a white plate
with a pattern of green leaves. 'There you are,' she said. 'That's
my chardquince pie. You just tell me what you think of that,
Brehon.'

Neatly she detached a triangular portion and slid it onto a
thin wooden platter and put it in front of Mara.

'Delicious!' Mara nibbled a little. The egg pastry, Joan's
speciality, melted in her mouth. The filling, though beautifully
cooked, was, in fact, a little sweet for her taste, but her mouth
watered at the thought of what a cook like Joan could do with
the silky smoothness of salmon flesh and the salty crispness of

the samphire. She would have to pay another visit to Galway in the early autumn, perhaps in September before the Michaelmas term started. If all was settled for Finbar it would be her duty to visit him from time to time and to see that he was happy, she told herself, and Sorcha was always begging her to come and stay and to have a complete rest from all her responsibilities.

'What's in it?' she asked and listened with half an ear as Joan related the quantities of mashed-up quince and the two cups of white wine, the sugar, the egg yolks, nodding wisely at the mention of the exotic spices of cinnamon and ginger, but her mind was working busily. *Samphire*, she said to herself. Surely this can be no coincidence. However, Mara's mind was a well-disciplined one and she was used to listening so she allowed no sign of impatience to escape until eventually Joan came back to the question of the new pie, wondering whether Valentine could get her some lemons on his next shipment from Spain.

'Would lemon go with the samphire, though?' enquired Mara innocently.

'Well, I can but try,' said Joan. 'It's no good making up recipes in your head too much, it's your mouth that needs to do the work and the great thing is that I can have as much samphire as I wish. I was telling you about the girl who came here, ate a nice apricot pie, well, she and her brother can supply me with as much as I want. Etain, her name was.'

'And she came in with the goldsmith?' queried Mara, seeing her opportunity.

'No, no, not with the goldsmith. I can't imagine him with a pretty girl like that. No, he was with someone else. Someone who spoke funny, foreign . . .'

'Spanish?'

'No,' said Joan with scorn. 'Not Spanish, nor French, not anything usual like that. Funny . . .'

Galway, thought Mara, was a very international place. Gaels, English, Spaniards, French, Portuguese and even Dutch traded there. Joan would probably speak a smattering of most languages. Where could this stranger have come from if Joan did not recognize his accent? What would pass as 'funny' in this sophis-ticated city?

'Could have been Greek,' said Valentine casually. 'We had a ship from Athens in here a week ago. Stayed for a few days; I think it may still be here, down in the docks, though it might have sailed last night.'

'From Athens!' Mara was startled. 'Where is it going?'

'Following the route of Christopher Columbus – lots do,' said Valentine with a shrug. 'The new world, they are calling it. Making Spain very rich! Doing well for Galway, too; lots of ships from Europe are stopping for a few days in Galway to get fresh water and provisions, smoked fish, that sort of thing. Christopher Columbus has done well for us. He came to Galway once, you know, Brehon. My father used to be telling me about it – no one knew then that he would get to be so famous afterwards, of course.'

'So the gold merchant may have been talking to a Greek merchant, perhaps something about gold,' said Mara after Joan had gone back to the kitchen. That, she thought, might be a reasonable explanation of the fact that Niall Martin had not taken off his wig in order to disguise himself from the fishermen of Fanore. Perhaps on this occasion he had visited Fanore in the company of this Greek merchant. Perhaps the gold had been found and Niall Martin had lost his life at the hands of the man whom he had thought of as a customer. It would be a neat solution and would absolve her of all responsibility since neither victim nor criminal was under her jurisdiction.

'Then it might be a crime that you should be dealing with, Valentine,' she said aloud and smiled at his raised eyebrows.

But it seemed to be an enormous coincidence that Etain O'Connor, sister of Brendan and soon to be married to Fernandez, had been in the pie shop on the Monday before midsummer's eve, at the same time as Niall Martin was conversing with the sailor from Athens.

And, if Nuala was right, and Mara had never known her to be wrong, then Niall Martin was killed at Fanore, probably, late on that Monday night or else in the early hours of the Tuesday that followed it.

So, she thought, after she had said goodbye to Valentine and ridden out through the city gates, followed by the now-silent

Finbar, Niall Martin perhaps got a fisherman from Galway, or even one from the Aran Islands who could drop him off at Fanore on his way back to the islands which stood about six miles west of Fanore across the sea.

Or else he went back with Etain O'Connor.

Ten

Oi Chetharslicht Othgabálae
(On the Four Divisions of Distraint)

If a person destroys a man's cliabh *(a wicker-frame boat) the fine is two and a half pieces of silver, or three milch cows.*

If a person destroys a náu *(a boat made from wood) then the fine is five pieces of silver or five milch cows.*

When Mara emerged from the mountain pass on the following morning she found that there was a group waiting for her. It was a misty morning and for a moment she had a fright, wondering whether something had happened. But then as she came closer she was able to count heads, seven of them – the two tall older boys, the MacMahon red-headed twins, still so alike, the sturdy, broad-shouldered form of young Art and her own son, Cormac, lighter, slimmer and slightly smaller than his foster-brother, and the seventh was, of course, not Finbar who was by her side, but Séanín who had been left behind by Brigid, ostensibly to help with the fish, but also because, according to Brigid, he was driving her husband wild with his non-stop questions about everything and his continual suggestions of a better way of doing things.

'You had a successful journey, Brehon,' said Domhnall politely.

'Very,' said Mara heartily. 'And Finbar had a nice time seeing over a pottery belonging to a friend of mine in Galway. You'll have to tell them all about the pots and the ceramic plates, Finbar.'

She said no more about the murder case just then because of Séanín. Though he had been informed about their treasure hunt by one of the younger members of the law school and she was fairly certain that the fishing community had guessed why they were all searching along the beach and by the riverside, she did not want to discuss other matters in front of him so she waited until she could get rid of him.

'Brigid has given me a bagful of goods for you, Séanín. She says you are to build a big fire and then when it's hot enough that you are to toast those pasties over it; the round ones have goat's cheese, the square ones have venison pieces and the long ones have minced pork in them. She says there is plenty for all.'

Séanín went off with the bag and a disappointed expression. He probably preferred going around with the scholars to cooking. However, once the smell of the savoury pasties arose from the beach then he would be the centre of attention and would enjoy patronizing all the young fishing lads. Mara herself was looking forward to the venison pasties. She had been up early, but Brigid had been even earlier, cutting the strips of venison into cubes, sprinkling them with pepper, boiling them in some vinegary wines, shredding them and stuffing them into the delicious pastry shells.

'We have a lot of things to show you, Brehon, when you have time to look,' said Domhnall as they followed Séanín down the road, the well-bred horse keeping a steady pace beside them. 'We have taken notes from all the boats of where they went on the days before the storm and perhaps you would like to read the result sometime. I have everyone's script here in my satchel.'

'Excellent,' said Mara and she meant it. This painstaking seeking of information was very usefully done by her scholars and it was only by fitting these things together that in the end the whole story could be known. Nuala had put the day of death as being probably on either Monday or early on Tuesday, and yet, on Monday Niall Martin, the goldsmith, was having an apricot pie in Blake's Pie Shop in the presence of Etain O'Connor, sister of Brendan the samphire-gatherer, who was talking to Joan at the time. She looked around her. The mist was thick, just a sea mist, but everything was very wet. She did not fancy exposing the map that she had borrowed from the goldsmith's premises to this damp.

'Where is Fernandez?' she asked.

Her question was answered by Domhnall with a smile that showed he had read her thoughts.

'I wondered, Brehon, whether it might be more comfortable for you to be indoors this morning until the mist lifts,' he said, 'and I had a word with him and he was delighted to lend you a room. He even gave me a key to it in case you wanted to leave any of your belongings there in perfect safety.' Domhnall seemed to feel this needed an explanation as he handed over the massive key and added, 'People are in and out of the Cathair Róis all day long, they take fishing equipment and nets and whatever they require. Fernandez encourages them to do this. The castle is for the clan, that's what Fernandez says, and he and Etain make everyone welcome.'

Fernandez sees himself as the new leader of the O'Connor clan, thought Mara as she accepted the key with thanks and walked her horse down the road towards the newly built Cathair Róis. The other scholars, she saw with pleasure, were pestering Finbar for details of his visit to Galway and there was a note of envy in Cormac's voice. He had never been to the city and continually pestered to be taken there. However, Mara had no intention of permitting the son of Turlough Donn O'Brien, hated by the English, declared to be the greatest enemy in Ireland by their Lord Lieutenant, the Earl of Kildare, to ever go there, just in case that he might be taken hostage. No, Cormac would stay safe within the Gaelic Kingdom of the Burren.

When Mara entered the castle of Cathair Róis, Etain was running down the steeply spiralling staircase. She greeted Mara with a wide smile and accompanied her into the room that had been set apart for her. Mara was touched and pleased to see that all arrangements had been made for her comfort. The young couple, Fernandez and Etain, had gone to quite a bit of trouble. A fire blazed in the hearth and there was a cushioned bench drawn up in front of it, and over by the window that at the moment just showed mist, but would once that cleared show the Atlantic Ocean and the Aran Islands, there was a solid table drawn up, with chairs and stools arranged around it. In the background, cut off by linen curtains, was a bed.

'We hoped that you would be comfortable here and that you will stay the night, if you need to, while your investigations are going,' said Etain and the note of anxiety in her voice made Mara immediately reassure her that all arrangements were perfect. There was even, she saw, a horn filled with jet-black ink and mounted in a silver stand. In front of it, on a long tray made from alder twigs, were a group of pens, the quills from eagle, goose, and crow neatly trimmed and sharpened to a point. Mara thought that if this mist persisted it might be sensible to send Séanín off after the midday meal to bring back a change of linen and perhaps anything that the scholars might need so that she could stay the night in this cosy room.

'I've been to Galway City,' said Mara sinking down upon the couch and stretching out her hands to the comforting flame of the fire. 'I don't think that I slept so well last night, so it's lovely to see everything so ready for me.'

As she had hoped, Etain took up the mention.

'Galway City – that's a long way on horseback,' she said.

'I'd have been better off to have gone by boat,' said Mara, shaking her head at herself. 'My scholars told me that. How long does it take you to sail across the bay?'

She only half-listened as Etain discoursed knowledgeably about wind, tide, sail and routes, waiting with a skill born of years of experience, to slip in a question without alarming the person in front of her or making them defensive.

'I suppose the people in Galway are surprised to see a woman sailing a boat by herself,' she said with a smile. 'I gave them a shock as a woman lawyer – and I suppose that a woman sailor would come as a shock, too. In fact, Joan in Blake's Pie Shop remembered you very well.'

'I think that she was more interested in samphire than in sailing,' said Etain without hesitation. 'She drove a fairly hard bargain, too. Wants absolutely prime quality. She's thinking of using some of it uncooked, so it has to be perfect for that. Whoever delivers it, whether it's Brendan or myself, well, they'll have to go there first of all in the morning.'

Etain's voice was quite unconcerned and completely natural. Mara nodded her appreciation of the point and went swiftly on to her next question.

'Did you see the gold merchant, Niall Martin, there?' she asked casually. 'He was there at the same time as you were.'

'No, I didn't.' Etain frowned a little, her black brows knitted together above her very brown eyes. She, like her husband-to-be, Fernandez, was almost Spanish in appearance, but then there were many along the coastline who had those sort of looks – whether from a mixture of blood from trading Spaniards or from an earlier race than the red-gold haired, white-skinned Celts. 'The place was full,' she added, 'she does a great trade there. I'd say that every table was occupied.'

'You wouldn't have noticed his bald head?' asked Mara innocently.

Etain's expression didn't change. 'Lots of them there,' she said briefly. 'Bald heads and large stomachs; that's the way that it goes when they are sitting at desks for most of the day and then eating big slices of pie in between. Now, I'll leave you to yourself, Brehon, and get on down to the beach. I want to make sure that those barrels are properly packed. Fernandez says that it would very bad if customers complained that the barrel was not completely filled.'

Her manner was completely natural and she had shown no sign of resenting the question or seeing any significance in being asked whether she had seen the murdered man on the day before his death.

And yet, when Mara looked across the room she saw that Domhnall's eyes were on her with an expression of curiosity in them. He, certainly, had seen the significance of the question.

'Come around the table, all of you,' she said and waited until her scholars had dragged stools from the corners of the room. Cormac, Art and Cian perched on the high windowsill, their legs dangling, and Mara took her place at the head of the table, bending down and taking the scroll from her satchel.

'I found this under the counter in the goldsmith's shop – just where Ardal O'Lochlainn saw him put it when a stranger entered.' She unrolled it as she spoke and hands came forward to hold the corners flat to the table. Eyes widened and she heard Slevin draw in a breath of excitement.

'It's very well drawn,' said Finbar.

'I was looking at it last night and wondering whether we were searching too near to the beach,' said Mara. She pointed to a spot higher up the hillside. 'Whoever drew this map seems to have made a sharp wiggle just here and that might well be a spot and look, he has drawn a small circle just near it. What do you think that might mean?'

'An enclosure,' said Slevin doubtfully.

'We'd remember that,' said Cael instantly. She did not look at Slevin, but peered earnestly at the small circle. 'Perhaps it's something else. I think that we should go and have a look.'

'In a minute,' said Mara. She sympathized with Cael's impatience. When she had studied the map last night in her bedroom she had known that if the beach had been beside her she would not have been able to help going down there and beginning the search.

'Anyone notice anything else of interest?' she asked.

'You see that little mark here, it's a little question mark, isn't it – it's right down on the sand, not on the dunes,' said Cormac. 'I think I recognize that place. I noticed it on the first day that we were here, before we ever found any dead bodies or things like that, when we were collecting driftwood for the fires. Do you remember, Art?'

'You said that it might have been a house once,' said Art.

'Looked like cut blocks,' said Cian.

'What! As near to the sea as that! No one would be as stupid as that, birdbrain!' Cael was definitely on bad terms with her brother – and with the others, also.

'Michelóg told me that his grandfather's house was a hundred yards nearer to the sea than his and that he worries sometimes in the winter storms it will be destroyed entirely. He said that his father built the new house, much further back, further away from the shore. Do you remember, Art?' said Cormac. 'Do you remember the way he was going on about how God created the sea before the land and that eventually the sea will take back everything – "*And the spirit of God was hovering over the surface of the waters*",' he intoned and Mara bit back a smile while Art and Cian giggled and Cael looked scornful and said:

'He's just making that up to sound important. You believe everything you hear.'

'It's true, actually, Cael. You're right, Cormac; Brigid was saying the same thing,' intervened Mara. 'She was saying that when she was young the sea did not come in at all as far as it does nowadays, and she, too, pointed out to me the old house belonging to Michelóg's father. She said it was right back on the sand dunes when she was a child, and now it's very close to the high-tide mark, so I suppose it's possible that there was another house, even older, down there at some time in the place that Cormac is talking about,' said Mara. 'I must say that I didn't notice any cut stone on the beach, but we'll certainly take a look.'

Privately she thought that Cormac was probably wrong about this particular house that he had discovered. It did seem too far down for a dwelling to have been built; it must be almost at the low-tide mark. It was probably not cut stone that he had found as the sea itself did very good work in shaping boulders. The limestone seemed to split evenly, often along seams of some clayey material – perhaps it was the rain that did that as miles away from the sea one could find these solid, square or oblong rocks, and then, of course, when it came to shoreline, well the force of the waves and the washing of the water smoothed and shaped those massive stones.

'So today we will have another search to see where the treasure, if there was a treasure, was hidden. But of course the most important thing has to be finding out who killed the man. We must never forget that. Someone took a heavy instrument, probably padded, and hit a man so hard that he killed him. And it's up to us, who uphold the law in this kingdom, to find out who did this deed.'

There was a moment's silence after she spoke and then Slevin said: 'Surely the two things are connected, Brehon. If the goldsmith drew this map of the shore and visited it here continually during the last few months, it seems likely, doesn't it, that there were some objects of value brought to him at his shop in Galway and that the coincidence of these fishermen coming from the same place on the Burren made him guess that there may be a source of treasure there. Does anyone disagree with that?' He gazed around him in a challenging way and after a minute was answered by shaken heads. 'So my case is,' he went on, 'that the murderer found Niall Martin at the moment that he discovered the treasure and then he murdered him and took the gold.'

'Makes sense,' said Cael dispassionately.

'The strange thing, though,' said Domhnall, 'is that no one, even knowing that a man has been murdered, is willing to admit that there have been finds here in Fanore, even that there have been rumours of finds.'

'It could be that people are afraid,' said Finbar in a low voice and then blushed slightly as everyone looked at him.

'I think that is a very good observation,' said Mara immediately. 'Fear is something that every Brehon has to take into account when investigating a murder. Death is fearful in itself and a secret and unlawful killing is something that upsets the whole neighbourhood.' The scholars, she thought, were taking this killing very much to heart. Cormac was quite a leader of the younger ones and to him Setanta was probably more nearly akin than his own father, King Turlough Donn, whom he only met four or five times a year. 'Now let me tell you,' she continued smoothly, 'about the man that Niall Martin dined with at the pie shop in Galway on the day before his death.' She looked all around and saw the alert, interested faces – and perhaps there was a hint of relief on them all. Understandable, she thought in Art and Cormac, whose father – stepfather and foster-father – was one of the fishermen. Cian was a great friend of Cormac and Finbar took his opinions from them. If only this murder turned out to be the act of a stranger, not someone known to Art and Cormac for the whole of their lives.

'Well, the woman who runs the pie shop thought that he sounded – she said "funny" – foreign in some way – perhaps speaking in a foreign language – or perhaps just with a strong foreign accent. I suggested Spanish or French, but she knew these languages and then Valentine Blake, the Mayor of Galway, suggested that it might be Greek, as there had been a ship from Athens in the docks up to a day ago.'

'Greek!' Cormac looked with wide, excited eyes at his friends.

'Unlikely to have much connection with the murder,' said Slevin while Domhnall frowned thoughtfully.

'There's quite a lot about gold in the *Iliad*, isn't there, Brehon? I remember noticing that. Wasn't there something about Zeus and his horses' manes threaded with gold and having a golden whip? And about armour made from gold, wasn't there? Perhaps

Greece is a place where there are large deposits of gold, what do you think?'

The scholars looked at him respectfully. Domhnall was the only one to study Greek at the moment – the others found English, Latin, Spanish and French enough for them. Domhnall, of course, had been brought up to speak both Gaelic and English fluently and had that advantage when he started at law school.

'So your impression, Domhnall, is that this Greek sailor might have been selling gold to Niall Martin, rather than being interested in buying it?' Mara was conscious that faces showed disappointment as she said that.

'I'm not sure, Brehon; both are possible.' Domhnall, as always, was cautious.

'But not a single fisherman here brought Niall Martin over to Fanore on either Monday or Tuesday, isn't that right, Cormac?' Cian had an aggressive tone as though someone was trying to cheat him.

Cormac nodded vigorously in support of Cian while Art looked apprehensively at Mara.

'It could, of course, be a fisherman from Galway who took him over. The Mayor has promised to make enquiries and to send a message if he finds anything useful,' Mara said in response and was pleased to see Art relax a little. He was a very sensitive boy and she wished that there was some way of excluding him from this enquiry, which seemed to involve his parents – and perhaps Cormac, also, though he seemed, according to his very different temperament, to be excited and belligerent. She would keep them occupied with this treasure hunt while she did some questioning by herself, she thought. She delved in her satchel and produced the pink linen tape that she used to tie up scrolls.

'Domhnall, could you divide up the map into three or four sections with some pieces of tape – use your knife to cut some of the right size. Then each of you could copy out the section of the map onto a piece of vellum from your own satchel. Be very careful. I want to be able to return that map unmarked.'

Once they were all busy, she got to her feet saying carelessly, 'I must go and find Etain and thank her.'

She had not far to go. Etain was indoors for once, standing looking disconsolately through the window on the stairs at the mist that seemed to be even thicker than ever.

'Look at that mist,' she said. 'I was up at six in the morning and gathered ten basketfuls of samphire and how can I get them to Galway? Not a puff of wind for the sails and even rowing would be dangerous in this weather. Brendan has taken his load on the horse and cart inland, but Galway is our big market.'

'Yes, when I was at Blake's Pie Shop yesterday Joan was telling me that she was going to get a regular supply of samphire from you. She's planning great ideas of pies with golden crust and pale pink salmon in a butter sauce and the samphire arranged like a trellis on top of it.' Mara watched the girl's face narrowly as she said this.

'And she's a new customer, too!' Etain showed no sign of alarm at Mara's reverting to the matter of the pie shop, just sounded disgruntled with the weather. 'What do you think, Brehon, should I chance it? It's slow to row the whole distance, but, who knows, the wind could blow all that away before midday and I could come back by sail. At least the samphire will stay fresh out in the mist.'

'It's no good asking me about the weather,' said Mara with a smile. 'You go and ask Setanta. He'll give you better advice than I could.' She pretended to peer out of the window and then turned back. 'By the way, Etain, I was going to ask you whether you noticed who was talking to Niall Martin, the goldsmith, when you were having that conversation with Joan Blake in the pie shop. Apparently he was there at the same time, was that right?'

'Was he?' Etain hoisted an indifferent shoulder and rubbed a finger over the diamond-shaped piece of glass. Her mind appeared to be on the weather, but it was difficult to be sure whether or not there had been a slight tension in her voice.

'Yes, he was sitting at the side table with a man that Joan thought was a foreigner. He was wearing his wig at the time.'

'I wouldn't have noticed him, then. I think I only saw him once in my life. He was climbing over the rocks and I asked Brendan who he was and Brendan said that he was an old fellow from Galway who liked to come and get some shellfish for his supper. I thought it was strange for him to come into a kingdom that was not his own, but Brendan said that the amount that one man took wouldn't make any difference to the rest of us.'

'Yes,' said Mara. 'The law allows a stranger in a kingdom to have one dip of a fishing net in the stream, a handful of hazel nuts, enough wood to cook a fire . . . and enough rods to make a bier, though that one always puzzled me as I couldn't imagine a someone coming into a strange land and being accompanied by a corpse,' she added and Etain laughed in an unselfconscious manner.

'It's strange, though, what you say,' said Mara, watching the girl carefully. 'When I heard that you were in Galway at the time when Niall Martin was eating his last meal, well I was fairly sure that you were the one who took him across to Fanore on that Monday, the day before midsummer's day.'

'No, it wasn't me, Brehon.' Etain sounded quite unconcerned as she explained again that she had only seen the man once or twice and that was at a distance. 'Better go and have another look,' she said, 'that's the thing about the mist near the sea. It can be here one minute and gone the next. I feel like trying it. I don't want to lose my market and Brendan is a bit of an old woman about going out in a mist.' She waved a careless hand at Mara and went running down the stairs to investigate the latest state of the weather.

Eleven

Cís lir foðla ríre?
(How many kinds of land are there?)

*Access to a 'productive rock', that is a seashore where the rocks bear
seaweed and shellfish, can add the value of three milch cows to a holding.*

Domhnall had sorted out the work for the scholars by the
time that Mara returned to the room allocated to her.
She glanced quickly over the grouping for the maps, noticing
to her surprise a different order to the usual. Cael was with
Domhnall, Slevin with Finbar, Cian with Art and Cormac.
She rolled up the original map from the goldsmith's shop,
wondered whether to leave it in the room, but some instinct
of the importance of confidentiality made her replace it within
her satchel and take it with her. There could, she thought, be
two keys to a door, no matter how securely the lock was
clicked into place.

Not the best of days for a search, she thought, as she strolled
down the road, well behind the eager footsteps of her scholars.
There was something quite different about mist by the sea,
something strange about the way that land and ocean seemed
to meld, a new world where the salt was on your lips and the
waves ceased to crash onto the rocks, but just became part of
an encompassing vapour, and there was something eerie
about the way that the mist muffled the sounds from the voices
on the shoreline.

When she came nearer, though, the orange flames from
Séanín's fire formed a glow within the universal grey and she
heard his cheerful voice assuring the scholars that he would
whistle when he had prepared their meal and that he would
guard their boots if they wanted to leave them there with him
so that they could run across the strand and splash in rock
pools without worry about the effect on the leather.

Mara thought of following them down towards the beach, but her good sense told her that the scholars' eyes were sharper and that in this mist, unfocused wandering would bring little result. She would be better off, she thought, just to go walking quietly along the road and consider the enigma of this man, Niall Martin. Often, she had thought, the root of a crime can be found in the personality of the victim and in the victim's relationship with those around him, but Niall Martin appeared as nebulous a figure as the salty mist that enveloped her. Even Valentine Blake seemed to have no idea how old he was, knew of no one who was friendly with him, was only able to give the impression of a rich man who spent money on clothes, on an elaborate wig, which was nevertheless unfashionably long and given the aged appearance of his skin, unbelievably blond in colour. He was called a goldsmith and there had been instruments on the shelves: steel scribing tools, pitch pot for repoussé work, small picks and clippers, but all of these had been covered in heavy dust. It seemed as if, perhaps with fading eyesight, unsteady hands, that Niall Martin no longer worked in gold, but put all of his energies into buying and selling objects made from it.

And, of course, if he were excited about the possibility of a hidden hoard of the precious metal on the 'golden slope' in the north-western corner of the Burren, then it was not surprising that he came to visit the place and came back again and again after each new rainstorm.

This murder, thought Mara, may well have been an unpremeditated killing. She could imagine the scene. The gold merchant had eventually found his treasure. He was perhaps loading it into a bag. Someone arrived on the scene. There could have been a struggle, a struggle that would easily have ended in victory for any of the fishermen of the area, with their muscles hardened by daily struggles with the sea from boyhood.

But the temptation to have no dispute over a hoard of gold might have been too great and the fatal blow could have been struck by design.

And what could have delivered the blow? Nuala had not thought that it was metal. The skin had not been broken.

Suddenly Mara thought of what every fisherman would have to hand when he walked up the slope from the sea.

The boat itself would be left moored to the pier, or drawn up on the strand, but the oars would always be carried on the man's shoulder up to the house to remain there in safety until the boat was taken out again.

And a waterlogged oar could perhaps have delivered that stroke that Nuala had described.

But then there was the next puzzling aspect to this murder. Where had the idea come from to place the body in an old boat with no oars and to launch it out to sea? Was it an attempt to get rid of the body by pretending that this was a judicial affair, the punishment for the crime of *fingal*? But Mara herself did not remember any case of it, certainly not during her time as Brehon, and not, she thought, during her father's time, also.

But there was, she thought, one fisherman who would have known all about this.

Setanta and Cliona were immensely proud to have their son Art attend the law school at Cahermacnaghten. It had been asked for in lieu of a fosterage fee, which, for the fostering of the son of the King, would have been a substantial sum.

And every time that Art came home, he had, according to Cliona, recited his lessons to herself and to Setanta.

So, one fisherman at least, would know that in the case of *fingal* the convicted murderer is placed in a boat with no oars and pushed out to sea and allowed to drift there at the mercy of the wind and the waves.

The sound of an axe coming from the area of the sand dunes attracted her attention, and she was glad to shelve the matter of Setanta for the moment. She had had complete faith in him in the past; she had never had a moment's doubt in entrusting the care of her little son to Cliona and himself. She could not think, she would not allow herself to think, that he could be guilty of the slaughter of a man just for some gold, which he might find it hard to get a price for. If there was anything that he needed, he knew that he just had to apply to her – she always felt that her debt was unpaid to them for their care of Cormac. Art was a pleasure to have at the law school, sensible, hard-working, intelligent and a great companion to her mercurial son – she would probably have been happy to waive fees for the son of a neighbour, even without the foster-ship relationship, and, of course, Cormac and Art had a very close relationship: *'foster-brothers of the same blanket and of the same cup and of the same bed'*, as the law put it. To accuse Setanta would cause a huge breach between herself and Cormac. Determinedly, she pushed her thoughts aside and followed the direction of the axe blows towards Michelóg's house.

Michelóg was an extremely powerful man. There was an enormous tree propped up against a low bank near to his house. Judging by the rope tied around it and by the tracks through the grey-green grass of the sand dunes he had dragged it up from the beach – some exotic tree with oddly shaped clusters of leaves, browned by the sea, and strangely scaled bark. The axe was high above his head and as she came closer it crashed down onto the wood, causing a spurt of water to shoot up and a large gash to penetrate at least halfway through the trunk. Once again the axe came crashing down and this time the trunk split into two pieces. Michelóg stopped to wipe his brow and then saw Mara standing there. An expression of belligerence came over his face and Mara could understand why. In a windswept kingdom of stone there were very few trees, except in some sheltered valleys. A find like this, no doubt come in from the sea, belonged to whoever owned the foreshore rights – Brendan the samphire-gatherer in this case. However, there were more serious things to think of just now.

'Cutting some firewood?' she queried politely and was secretly amused at the look of scorn that he cast at her. Of course a huge tree like this would be far too valuable to be used for firewood. There was a large peat bog in a hollow between the peaks of Sliebh Elva, owned by the clans that lived around it, including her own clan of O'Davoren. It was only a few miles away from Fanore and with a few days' work as much turf could be cut as was necessary to fuel the fires for a winter. This tree would be used to make a boat, or perhaps a table or something of the sort. She wondered whether Brendan knew of this find and whether there had been any dispute over the ownership.

'You own a boat, do you, Michelóg?'

'I do, indeed, Brehon.' He swung the axe again, now

trimming the rough edge. He wiped his forehead, and stood, obviously waiting for her to go.

'I wondered whether you had ever ferried Niall Martin, the man that was found dead, in your boat; or anyone else from Galway here and back again.' Mara allowed the sentence to hang in the air as he stood thinking about it, meditatively swinging his enormous axe to and fro.

'I might have done,' he said eventually.

'So that's a *yes*, is it?' she said smiling at him and wishing that people would be more straightforward. There was a caution about these shore-dwellers, an instinctive dislike about betraying their affairs to outsiders. 'When was it?' she continued briskly.

'About May,' he said reluctantly and then suddenly and unexpectedly became loquacious. 'It was like this, Brehon,' he said. 'I had a piece of well-tanned ox hide and I took it to Galway to sell to a leather merchant there. This goldsmith was in there to bespeak a leather case for a ring and when he heard me speak Gaelic he asked me where I came from – spoke good Gaelic himself – and when I told him from Burren, he asked all sorts of questions and he asked me if I knew of anywhere that he could sleep for the odd nights that he spent by the sea. He had some sort of problem, so he said, where the doctors thought it was good for him to sleep by the sea on summer nights, so I told him about my grandfather's old house and to cut a long story short, Brehon, I had a word with Brendan about allowing the goldsmith the use of it – it's safe enough in the summer months – and I put a load of clean dry hay up in the loft so that he could sleep there overnight whenever the mood took him.'

'I see,' said Mara. This, she thought, explained a lot. She had been puzzled about this coming and going to Galway. It would be unusual to make the journey twice in one day, but if Niall Martin came over with, say Brendan, or Etain in the afternoon or the evening of these long summer days, then he could go back in the morning. I bet that the entire population knows of this arrangement, she thought with irritation, but she said no more. They were a cautious set of people and she had to take them as they were, just go on probing the cracks and gathering information.

'So did Niall Martin spend midsummer's eve in the old house by the shore?' she enquired.

Michelóg shrugged his shoulders. 'I couldn't tell you, Brehon. The hay was there for him and a roof over his head and it was up to him to use it when he wanted. I'm not a man to probe into anyone else's business.'

'Did you take him across from Galway last Monday?'

'Do you know, Brehon, I didn't exchange a word with him since that very day that I was telling you about, in Galway. And you can ask the leather merchant there, if you want to know if I'm telling the truth about that conversation. He listened to every word that we said.'

'And he was wearing a wig that day, I presume. So I'm surprised that you did not immediately recognize him when you saw the dead body.' Mara rushed her two sentences together to prevent a denial and, as she expected, there was a short silence while he thought of what to say. When he did speak, what he said was unexpected.

'To be honest with you, Brehon, everyone knew who it was once young Síle found him. A wig on, or a wig off, doesn't make too much difference to a person that every man, woman or child had seen hanging around this place for almost a month. Everyone recognized him, but seeing as he was in that old boat belonging to Séan the Shark Slayer's grandfather – well, no one wanted to have anything to do with it.'

'And where is Séan's grandfather now?' Mara heard the irritation in her voice and mentally reproved herself for it. Nothing could be served by showing impatience and by allocating blame. The community had closed ranks – just like a herd of long-horned cows confronting a hungry wolf from the mountain, they had drawn together and presented a solid and unbroken front to her questions. There was, she noted, a slight look of triumph in Michelóg's eyes. He would often have been excluded from the affairs of the fishermen. He allowed a long moment to elapse before answering her question and then pointed dramatically to the hillside where the little church stood.

'Up there, Brehon, up there, he is buried under six foot of good earth.'

Mara nodded at this, but lingered. Michelóg was enjoying his role and she might get some more useful information from him. This rock-solid wall of denials which had met her from the start of this enquiry seemed to have been coordinated in some way, but Michelóg was a farmer, not a fisherman, and he, though of the clan, did not have a close relationship with those who took their living from the sea.

'So was it Setanta who thought it might be best to deny everything?' she enquired, bending over to feel the knobbly surface of the tree bark. Where had it come from? she wondered. She had never seen a tree like that in her life and the heart-wood exposed by Michelóg's axe was a startling shade of bright orange. The westerly gale had perhaps carried it from one of the countries discovered by Christopher Columbus, that intrepid Italian explorer who had made Spain rich and had honoured the city of Galway with a visit at the time when Mara was four years old.

'No, no, not Setanta; it was Fernandez who told them what to say,' said Michelóg with an air of scorn for her naivety. 'He said that we didn't want any trouble. He just went from group to group when your young lad, Domhnall, is it? – well, when he set off, Fernandez arranged it all, told everyone to say nothing. The other scholars were down by the body, they didn't hear a thing – watching the body, they were, and him stretched out in Séan's grandfather's boat, like on a bier.'

He chuckled merrily to himself and then went into the house and came out with an enormous saw.

'If you'll excuse me, Brehon, if you've finished asking me questions, I'd better get on with this. The quicker I get to work on this, the easier my job will be.'

'Just one more question, Michelóg,' said Mara, refusing to be hurried. 'Has there been much speculation about what brought an elderly gold merchant from Galway here to wander around the seashore and to sleep uncomfortably on a bed of hay in the loft of an old damp house?' She laid a slight emphasis on the word '*gold*', but his face remained blank.

'I couldn't tell you, Brehon. The folk around here are not too friendly to me. You know that yourself. They keep their counsel and I keep mine.'

'And what did you, yourself, make of this strange notion. Did you think that he was looking for something?'

He hesitated for a minute and she thought that he might be going to say something, but then he cast a quick glance over his shoulder, almost as though he thought he would be overheard, and picked up his saw and began to trim the bark from the trunk.

'I didn't think anything, Brehon. I'm too busy minding my own affairs for thinking about other people's.' Once again, he cast a look over his shoulder and when Mara left him and walked back onto the road, she understood why. She could hear the sound of a stone hammer and guessed that Brendan was mending the stone wall that stood between his land and Michelóg's holding. In the pauses, it would have been possible for him to overhear the conversation on this morning when no wind blew and the sound of the waves was muted by the mist.

There was no doubt that Michelóg, the farmer, was an outsider in this community, and that he was at odds with the others of the neighbourhood who took their living from the sea, rather than from the land. No one would be sorry, she thought, if the blame for this secret and unlawful killing could be shifted onto his shoulders – and Michelóg himself knew that feeling.

That was, she thought, why he had been so open with her and why he had pointed the finger at Fernandez as the co-ordinator of the blank response to her questions. But what about Brendan? He and his sister were the ones that went to and from Galway almost daily. If anyone had ferried the gold merchant to Fanore on that Monday of his death, then the chances were that it was one of the samphire-gatherers who brought him – and, probably, the arrangement would be that they would take him back again on the following morning.

But no one had missed him, apparently. Surely someone would have gone to see whether he was all right? The body did not turn up on the beach for three more days.

Twelve

When it comes to assessing the extent of the damage inflicted by trespassing cattle the Brehon's judgement as to the harm done is assisted by the evidence of a neighbour of good standing who is respected by all and whose knowledge of the land and of the possibilities of either recovery or permanent harm to a piece of pasture is well known.

It was, thought Mara, as she walked in the direction of the tapping on stone, surprising that Brendan had no cows at all on his land. Admittedly his acreage was small and the land was even nearer to the sea than Michelóg's, but then from time immemorial his family had owned the seashore rights and that meant, as well as laying claim to anything washed down from the mountain and onto the strand, Brendan could graze his cows there and let them eat the seaweed from the rocks and no one could deny him those rights. She put the question to him when she arrived at the boundary wall and saw him blink with surprise.

'You know, Brehon, I never did get on well with cows; I don't like them much at all,' he said after a moment. 'It's a chancy sort of business. You wouldn't believe the amount of illness cattle get and then you reckon on having six calves born and then next thing you find is that one of the cows was barren, one miscarried and the rest of them all had bull calves which are not worth the same at all as little heifers. And then they slip and slide on the stones and break legs – at least mine did. I had no luck with them at all so in the end I could see how Etain was doing well with samphire so I joined with her and we started to go to Galway market and then to the inns and now it's all going well.'

'So you didn't mind Michelóg grazing his cattle on the foreshore?'

Brendan's face darkened. 'I didn't like it,' he said bluntly. 'I never gave him permission to do so; I just didn't want any trouble with him – he'd knock you down as soon as look at you, a very handy man with the fists and the stick, too; so I thought to myself, well, it's not doing me any harm and I didn't think it would cause trouble because the rest of the people around here were just in the fishing line and it didn't matter to them, then, though a few complained about the cows fouling the seaweed, but when it came to letting that vicious bull of his stalk up and down the strand and frighten the life out of the children, well then I had to go to law and he has his knife stuck in me ever since – so as to say,' he added hastily.

'I remember the case,' said Mara. She remembered now that Ardal O'Lochlainn had been called in to assess damage and had been rather dismissive about the amount of harm that cows could do on those sandy dunes, as compared with the heavier richer land of the valleys between the mountains, where Mara's land and Ardal's own land were situated. She had imposed a fine on Michelóg, though, because of the bull affair, and had banned him from allowing his cows onto the foreshore again, recommending Drendan to keep his walls in good order.

And this was a magnificent wall that he was working on, watched by a golden brown blob of an active, square-tailed wren. It was one of the ancient shore walls, large round boulders piled line upon line, with each smoothly curved stone bridging the gap beneath it and then the whole wall capped, at waist-high level, with a series of oval slabs. In the morning mist, the stones were dripping and coloured dark grey, with just glimpses of the orange sand showing in the spaces between the smoothed outlines, but on a sunny day it would gleam a pristine silver-white.

Brendan, frustrated perhaps by his inability to get to Galway in the thick mist, was building a stile here so that, as he explained to Mara, he could easily take the heavy baskets of dripping samphire over the wall to the pathway without knocking the stones and then load them straight onto the cart, avoiding having to drag the heavy weight across the sand and rooting up the superficial coating of marram grass.

Mara admired the workmanship. He was using the squared-off oblong slabs of black limestone from the beach and like every native of the Burren he had an instinctive appreciation of which stone he needed next, as with only a glance he selected one from the pile on the grass verge – the largest and longest was already in position, well settled with a few taps of the stone-worker's hammer, and then came the next, just the length of a man's foot shorter than the first, then another – this one, a little too short, had a small piece tucked behind it and then the top stone, by now the stile was three-quarters the height of the wall so Brendan took off one of the stones, balancing its massive weight with ease and replaced it with a finger-thick slab that could be stepped over with ease and then he turned to Mara with a grin.

'Well, that's done and all to do again on the other side,' he said.

'And it will be there for your sons and your grandsons and your great-grandsons that come after you,' said Mara looking at the perfection and solidity of the work.

'Etain's son before mine,' said Brendan. 'There'll be a baby in Cathair Róis by the feast of Imbolc.'

'That's lovely,' said Mara warmly. The priests were trying to call the first of February St Brigid's Day, but on the Burren it was still known as Imbolc and was one of the four great festivals in the Celtic calendar. 'Fernandez and she must be delighted,' she finished and hoped that this business of the gold merchant was not going to mar the happiness of the young couple. She watched him for a few minutes as he worked on steadily, checking the stability of the steps, selecting and then inserting a few small stones from the pile beside him underneath the massive slabs. For a moment she envied him. It was a simpler and easier way of life than trying to tread a path through the labyrinth of the human mind and human emotions. And then she smiled to herself as she remembered the huge intellectual satisfaction of her work. She would, she knew, not willingly swap places with anyone in the three kingdoms. To a certain extent, she thought, she also built walls, as she balanced the relationships between neighbours, sometimes inserting the small stones of conversation, compliments and understanding, but all the time relying on the massive solidity of the law to provide the frame-work for peace in the kingdom.

'Look,' he said, breaking into her thoughts and he pointed over her head so she turned and looked. The heavy dark cliff-edge of the mountain that towered above the River Caher was beginning to emerge from the mist and there was a faint brightening in the sky.

'Etain will be able to get to Galway after all,' he said with satisfaction.

'And you?' asked Mara. She was unwilling to delay a man who wished to seize the tide, but he shook his head. 'Not me, I've started so I'll finish. This is my task for the day, that and making a proper path up from the beach through our land. There are plenty of slabs lying around and I can bed them down into the sand. And then we can roll up the baskets on a turf barrow and carry them across the wall and load them onto the cart – easier when they can go by boat, of course, but the winter is long and the sea has its storms. And I enjoy building things.'

If Séanín was not needed to go and fetch her overnight linen she would have offered him as an assistant. Perhaps the boy could stay overnight in one of the scholars' tents and then help on the morrow. Brendan was obviously a past master with stone building and a skill like he possessed was always a useful one on the Burren. The work on her own farm, with the hay already saved and the turf drawn, had slackened off and wouldn't gather pace again until the oats ripened. In any case, Cumhal and Séanín were at odds with each other – Cumhal preferred the quieter and more respectful boys, so Séanín might learn more readily from the younger and more easy-going Brendan.

'If you wish, Séanín could work with you tomorrow, Brendan,' she said. 'I'd offer him to you this afternoon if I didn't need him to go across to the law school – but tomorrow he could spend the day with you.'

He thanked her so cordially for her offer of a helper that she seized the opportunity of the warmth between them and said in a friendly way, 'Brendan, tell me, why was everyone so secretive about the identity of the goldsmith? You must all have known him, wig or no wig, and everyone must have been wondering for the last couple of weeks what on earth he was doing here, pottering around and then sleeping on a load of hay in that old house down by the shore.'

She could have sworn that the steps he had built going up to the stile were as firm and as solid as the steps in the Brehon's house at Cahermacnaghten, and the wall behind them had probably been in place for hundreds of years, but he seemed to move, almost to stumble and then he shouted, 'Stand back, Brehon!' and one of the smaller rounded stones tumbled from the wall and fell almost at her feet.

It took him quite a few minutes before he rebuilt the wall and by then, she reckoned, he had a story ready. He was, she thought, observing him narrowly, extremely uneasy, and her question had brought sweat to his brow, which had not been there when he was handling the enormous slabs of stone – all of them at least the thickness of a man's foot.

'Well, it's like this, Brehon,' he said with a false air of confidentiality. 'This man was searching for something and no one quite knew what he was about. You could say that he was causing trouble between neighbours. No one knew if he was working with someone around here or if he was working for himself. And then when he was found dead, well, no one liked to point the finger. And when it came down to it, I suppose,' he said, throwing his hands wide open in a gesture of candour, 'when it came down to it, there were people around here who guessed what he was looking for. They've been rumours, you see, Brehon.'

'Pieces of gold had been found.' Mara had found on many occasions that a statement worked better than a question.

'Not by me,' said Brendan quickly. 'Not up early enough in the morning; but there have been rumours. Someone would be in the money. A pair of oars here, a fancy gown from Galway there . . .' He let the sentence tail out and nipped neatly through the gap in his wall and began to build up the steps of the stile on the other side. 'People don't always let neighbours know of good fortune, Brehon, but, of course, envy begins to creep in and causes bad blood.'

'And Fernandez thought that it might be best if no one admitted to knowing who he was, and that he would be just an unknown corpse washed up on the beach.'

He made no reply to this, just bowed his head and looked uncomfortable, so she reverted to the questions about the treasure hunt.

'And if a fisherman coming down to beach early one morning, or even returning on a moonlit night, caught a glint of gold and found that he had a bracelet or a ring, or a brooch, would he know what to do with it?'

'That would be an easy matter, Brehon. Don't they say that the streets of Galway City are paved in gold? That would be the first place that they would take it – and easy enough it would be to go there by boat, without causing any talk – the fish market there is open to all.'

'So during the last few years fishermen have been finding things here on Fanore – nothing too big, that would have been noticed – and they have been secretly selling their finds to the gold merchant at Galway – and there was only the one man there, and that was Niall Martin, so quite a few would know him. And Niall Martin puts two and two together, then he starts to come over here, coming in the evening, staying the night in an old house and then returning on the following morning.'

'That's right,' said Brendan, 'and I can tell you, Brehon, there have been a lot of wasted footsteps on the strand and up on the dunes, just the way that your own scholars have been searching for the last few days.'

He laughed merrily at the thought and then stopped, tilting his head to one side. The sounds of blows came clearly through the still, damp air.

'What is he at, at all, this morning? He sounds like he's breaking his house down.'

'Michelóg, you mean?' asked Mara. 'When I passed by there he was chopping an enormous tree trunk – one that came in on the tide. Not a tree that you would find anywhere around here; came from across the ocean, I'd say,' she added hastily, remembering that she was speaking to a man who held rights over everything found on the beach that had not come from *'beyond the ninth wave'*.

'So that's what he was doing the other night – must have been Monday night,' muttered Brendan. 'I heard him at something, heard a thud.'

Mara stiffened slightly, but she tried not to let her reaction be noticed. Monday night or early Tuesday morning had probably been the time when Niall Martin had been killed. *A thud*, Brendan had said. That could have been a tree trunk falling to the ground, or it could have been a man's skull struck hard enough to cause death. In either case, it was time that she had another word with the farmer.

'I'll leave you in peace, Brendan,' she said. He had, she thought, been honest with her, apparently, anyway; while still distancing himself from any involvement in gold or in knowledge of the man who dealt in gold.

Michelóg, also, she thought as she made her way back to where the thud of an axe still sounded, had, in the same way, appeared to be honest, but people, she knew from long experience, did not always tell all of the truth, even when they appeared frank and open.

'Just wanted to check on something, Michelóg,' she said when he paused with uplifted axe at the sight of her, 'You were heard out on Monday night dragging that tree back to your yard. I wondered whether you saw any activity on the beach that night.' It must have been quite a task for one man to have dragged that back from the waves, she thought, looking at the coil of extremely thick rope lying beside the tree. Michelóg had left it propped up on its branches and the ground beneath it was red and rusty-looking from the salt water that had dripped from it and scorched the grass. Even bone dry the tree would be an immense weight, but saturated with sea water it would have slow and difficult task to drag it over the sand. Mara could see how the marram grass had been uprooted and a track scored into the sand. Not an undertaking that would have been quickly achieved.

'It must have taken you at least an hour to haul that up from the beach on Monday night,' she said. 'You would surely have noticed if there had been anyone around.'

He gave a short laugh. 'I don't suppose that there would have been anyone out on a night like that, Brehon. You must sleep very sound if you did not hear the thunder and the lightning.'

He had not denied that it had been Monday night when he was out, noticed Mara, and she just smiled a response.

'Indeed,' she said. 'It took a brave man to go for a walk on that night with the lightning flaring and the roar of the thunder, though I think it all died down by dawn. I woke once in the darkness of the night and was glad to be in my warm bed and under a good roof.' She had lain awake for a while, she remembered, thinking of her scholars and had hoped that Fernandez was trustworthy.

'God bless you,' he said and she could see that he bit back the words: *Isn't it fine for you.* 'Of course, for a poor man like myself, the chance of getting a tree like that was too good to pass up on. I'll tell you how it was, Brehon,' he said, suddenly becoming so loquacious that she grew suspicious as he related how he had been sitting up late with a cow and it had been a hard calving and then when eventually the little heifer had been born he had walked down to the sea to wash the muck from himself and then he had seen the wave throw something long and dark up onto the sand and with another flash of lightning he had seen that it was a tree.

'Well, I said to myself, Brehon, *if I don't take it now there won't be a splinter left in it by dawn,* so back I went to the house and got that rope there,' he pointed to the evidence of the rope, adding the usual *'and that's the God's honest truth,'* just in case the rope denied the matter.

'How long did it take you to bring it back?' asked Mara and then knew that was a stupid question, addressed to a man who ruled his day by the sun and not by sand clocks or new-fangled timepieces.

'About the time that it would take to milk a cow,' he said, unexpectedly cooperative.

'Pretty tough going, I'd say – and no one to help you, was there?' To milk a cow would take about fifteen to twenty minutes, she reckoned. He gave a flicker of a grin at her question about assistance. Nothing, she reckoned, would have persuaded him to share his booty with another. It was, she thought, fairly unlikely that anyone else would have been out walking the strand on a night like that one. Michelóg's story made sense. Why use well water, very precious in this sandy part of the country, for cleansing purposes when salt water in abundance was available only a couple of hundred yards away?

While she was deciding whether to leave him or to try another few questions, he suddenly went off into a small stone shed beside his house and came out with a heavy hammer, its head swathed in a piece of an old woollen cloak. Working delicately and methodically, he tapped the bark of the tree, moving up and down the length of it, muttering something about loosening the bark, and then he straightened his back and looked at her.

'Gold doesn't mean much to me, Brehon,' he said unexpectedly. 'I'm getting old and I have neither wife nor child. I don't want any more cows – the land wouldn't bear them – and I wouldn't fancy, at my time of life, to move somewhere else, even if the *taoiseach* would find me something else. You're wasting your time with me. Why don't you go and talk to the man on the hill up there.' He jerked his head towards where the white rounded shape of Cathair Róis was beginning to materialize through the mist. 'Now that's a man,' he said with emphasis, 'who could make good use of a pot of gold.'

Thirteen

Brecha Comaithchesa
(Laws of the Neighbourhood)

*Failure to maintain a field-boundary can be punished by the imposi-
tion of a fine of one of the tools used for that purpose. Any one of
the following tools can be taken from the offender and given to the
man who has suffered a loss because of his carelessness:*

1. The spade used for the trench-and-bank.
2. The iron spar-pin for the stone wall.
3. The mallet for the breaking of the stones.

Brigid's food was much appreciated and Séanín was given
many compliments for the way it was heated up and
served. Mara noticed that despite a lack of success, her scholars
seemed to be in good humour. Smiles and giggles came from
the younger ones and Mara was glad to see that Cael was once
more one of the gang and that they were all sharing jokes as
usual. The two eldest boys were deep in discussion and when
it finished, with a nod of understanding from Slevin, they
turned their attention to their food. Domhnall, in particular,
seemed to be anxious for the meal to be over and swallowed
his pasty with great rapidity. Mara surveyed the crowd. Etain
was not there, nor was her brother Brendan, nor, indeed,
Michelóg, but the fishermen were all present, discussing the
next venture, and Fernandez was the centre of attention,
directing the next location to be fished, and helping to spread
out the large net to make sure that there had been no holes
torn in it during the last outing, discussing how they would
go in a large bunch and rent a stall at the fish market in Galway
next week when they had plenty of barrels of smoked fish to
sell. He was generating a huge excitement and, young, clever,
good-looking and full of ideas, was demonstrating to the clan
that he could be an ideal leader of the O'Connors when the

present *taoiseach* passed on, or gave up the post. Yes, Fernandez would make a good *tánaiste*, he would be an heir who consolidated his position while he was in waiting, rather than wasting his time in drinking and pleasure-seeking like Tomás O'Connor, who showed no interest in the lowly members of the clan. Fernandez would be a change for the better and as the descendant from the same grandfather had equal rights to the position.

But not, thought Mara firmly, if he was guilty of the crime of murder just in order to get hold of the treasure which would finance all his projected enterprises. If that were true she would never consent to his election and would make the King understand the impossibility of a man who committed a secret and unlawful killing and who frustrated the cause of justice should hold such a position. She watched Fernandez carefully but he showed no signs of guilt or even seemed aware of her steady gaze.

When the meal was over Mara went up to tell Séanín about his journey to Cahermacnaghten.

'Bring back the cart so that you don't overburden your pony. Brigid will know what I want,' she told him and then called her scholars to see whether they needed anything other than fresh linen. Cormac wanted his throwing knives, but when she said no to that the younger ones compromised on their hurleys and a ball. Domhnall wanted his copy of the *Iliad* and told Séanín that he would find it on the shelf above his bed, describing it so carefully that Mara reckoned he must have other books there. She half-thought of persuading him to enjoy the holiday without adding extra study, but she understood that he now wanted to look up the reference about gold.

Séanín was a bit downcast about the journey back to Cahermacnaghten and to cheer him she told him that when he returned he could stay overnight at Fanore in one of the tents and how she had arranged for him to spend tomorrow helping Brendan with building a stone path. To her surprise he did not seem enthusiastic and she caught him exchanging glances with Cormac, which showed that he had planned to spend the afternoon with the scholars on the treasure hunt, which was still filling them all with excitement. Cormac, also, looked rather thwarted and she saw him eyeing Séanín with disappointment as he reluctantly retreated at her gesture of dismissal.

'You'll enjoy helping Brendan,' she said bracingly to Séanín when Cormac had gone down towards the beach. 'And then when you have learned the skill you might build me a path through my woodland garden when we all return home.'

'But Cormac promised that I would help to find the treasure this afternoon,' he muttered. 'We were going to be partners and help solve the murder case for you.'

Mara grimaced slightly. She was pleased that Cormac was so open and friendly with everyone – like his father in that, she thought. Turlough made friends wherever he went and it mattered very little to him whether a man was an innkeeper, a shepherd or a *taoiseach*. On the other hand, she would have preferred this search to stay as confidential law school business. Still, common sense told her that every fisherman, wives, children, all knew that they were looking for gold – though she herself was fairly convinced that the gold had been removed when the man had been murdered.

'I'll see you later on, Séanín,' she said briskly and left him to mount his pony and set off back to Cahermacnaghten. She hoped that, in the midst of his disappointment, he would not forget all of his instructions.

When she went back to her scholars they told her, as she had guessed, that they had discovered nothing during the morning, but that it had been decided that the areas allocated to each would be swapped and that they would commence a more thorough search during the afternoon.

'The mist was terrible this morning,' said Cormac. 'It was like trying to find a mouse in a pile of sheep's wool. It's lifted now and so this afternoon it will be better. But it's boring searching the same places over and over again. Why don't we go higher up towards the mountain?'

From Domhnall's dubious-looking face it appeared as though that was not a good idea and she agreed. If the treasure trove was further up the mountain it was unlikely that the articles ended up in the places that the goldsmith had marked on the map. However, it was her policy to allow the head scholar of the school to sort out tasks like this. She decided to leave them to it and go in search of Fernandez.

He was down at the pier with the others when she found him – not a good place for questioning him in private, so she just stood and watched. He was, she thought, a natural leader. The fishermen, all experienced at their craft since babyhood, were listening to him with the greatest respect. They would follow him through thick and thin and that was what made a good leader. Her husband, King Turlough Donn O'Brien, was a man like that. A man who was quite unassuming, a man who had no pretensions to scholarship, or to any particular outstanding skill, but nevertheless a man to whom all turned when danger threatened; and a man who had never let down his followers. Turlough would like Fernandez, but did that mean that Fernandez was to be trusted? That was something which she did not know yet, and until she was certain of that she would not mention his name with approbation to her kingly husband, she thought as she waited patiently for him to finish his instructions. It was difficult to make time to have an uninterrupted chat with him as his opinion and his decisions were being constantly sought by the fishermen.

'Brehon, did you want me for something?' Fernandez broke into her thoughts, coming across the rocks to where she stood.

'Yes,' she said gravely eyeing him to see whether he showed any signs of guilt, but he rushed on, repeating his Etain's invitation to stay the night in his castle and telling her that it would give her time to question everyone, and certainly himself, as they would all be back by sundown. It was so apposite that for a moment she could only stare at him and he said quickly, 'You'll be worn out riding back and forth every day. We can send your young lad, Séanín, back to the farm with a message to say that you will be here and then no one will worry about you. We have a comfortable bedroom for you, and your scholars will be glad to have you within reach. They were worried about you when you went off to Galway.'

Mara doubted that, but assured him that she had already accepted his hospitality. There would be a good opportunity for an uninterrupted talk with him as Etain would no doubt be late home from Galway.

When she went back up the beach she found that her scholars had already worked out their afternoon tasks.

'Cormac suggested that we swap maps so that a different pair searches the area for a second time and I thought that was a very good idea,' said Domhnall, as always willing to give credit to a younger member of the school. 'So Slevin and I are going to search the area where Cormac, Cian and Art searched this morning, just north of that circle on the map. We've found it that it is called Lios na hAbha . . .' He went on detailing the new groupings and the various places but Mara's attention was caught by the name that he had mentioned – it meant *the fortified place by the river*. She had not known that there was an ancient enclosure there where the river made a slight turn. She was glad that Domhnall was going to search that place now. Cormac got bored easily and he would be very much the leader of Art, and Cian was definitely the more idle and less intelligent of the MacMahon twins. Domhnall and Slevin would make a thorough exploration.

These old enclosures, she thought with a sudden feeling of excitement, often had underground rooms and passageways – whether for shelter from enemies or purely as cold-storage areas – but, also, an underground room could have been a place where treasure trove was hidden. When she thought of that she decided to join her eldest scholars by the easier route, crossing the sand dunes, she thought, and then coming out beside the river at the spot where they had climbed up.

She had only gone about halfway across when she saw the figure of Cormac running and jumping from sand hill to sand hill with the exuberance shown by her younger scholars when they were allowed out of the school house for a break.

'It's definitely an old house, Brehon,' he said breathlessly when he came up to her. 'Come and look at it.' He did not wait for an answer but went flying down to the spot where Cael stood beckoning to her.

'Look what I found, Brehon!' The girl was bursting with excitement. They had shifted a slab – Mara could see that all the blobs of dark brown sea creatures that had been firmly glued to the underside of the slab were now squirming with distaste at their exposure to the upper air.

But sunk into the ground was an ancient iron pot, its bottom dissolved by rust, but the curved sides and even the handles still intact. It was just the sort of pot that Brigid kept hanging over the fire in the kitchen with bones simmering in it and handfuls of vegetables thrown in from time to time so that there was always hot soup available for any of the scholars who wanted a quick snack, or who were, in Brigid's opinion, looking a little pasty-faced.

'I'd say you're right, Cormac,' said Mara, glad to see that he and Cael were so friendly again. 'It just goes to show that the sea at some stage was a long way further out than it is nowadays. This was undoubtedly a house at one time.'

'We were wondering whether the treasure could have been hidden in this pot,' said Cael excitedly. 'That's what we think.'

'Do you reckon that slab has been lifted off recently?' Mara watched the squirming blobs. One of them was already moving, seeking the underside of the stone. Instinct was a wonderful thing, she thought, once again. Although the mist had lifted, it was not a sunny day and yet the sea creatures knew that they dare not remain in the open.

'Could be,' he said. 'It came away very easily.'

'Do you know what you should do now, my two investigators, you should take out that pot and go through the sand under it very, very carefully. You see gold does not rust, so when the bottom of the container rusted, then something very small, like a finger ring, might have sunk into the sand beneath. If you could find that, it would prove the matter.'

She left them at work, assuring Cael that she would tell no one else of the discovery, but allow them to work in peace.

Mara suspected that this was an unlikely place, out in the open beach, for the murder to have taken place. Despite Cormac's optimism she doubted whether that slab had been moved and then replaced. Although all was possible it seemed to her that it might be more likely that a treasure would be concealed within one of those ancient fortified circular enclosures.

However, as soon as she arrived there she realized that it was too far from the river for a flood to have swept through it, no matter how much of a storm occurred. Domhnall and

Slevin, however, emerged from the underground passage with triumphant faces. In Slevin's hand was an expensive-looking tassel of purple silk. He held it aloft and blew a triumphant whistle and the other scholars came tumbling up.

'Definitely his,' said Cormac instantly. 'Look how new-looking it is. That has not been there long. Don't know how we missed it this morning.'

'Just the sort of thing that a man from Galway would have worn.' That was Cian's contribution.

'Very fine,' said Art.

'It does look like something belonging to the gold merchant, doesn't it, Brehon,' said Cael.

'So he went in here, into the underground room, and then where did he go?' Domhnall was considering the matter.

'You don't think that the treasure was here?' Cael was more pleased than disappointed. Both she and Cormac were pinning their hopes on the ancient house on the beach, with its conveniently placed iron pot.

'I think that Niall Martin came here, looking for the treasure, but I'm not sure that he thought it was the right place.' Mara cast her mind back to the map that the gold merchant had drawn. Certainly Lios na hAbha had been marked on it, but when the man realized how far from the river it had been placed – well, he would surely have known that no flood could have swept any gold from that underground chamber.

'I wonder where he went next; what do you think, Cael?' asked Cormac, showing an unusual deference to another scholar's opinion. He looked all around, starting from the far side of the strand where the boat with the body had been beached, moving past the pier and the up beyond the high-water mark and then focusing on the broad sweep of the dunes that fringed the golden slope.

'What about there,' said Cael, instantly, pointing to the far side to the river, to the place where the Farmer Michelóg's land began.

'I'd say you are right,' agreed Cian. 'Have we searched that side of the river properly? Has anyone gone there? If we haven't then we should start on it straight away.'

'Cael and I will do it,' said Cormac. Mara was surprised that her son wanted to give up on his special discovery of the old house with the pot beneath the slab. However, it was typical that he got bored easily. Sifting endless grains of sand was not an occupation that appealed to him, though, she thought, if they persevered they would have come to bedrock. No one would have built a house on sand. And then when she thought about the building of the house, she remembered the custom on the Burren, when building a new house, of placing a broken iron pot beneath the flagstone in front of the fire. Then during a *ceilidh*, the best dancer would be given the honour of that particular spot where the sound of his or her feet echoing above the music of pipe or fiddle would keep the time for less accomplished performers.

That would, thought Mara, be the explanation for the pot beneath the slab and she was glad now to see Cormac directing his attention in another direction. She seated herself on a rock, taking out Niall Martin's map again and studying it carefully and then looking all around her, trying to picture the gold merchant's last hour.

Not night time, she thought. Even moonlight, adequate for fishing, would not be enough for a search for buried treasure, but sunrise would be an ideal time, and, no doubt, a bed of hay in the roof space of an old house would not be a great place for an elderly man to spend the night.

And why did he do it?

Michelóg had said to her with an appearance of candour that gold was of no interest to him, that he had neither wife nor child, and wanted, in the way of cattle and land, no more than he already possessed. But surely if that was true, the same applied to Niall Martin.

Or did the glamour and lure of gold act upon all men, irrespective of whether they needed it or not? Mara was inclined to think, despite Michelóg's words, that it did.

So Niall Martin emerged from his uncomfortable sleeping place at night, came out upon an immaculate beach of orange sand, made his way to a place not yet searched, and found the gold, stood contemplating it. And then? And then, another person who could not sleep, so far faceless in Mara's mind, came upon him and struck him down and fled with the gold.

But who was the person appointed to take him back to Galway? It was ridiculous that she still had not found that out. It would not have been Michelóg, she guessed. He would not undertake long trips to Galway when he had cattle to see to, so it must have been one of the others.

At that moment there was a shrill scream from Cael, followed by a whistle. Mara got to her feet quickly. Domhnall and Slevin emerged from the underground passageway of the ruined enclosure and Finbar, Art and Cian came running down from the promising bend in the river that they had been investigating.

'I saw the footsteps,' shouted Cael. 'I was the one that saw them first. And Cormac thought that they were just belonging to Michelóg, but I said that they were too small and they have no hobnails in them like farmers always have and the fishermen don't wear boots – they wear *cuaráin*.' Cael, as usual, presented her evidence in a cool, succinct manner. Only the glow of her eyes showed her excitement. She waited until everyone's attention was on her and then said, 'But that is not all. Look!' Walking carefully well to the side of the footprints she made her way up the steep slope towards Michelóg's farm. As they got nearer they could hear the muffled thump of the hammer on the bark of the exotic tree trunk, but no one spoke and the noise went on without hesitation.

Outside the farm, just at the spot where there was a field of delicate grass, just where the land was watered by the River Caher and enriched by thousands upon thousands of baskets of seaweed, heaped over it by generation after generations, there was a bank that formed the boundary. It had been dug to form the base for a wall and a ditch showed where the sandy earth had been taken. Part of it looked newly turned over, but the section where Cael was now scooping over with her hands was heaped up with a pile of sand that looked as though it had been taken from the nearby dune. It only took her a moment to move it aside.

And there was a pile of clothing and a small empty leather bag with two handles and a lock. There was a hat of black silk – and it had two purple tassels remaining on it. There was a tunic of black broadcloth, thick and expensive, and trimmed with velvet, finely knitted black nether hose, and a pair of

smallish leather boots with smooth soles. Typical clothing for
a well-off merchant. Mara had little doubt that she was looking
at the garments worn by Niall Martin on the morning when
he was murdered. And, of course, Cael was right. The fishermen wore these light foot coverings, made from a piece of
raw cow hide or bull hide, still with the hair on it – these
were comfortable when kept wet and were perfect for their
work: light in the boats and flexible as bare feet on the rocks.
No fisherman wore boots.

So who had buried the clothes here? Mara looked specula-
tively in the direction of the farmer's house. The dull sound
of blows had ceased, but a minute later the snarl and squeak
of a saw filled the air and drowned the voices of the scholars.

'Was the gold near here, then, Brehon, do you think?'
Domhnall kept his voice low and gestured with a downward
motion of the hand to Cael when she began to speak in a
high, excited tone, and she immediately obeyed him despite
her exhilaration, clapping a hand guiltily over her mouth.

'It all makes sense, Brehon,' she whispered then. 'Look,
that's the place over there, across the river, where Séan's
grandfather's boat was dumped, just there between those two
sand dunes. The murderer stripped the body of his English
clothes, carried the boat over, wedged it with a stone, perhaps,
and then lifted the body in and launched it at high tide.'

Mara looked at her only girl pupil with respect. That was
quick and clever reasoning from a twelve-year-old.

'When was high tide on midsummer's eve?' Automatically
Slevin looked at Art who immediately said: 'Would have been
about an hour before midnight.'

'And that was the night that there was all the thunder and
lightning. Etain was worried about you lot out down in the
dungeons. I heard her talking to Fernandez. And there was I
stuck in that wall chamber with dear little Síle,' Cael added
with disgust.

'Pity that we were so far away from the river,' said Cormac,
'otherwise we might have caught a murderer red-handed.'

'Except that there was no blood,' said Cian smartly.

'Let's go back to those clothes,' said Mara. Art looked a little
pale. When he was younger the sight of blood always upset

him and though she thought he had outgrown this, it might be still there, though hidden through shame or fear of teasing. 'I think that Michelóg and Brendan must be asked about them. They are just on the boundary to Michelóg's land and Brendan's is not far away. Domhnall and Slevin, would you go and ask them, very politely, to spare me a moment. Michelóg, first, I think, Domhnall and then when he is on his way with Slevin you can go across to Brendan's place.' She need say no more, she knew. Domhnall would guess that she wanted to space out the interviews – to confront first one man, and then the other with the sight of the dead man's clothes and to note their reactions.

Michelóg, she could have sworn, was stunned at the sight. Stunned and slightly frightened, she reckoned. He was a man who, like the fisherman, had a deeply tanned skin even during the winter and now, in midsummer, was a dark mahogany brown. But he definitely paled at the sight, his skin turning a dirty shade of yellow and his faded blue eyes staring with horror.

'Someone is trying to get me into trouble, Brehon,' he said eventually and she had a feeling that he was almost pushing the words out. 'They're trying to blame me for that death. They deliberately buried the clothes on my boundary. I swear I had nothing to do with it, they've got it all stitched up between them. They want me to be forced to sell up this place in order to pay the fine – what would it be, you tell me that, lad, you'll know?'

He addressed his question to Finbar who turned red, then white and then said shakily, 'It would have been twenty-one milch cows if you had acknowledged it within twenty-four hours, but now that has doubled and you would have to pay forty-two cows and the man's honour price added to that . . .' He stared dumbly and miserably at Michelóg who immediately retorted:

'Well, there you are now. My entire herd is only twenty cows. How can I pay that without selling my land and my house and all that belongs to me?'

'No one has accused you of anything at this moment, Michelóg,' said Mara crisply. 'What I have asked you is whether you have any knowledge of how those clothes came to be buried here in your boundary ditch?'

He stared at her with the baffled and angry look of a tethered bull. 'You know I don't,' he said. 'Why not ask those fishermen? Or Brendan?'

'I certainly will ask everyone,' said Mara mildly, 'but now I am asking you. And do I take it that you deny all knowledge of how those clothes got here?'

He seemed subdued by her tone and nodded his head. 'I swear I know nothing about them, and nothing about the killing of that man from Galway.'

She thanked him gravely and watched him walk away. He wore, she thought, the demeanour of a worried man, but not, unless her instinct failed her, that of a guilty man. Her eyes met Slevin's but it was Cael who said, rather unhappily, 'I don't think he did it, Brehon. I think he is stupid and stupid people lie in a stupid way.'

'Perhaps,' said Mara and then she hushed them as she could hear Domhnall's voice chatting about the samphire season in an amiable, but slightly loud tone of voice. She smiled to herself. He was certainly quite a diplomat. He was giving her warning of their approach and the chance to formulate her questions. This time, she thought, she would have a different approach, a different approach for a very different man.

'Stand in front of the ditch, all of you,' she said quietly and immediately they all lined up: Cormac, Art beside him, then Finbar, then the MacMahon twins, with Slevin standing slightly ahead of the others and taking the eye with his tall figure.

Brendan, she thought, was puzzled. He eyed the line of scholars and then looked at her interrogatively.

'Yes, Brehon,' he said. 'Your young lad said that you wanted me to look at something.' He gazed all around, looking she thought, over at the other side of the river in a slightly furtive manner.

'That's right, Brendan,' said Mara. She turned and then appeared to be surprised at the line behind her. 'Stand aside, all of you, please,' she said mildly and then watched him intently when the scholars moved away.

Well, she thought, he's surprised, but he's not in any way

as surprised and as shocked as Michelóg had been. She kept
her eyes on his face and seemed almost to see his mind shut-
tling through ideas and coming, she was puzzled to note, to
some conclusion. Then he said blandly: 'Don't tell me those
are the clothes of that poor man.'

'I was hoping that you would tell me since you have often
taken him from Galway to Fanore,' said Mara coolly. 'I'm sure
you remember his clothes.'

'He dressed very fine; I don't remember these, but they
could be the sort of thing that he would wear,' admitted Brendan
with an air of one who is willing to tell all that he knows.

'So you don't recognize them, but you think that they may
have been his,' stated Mara.

'That's right, Brehon. They look like the sort of thing that
he would wear,' repeated Brendan. He seemed at a loss for a
moment and then bent down and touched the boot. 'And I'd
say these might be his; I remember thinking once that he had
very dainty little feet for a fairly tall man, God have mercy on
him,' he finished piously.

And, at that moment there was a sound of loud deep barking
and an enormous dark grey wolfhound came flying across the
dunes, cleared the river with one bound and launched himself
at Cormac, barking hysterically and licking every inch of bare
skin he could discover.

And after him, breathless and apologetic, came Séanín. 'I
didn't mean to bring him, honest, Brehon, I didn't mean it,
I just couldn't get him to go home again. Every time I chased
him away, he just took a shortcut through a field and there he
was again, running behind the cart. I did everything I could,
but in the end I just had to leave him, or I wouldn't be here
for a month of Sundays.'

'Oh, Dullahán, Dullahán,' said Cormac fondly. 'You've been
missing me, haven't you? You're such a faithful boy. It's great
that he's here, Brehon, isn't it, because me and Art have been
training him as a tracker dog, haven't we, Art. Dullahán will
find anything you tell him to look for.'

Mara stared at the dog with exasperation. Dullahán was now
almost two years old and she had almost given up hope that
he would ever turn into a reasonable dog, never mind a highly

trained one. He had been originally named Smoke by Cormac, but in a moment of fury, when witnessing a row of flourishing cabbages uprooted by a pair of flying paws, Cumhal had named him Dullahán, a wicked god of the Celts, and the name had stuck and suited him.

As for his ability to find objects, well, if the amount of large holes which he regularly dug in her beautiful garden was any indication then Cahermacnaghten must be filled with buried treasure, which Dullahán sought with immense industry and perseverance.

Fourteen

Conslechto
(Dog Sections)

1. *Any man who kills, without justification, a dog who guards a man's flocks must pay a fine of five cows, supply a dog of the same breeding and also replace any livestock killed by wild animals until the end of the year.*
2. *He who kills a dog of 'four doors', that is a dog which guards the dwelling-house, the cow-shed, the calf-pen and the sheep-fold, must pay a fine of ten cows and supply a dog of the same breed.*
3. *A man may divorce a woman who neglects her husband's dog and does not feed it, thereby imperilling its life.*

Wednesday dawned fine and heralded by a bright and clear sunrise without a trace of red in the blue sky – giving the promise of a dry day. Mara rose very early, washed and dressed and went quietly down the spiral staircase, opened the large oaken door and went out into the clear morning air. She was not the first up in the castle. Etain she saw in the distance clambering over the rocks in search of samphire. It had been a late night of celebration at the castle. Unfortunately Fernandez had invited several members of the clan and their wives, their sons and their daughters to an elaborate feast in her honour and there had been no opportunity for her to talk in privacy with her host. She reminded herself to return to the castle before Fernandez left it. Etain, she thought, must have sensibly slipped off to her bed when she returned from Galway and now was up early and hard at work. Today would be Brendan's turn to make the journey. What would Brendan do when Etain's pregnancy advanced to a stage when she was unable to climb rocks and sail a boat? He would have to get someone to help him with the budding industry that brother and sister had set up. Síle was still too young to be much of a help. In fact, thought Mara, compared to the fishermen's children, Síle was rather spoiled by the two who had been mother and father to her.

Mara stood for a moment after she had quietly pulled closed the door behind her. There was a wonderful view out to sea from the steps to the castle. She could see the tide coming in and the orange strand half covered with lazy, rippling waves, as she strolled down the steps from the castle, breathing in the very fresh air. She noted that the tents snugly situated in the hollow between the sand dunes were still closed up and that none of the stone fireplaces in front of them were in use. There was one extra tent and a long paw stuck out from it and Mara smiled with amusement, imagining how little room there must be for the original occupants of the tent now that the enormous Dullahán had joined them. Cormac may have been politely requested by the others to take himself and the dog off to the new tent and allow the others to have a more peaceful night.

And then she frowned with concern. There was one boy not in a tent. He was walking along by the seashore, kicking moodily at the waves, and she recognized the thin form of Finbar. If it had been any other of the boys, if it even had been Cael, escaping from the childish chatter of young Síle, she would not have felt uneasy, but she had been anxious about Finbar all of yesterday. When she looked back on the day, he had hardly said a word, although he had been excited and pleased by his visit to Galway and had been full of talk for the first few minutes when he met his fellow scholars, but then for the rest of the day he had been silent. She wished now that she left him to stay in Galway. However, her duty was to inform his father, who had placed the boy in her care, and get parental permission for this big change in the son's life.

She wondered whether to abandon her plan and to go down to the beach to join him, but decided against it. There was something about that hunched back and the bent head which showed that he did not want company. There was nothing more that she could say, which she had not said already. No one could alter the fact that this boy's father had disowned him for something which was not his fault. In her reports she had always emphasized to the Brehon of Cloyne that Finbar worked as hard as he could; the ability was just not there. She felt impatient with the man. He, like she, must know that only the exceptionally clever scholars, those blessed with excellent brains and retentive memories and powers of logic, reasoning and understanding, eventually managed to qualify after the long and arduous years of study. There was no disgrace in not making the grade. Better to find this out early enough to make the change to a less demanding way of life.

Finbar, Mara decided, would be all right once he began work in Galway – that's if his father gave permission – and in the meantime he was better with the exuberant company of the younger scholars, not to mention the lunatic dog, Dullahán, who, no doubt, would soon rouse the sleeping camp. She decided to give Finbar his privacy and she turned her attention towards the mountain that rose up behind Fernandez's castle. The River Caher wound its way around this mountain, flowing through a small valley, rich in flowers and sweet grass. The climb was not a difficult one. The slopes of the mountain were terraced, by the hand of God, people around said reverently, and, indeed, it would take a God-like power to move those heavy boulders, to chip and sculpt the limestone slabs. Here and there, though, man had added to the work of the deity, placing stones to help to make a stair-like progression up the hill. The neat, small cattle of the locality used these as well as men, and the goats, with their kids, wandered at will, relentlessly devouring any embryonic hazel sapling or holly bush that dared to spring up in the earth that collected in the grykes.

Still we must have been a giant race in the past, though, thought Mara as she clambered up the steep slope and looked at some of the man-placed steps. How could mortal men have managed to shift those stones, many of them the size of a small house? And then there were the walls. Running the length and breadth of the mountain there were miles and miles of stone walls, most of them formed by leaning slab against slab, though some, she noted, were more elaborately built with a double row of the stones, filled in the centre with smaller stones. Every one of them had their own crossing place. A stranger would have found it difficult but Cumhal had taught

Mara how to look for the built-in stile, sometimes a gap filled with a rounded stone of granite, not limestone, arrived from where, only God knew, and which could be rolled out of the way and then replaced and sometimes a slab jutting out horizontally to form a step, decorated by a grayling butterfly; some just a gap in stacked uprights, cleverly made part of the wall; others a v-shaped notch, too high for a cow. Mara recognized all of the crossing places and she progressed, hand resting lightly from time to time on the sun-warmed stone, until she had attained enough height to look down into the Caher Valley and to see the river as the birds saw it – just a twisting line that snaked in and out. From here, she thought, she could make a better map and regretted that she had not thought to bring with her the satchel that contained her pens and her securely stoppered inkhorn. The scholars, of course, also had their satchels with them and she wished now that she had asked Domhnall and Slevin to come with her. Still, they may have been awake late the night before – she had seen the embers glowing and heads close together in the firelight from the dunes when she herself had gone up to bed.

Mara seated herself on the ledge of an enormous boulder, carefully avoiding the wiry black stems and tender green leaves of the maidenhair fern, and looked down. This twist in the river that was directly beneath her was higher up the valley than any of them had searched before. Her mind, and the minds of her scholars, had been fixed on the idea of the sea and the sand, and the fact that the boat had been lodged between two sand dunes close to the beach had misled them all. And then, of course, there was the find of the dead man's clothing, once again near the beach. If Fernandez's castle had not been so near to the side of the mountain she would not have thought of coming up here and would not have looked at that part of the river.

But a boat, she reminded herself, could be almost as easily dragged upstream as downstream. The difficult thing was the body, but if the boat were taken to the place where the body lay, then loaded, the water would bear the weight of the dead man. The clothes could have been dealt with afterwards, once the boat was safely floated down on the river water and launched upon the outgoing tide. She stood for a moment staring down to where the river wound around the base of the mountain. The sun was getting stronger every minute and its light shone down and suddenly she saw below her, on the bank of the river, a glint, a gleam of silver.

After a moment she realized what it was. There was a seam of calcite in the limestone rocks down there and the light had picked out the mineral – an odd seam, a strange streak, shaped like an arrow, or a lance head, which she felt she would recognize when she saw it again. An idea suddenly came to her. This treasure of gold would have been hidden in a time of unrest, a time of clan warfare, but it would have had to be hidden in a place where it could easily be found again – after months, or even longer. If that was the hiding place, the person who had buried the treasure could have memorized that odd streak of calcite; it would have formed the marker for the place where the treasure lay, a place to which, perhaps, he never returned. It could be that he was killed in a battle, died before he could reveal the secret. The treasure could have stayed hidden there for centuries upon centuries.

Until it was uncovered in times of storm when the river flooded.

Not completely uncovered, but little by little, a ring perhaps, such as she had found lower down, or perhaps most wonderful of all a torc, that gold necklet so prized by the Celts in the legends and stories. More likely, she thought, some small articles.

But what if, after that tremendous rainstorm on the Sunday night before midsummer's eve, when the downpour had been so heavy that, unusually, even the porous limestone of the Burren land had flooded and its fields had turned to temporary lakes. What if, on that night, the little Caher River had thundered down, slicing through the meander around that bend where now it flowed so placidly, scouring out the earth and the stones as it took a left-hand turn to travel on down to the beach, what if then it had uncovered the whole of the treasure, something carefully buried, perhaps a thousand years ago?

And, her mind went on, busily picturing the scene, trying to picture someone who walked where she walked now, someone who could have seen down into the river valley by the light of the sun, moon, or even by flares; she cast her mind back to the night when Niall Martin had been murdered. There had been a full moon on that night, but there had also been sporadic rumblings of thunder and flashes of lightning. No torrential rain like the night before, a night without rain, a night when one might risk walking under the beam of the moon and surveying the landscape beneath.

And perhaps, Niall Martin, having sought his treasure up the length and breadth of the Caher River beside the sand dunes, had decided to go a bit further up and into the valley between the mountains and had seen a gleam of gold at that spot, that outcrop of rock which the river encircled?

But his presence there at Fanore had not gone unnoticed. A watch had been kept on him and he had been followed – was it by a man or by a woman? By the murderer? Whoever it was may have come up here in order to keep an eye on where the man was searching, an unobtrusive, unseen eye, because what man, looking for treasure, raises his eyes to the sky-high mountain? So had the murderer looked down upon Niall Martin's progress, seen him scrabble amongst the rocks and then suddenly seen the flash of gold? The way down to the river valley would be steep and precipitous but the glow of gold would lend urgency and extra strength to the murderer's feet. Murder may not have been intended, just a lust for gold which perhaps led to a fight, and then the fatal blow.

Or had it, she suddenly thought, been the other way around?

Mara took careful note of the site and turned to go back down to the castle. It was, she thought, significant that access to the mountain path that she had taken this morning led through Fernandez's land and that the mountain reared up behind the castle walls.

Her scholars were all awake by the time she got halfway down. One of them was still down at the water's edge. Poor Finbar, she thought, with a sigh. Even from a distance he had a lonely, miserable look. Then she heard little Síle's high, childish scream, half-fear and half-delight, and Cormac's voice shouting reassuringly: 'Don't worry, Síle, he's a very friendly dog!' Since Dullahán was the size of a small pony that, thought

Cormac's mother, was hardly reassuring to a nervous eight-year-old, who had probably been roused from her sleep by an inquisitive muzzle inserted under the canvas of the girls' tent. She raised her own voice in a shout, calling authoritatively, 'Dullahán, come!' and remembering with regret her own beautiful and well-trained Irish wolfhound, Bran, the son of her father's faithful companion and who always did what he was told and was, from puppyhood, a calm and obedient dog.

Dullahán occasionally did obey her and this time, whether it was because he liked exploring new environments, or whether he was, for once, in a compliant mood, he seemed to be coming to her command. Síle's screams stopped and she heard the skidding of stones on the mountainside and waited, hoping that there were no sheep nearby. Dullahán's nature was amiable and he was well used to farm animals, but his exuberance and the suddenness of his movements frightened animals not used to his rambunctious personality.

However, all was well. No sheep, not even a goat appeared. Dullahán came at full speed up to her, suddenly remembering that she did not like to be jumped upon, skidded to halt and sat, panting heavily, showing a fine set of gleaming white teeth, which had probably frightened the life out of Síle, roused from her sleep.

'You bad dog,' said Mara severely. 'You are, let me inform you, the worst dog in the world.'

Dullahán wagged at her merrily, but she was conscious of a feeling of slight irritation. It was, she felt, rather a reflection on her dignity as Brehon to own such an unruly dog. When Cormac came up, scaling the mountain with ease, laughing and calling to his pet, she said to him severely: 'Cormac, you promised to train that dog and he is getting wilder and wilder.'

'I do,' said Cormac defensively. He scratched the soft hair behind his pet's floppy ears. 'Me and Art have been so busy training him to track that we haven't had time for all this "*come*" business. I'm going to set him to look for that gold this morning and I bet you anything, Brehon, that he's going to be the one to find the clue.'

'You'd better keep him away from Etain's samphire or he'll dig the lot of it from the rocks while you are calling him to come,'

said Mara, but she could not help a smile at the picture of her
son standing outlined against the silver-grey of the limestone,
with his gold-red hair and the enormous dog beside him. They
looked like a legendary Celtic boy hero with his wolfhound.
'That smells good,' she added as they came further down and the
unmistakable smell of frying fish rose up in the morning air. And
then she thought of the solitary dejected figure at the water's
edge and said impulsively:

'I think I saw Finbar down by the sea, Cormac. You and
Dullahán go on down there, bring him back for his breakfast
and I'll make my own slow way down.'

To give Cormac his due, she thought proudly and tenderly,
about her scapegoat son, he was a great friend – the concerns
of the other scholars were always important to him. He suddenly
looked very worried and left her instantly, sliding rapidly down
the slippery stones, followed by his four-footed accomplice in
crime barking excitedly at the prospect of a chase.

Mara followed, seeing thankfully how Finbar, in the distance,
turned at the sound of the barks that echoed off the rocks and
drowned the noise of the waves. No one, she thought, could
be depressed and anxious in the company of Cormac and
Dullahán. Together they exuded an air of excitement, pleasure
and joy in life.

Fernandez was swallowing a mug of beer and chewing on
an oatcake when she came into the small kitchen beside the
hall in the castle. He had the look of one who had taken a
little too much to drink the night before, but he immediately
exerted himself to provide her with breakfast, offering to go
down and get some fresh fish for her as he knew that Setanta
had planned to go out soon after midnight, before the tide
was too low for the use of the pier. She refused the offer,
declaring herself content with an oatcake, and spread it with
some butter.

'Have you any milk?' she asked. Fernandez, she noticed,
had no servants. Strange, but, she supposed, indicative of the
fact that any silver that he had with him on his return from
Spain had been used in the building of his castle. This was,
indeed, a man who could use buried treasure to great effect,
a man who would know where to sell it and how to do it

unobtrusively. He had, after all a fine ship, big enough to sail to Ireland from Spain, so he could easily go off in it, on a feigned fishing trip, and could sell the gold anonymously in Limerick, Cork, Waterford or even in Dublin itself, where he could easily pass for a trading Spaniard. He looked relaxed and happy, she noted; a man at peace with the world and at ease with his legal guest as he readily answered her query about milk.

'Yes, Michelóg filled our barrel this morning – brought some news, too. I hear that you've found the dead man's clothes.'

'Yes, we did. At least I think we might have. It was a black hat with purple silk tassels, tunic of black broadcloth . . .' She went on detailing the clothes, and the boots, finishing up by saying carelessly, 'Would that be what he was wearing?'

If he saw the small trap, he made no acknowledgement of it, merely remarking that he had never seen the man in his life and then going on to say: 'Well, he's buried and will soon be forgotten. We may never know what happened to him.'

'That's not really good enough for me,' she remarked. 'I can't look at it as a piece of inconvenience to be tidied away. A man was killed and someone tried to disguise the facts about his death. As Brehon, representing the King's justice, I cannot allow this event to go without doing my best to discover the culprit and to impose a penalty.'

'He was an outsider. You owe no duty to him.' His voice was harsh and abrupt. She had never seen that side of him before.

And, to a certain extent, he had justice on his side. The original Brehon laws were indeed administered to right a wrong done to a member of the kingdom, to settle disputes between them and to give impartial judgement on matters concerning property and livestock. However, Mara felt firmly, and knew that others of her colleagues felt like this, that, they had to uphold justice for all, not just for those who could pay the lawyers to enforce it, if they were to resist the criticism levelled on them by the English, that their laws were barbarous and fit only for savages. The man had, as far as they knew, done no harm in coming into the kingdom and taking a few shellfish for his supper – the question of the buried treasure was, perhaps,

a different matter, but the facts remained that he came to the
Burren, spent some nights in the old house, rooted around on
the beach, uncovered some sand piles and then was killed.

'I am determined to solve this murder, Fernandez,' she said
aloud and with great firmness. 'I do not like the thought that
a murderer is loose in this kingdom. One death can lead to
another and I expect every inhabitant of the Burren to assist
me in my task.' And then she paused, looked at him very
directly and said: 'On the night of the murder, Fernandez, on
the night when you were good enough to house my young
scholars in the castle, did either you or Etain climb the mountain behind the house – it would perhaps have been some time
after midnight or in the early morning.'

He gave her grin which, somehow, she thought was forced.
'Etain and I were otherwise engaged at that hour, Brehon.'

'And yet, Etain, at least, must have been up at sunrise,' she
said sharply. 'I understand from the woman in Galway, Joan
Blake of Blake's Pie Shop, that Brendan delivered a load of
samphire to her early on Tuesday – that would have been
midsummer's day.'

'No, you're mistaken, Brehon,' said Fernandez. 'It was
Brendan himself that picked that load and he was off before
we were up, before any of us was up. Etain went with the
second load after midday.'

'I see,' said Mara. 'So if I were to tell you that a figure had
been seen climbing the mountain, who would you guess that
it could have been?'

Fernandez shrugged. He didn't appear to be alarmed, but
there was a slightly wary look on his face. 'I'd say it could be
anyone, Brehon. I put up no barriers; have no savage dogs
guarding the place. I say to all of my clan to treat this place
as their own, to come and to go as pleases them. All are
welcome.'

Fifteen

Bretha Comaithchesa
(Laws of the Neighbourhood)

An owner is responsible for all damage caused by his dog.
A fine must be paid if the dog digs under another's house.
If a dog defecates on another's land, then the owner must remove the faeces, and give the landowner the weight of it in curds or butter as recompense.

When Mara came down onto the beach after her breakfast, Cormac, Art and Cian were running up and down the uncovered half of the strand and over the rocks, shouting, 'Seek! Seek!' while Dullahán, barking hysterically, his very deep-throated voice sounding oddly ill-fitted to his puppy-like behaviour, raced from one end of the beach to the other, splashing into the sea and skidding on the dark strip of black limestone which slanted across the orange sand, then turning to follow the others up beside the Caher River. There was no sign of Síle, but Cael was standing beside Domhnall and Slevin listening to the two older boys respectfully and ignoring the three younger ones. From time to time, the dog was encouraged to dig in various places, but all that seemed to be achieved were flying sandstorms and shrieks of laughter. Whenever Dullahán got tired of being directed to do these incomprehensible searches, he turned his attention back towards his primary purpose in life at the moment, which seemed to be to rid the beach of seabirds, even putting to flight a pair of black, hunch-backed and sharp-beaked cormorants, who shrieked rusty, broken sounds of rage over his head for the next few minutes.

Mara watched the dog tolerantly. There was always a hope, she thought, that Dullahán was a late developer and that he would turn into a reasonable dog who could manage to walk quietly and to bark only when strangers arrived. At the moment, though, honesty forced her to admit, that there was little chance that he was ever going to be of the slightest use, other than to keep Cormac and his friends amused and to reduce gardeners like herself and farmers like Cumhal to a state of near apoplexy. Still, she had other more serious matters on her mind so she walked away and began to consider the problem of Fernandez. The thing is, she thought, I know so little about him, other than the fact that his father was in all probability the brother of the present *taoiseach*. Other young men of the neighbourhood she had seen grow up, had watched them turn from engaging boys into troublesome adolescents and then mature into adults. Fernandez had arrived fully made, so as to speak, full of charm and self-assurance. But what was he like in reality, what were his hopes, his inner dreams and his ambitions? A man who could use some gold treasure, according to Michelóg, and Mara had to acknowledge that there was a lot of truth in that. Fernandez, she thought, was a man full of ideas and such men are ambitious – and ambitions such as his had to be financed.

So, she thought to herself, *make the case*, as she would tell her scholars to do.

The case against Fernandez was that he could have been roused by the early midsummer dawn, could have got out of his bed in the castle, seen only by Etain who would certainly have been devoted to his interests. He could have slid past the door leading to the great hall where the scholars slept, could have noiselessly opened the unlocked front door, then could have climbed the mountain to see what Niall Martin was up to. And then, by a piece of luck, he may have seen the old man, finally on the right track, whether by the chance remark of a Greek sailor, or whether by sheer luck, but whatever it was, Niall Martin may have uncovered the treasure trove, enjoyed his triumph for a few minutes, holding up a necklet to the morning sun, perhaps, then was attacked by a determined young man. What did he hit him with – well, Mara guessed the answer to that. Standing just inside the door of the castle there was a bundle of sticks, stout ashplants, useful for climbing mountains, and perhaps lethal if brought down on the head of an old man. Mara shook her head. She had made her case and it was a good one, if – and she did not know the answer to this 'if' – if Fernandez O'Connor was ruthless and evil and would take a life to get his hands on some gold. Somehow, her instinct seemed to tell her that he was not like that, but the possibility lay there.

And at that moment there was an excited scream from Cormac. She had been aware during her musing that the boys were still chasing after Dullahán the Wild, endeavouring to block him as he dodged between outstretched arms. He had fortunately stopped that ear-splitting barking and seemed to be getting enough amusement from eluding his pursuers.

'Dullahán, sit!' yelled Cormac.

'Dullahán, give!' tried Art.

'Dullahán, come!' The commands filled the air and several seagulls drifted overhead to see what was happening, associating a lot of shouting with the landing of a catch of fish, perhaps. The women tending the fires and packing away the smoked mackerel stopped their work to stand and laugh at the scene.

'That wretched dog's got something in his mouth,' said Cael, appearing by her side. She sounded elderly and disdainful.

'Probably a dead and very stinking fish,' said Mara with resignation, thinking that at least the dog could be led into the sea afterwards.

'No, it's not,' said Cael. 'I can see what it is now. He has one of our maps. It's a leaf of vellum. Dullahán,' she yelled crossly, 'give that to me.'

Whether it was because Dullahán bowed to the note of irritated authority or whether he had got tired of running around the beach, but he came up to Cael with his long, whip-like tail wagging and sat down, panting heavily and allowing her to take the partially-chewed piece of vellum from his slobbery mouth.

'Y . . . y . . . yuck!' Cael dropped it on the sand and dipped her fingers into a convenient rock pool.

'That's a piece of vellum that he had,' shouted Cormac, running up. 'Perhaps it's a clue. Don't throw it down, birdbrain. He'll take it again.'

'Is it your map, Cormac?' asked Mara, though she thought that the leaf looked too small for that.

'No,' said Cormac picking it up and frowning at it. 'That's not our map. It is a map of Fanore beach, but look it's got strange signs on it. No . . .' he said, his voice high and excited, 'no, not signs!' Suddenly he stopped. And then he turned to where the two older boys were talking and he yelled out: 'Domhnall, come here. Come quickly. Come and look at this.'

'What? What's all the excitement about?' Domhnall was smiling, though Slevin looked rather irritated by the interruption. His eyes widened though when he saw the piece of vellum that Cormac was holding up.

'That's a Greek letter, a word in Greek. They're Greek letters, aren't they, Domhnall,' he said. He took the leaf from Cormac and held it out towards Domhnall. This was too much for the wolfhound, which snatched it neatly from him and set off, ears flying behind him, racing towards the sea with the vellum held firmly in his mouth.

'Cormac,' yelled Domhnall. 'Get it from him quickly. This could be important. That was definitely Greek, wasn't it, Brehon? Could you read it?'

'I think,' said Mara slowly, 'that I might have seen the word "gold". Of course, it might be my imagination, but I don't think so. It definitely started with the X – oh that wretched dog. Cormac, get him back.'

Cormac was running at full tilt and Cian was aiding him as much as he could, trying to corner the enormous dog which twisted and turned and leaped over rocks. Art and Finbar joined in, though in a slightly half-hearted fashion of those who felt that this was not going to end in success. There had been many a chase after Dullahán back at the law school when he had got hold of a hurley ball, a sandal or even a leather satchel. Whether the sketched map would ever be readable again was another matter. Each time that one of his pursuers approached Dullahán he seemed to pull some more of the vellum into his mouth until now only a small edge of it dangled from his teeth.

'Dullahán, come,' shouted Mara in a voice which she had never used to her beloved Bran, but Dullahán had a different nature to Bran and her intervention seemed to spur him on to new levels of complete disobedience. He dodged Art's outstretched arm, flew past Finbar and plunged into the sea, his long legs moving effortlessly through the water. Cormac went after him, but in a moment Dullahán was swimming fast, heading out to sea. Then Cormac stopped and stood very still, and despite her fury, Mara shared his anxiety for a moment. It would break Cormac's heart if anything happened to his unruly pet.

However, Dullahán, once he had outdistanced his playmates, had turned and began swimming strongly towards the rocks. The tide was now almost full and the water lapped on the edge of the pier. Dullahán placed one paw on a rock and then a second and heaved his streaming hindquarters out of the sea and onto the pier. He shook himself violently two or three times and then ran back towards the beach, prancing up to his master with the expression of angelic obedience on his hairy wet face. Mara strode grimly down to the water's edge and stood waiting while boy and dog did a little dance of joy. One glance had been enough.

'He's dropped it somewhere in the sea,' she said and wondered whether there was anything in Brehon laws about the punishment due to disobedient dogs. However, it was, she knew, her own fault. A large dog like a wolfhound should have been trained from the moment it came into her house and Cormac had been too young really to train a dog. She should have taken matters into her own hands. And yet, that wouldn't have worked. If she had trained the dog, then it would no longer be Cormac's dog and the whole point of getting him something to make him feel special and very loved, of making him feel that his birth parents, whom he normally referred to as 'Brehon' and 'the King', wanted to buy him something precious, would then have been completely lost. She sighed and took a hold on her temper.

'Never mind, Cormac,' she said. 'You did your best. And I did see the Greek word on it and taken with the fact that Niall Martin was probably talking with a Greek sailor on the day before his murder I think that Dullahán's find was really quite significant, and who knows,' she said, trying to sound cheerful, 'when the tide goes out we just might find it again. It would be a good idea to come down to the beach tomorro morning very early, as near to daybreak as possible, at dead tide, and have a look.'

She wasn't sure whether the writing would survive a twenty-four-hour immersion in the salty sea. If it had been written with carbon ink the vellum would be wiped completely clean, but if it was iron-gall ink, then there might be a chance. In the meantime, however, there was something that needed to be done.

'Domhnall and Slevin,' she said, 'I wonder could I ask you to ride to Galway for me. I want a letter delivered to the Mayor, to Valentine Blake. You should stay overnight in your father's house, Domhnall. I'm sure that he and your mother will be delighted to have the two of you. Come up to the castle with me now and I'll write the letter and seal it and give it to you.'

They left Cormac lovingly rubbing his pet's wiry coat with the hem of his *léine* and went up towards the castle. Fernandez was coming down to meet them and Mara explained the matter about the map to him. He was highly amused and offered to ride to Galway himself, but Mara refused the offer.

A letter, she thought, could be unsealed, and then resealed, by someone with a candle and plenty of patience. And she had in her mind to ask Valentine to check up on some matters other than the question about whether the Greek ship was still moored in Galway's docks, and whether the sailor who ate the pie with Niall Martin could be traced.

There were some other questions that she had for Valentine Blake – simple questions, but of vital importance to her quest for the truth in the matter of this death that she was investigating.

Did Etain deliver the samphire on that Monday when she was at Joan Blake's shop, or did someone else, her brother Brendan, come back with it?

Who delivered the next lot of samphire on the morning after the death of Niall Martin?

And had Fernandez O'Connor ever appeared in the company of Niall Martin, the goldsmith?

'You see,' she said, looking intently up into the intelligent ⸰ces of her two oldest scholars, 'I suppose it would be a good solution if this Greek sailor had in some way heard of the finds here in Fanore, had drawn a map, had inveigled Niall Martin to come with him, had rowed or sailed the boat over to Fanore, but you know,' she said, impatiently putting her pen down onto the tray, 'it really does not make sense to me. What do you think?'

'I'm a bit doubtful, myself. Well, first of all the Greek sailor would not have easily found a small boat to take him here to Fanore. And this coast is very tricky. It's hard enough for the fishing boats to land here; they have to wait for high tide. And then there are terrible rocks stretching under the sea at Black Head, just before you come down the coast to Fanore. I can't see a stranger able to take a small boat past them safely unless he had a very good guide.' Slevin made the point but then looked at his friend.

'What I was thinking, Brehon,' said Domhnall slowly, 'as well as Slevin's points about the difficulties of the boat, is that no Greek sailor would have knowledge of our Brehon law. They would not know about *fingal*, about casting a man afloat in a boat with no oars. They would not know how to set up an appearance like that, to simulate death by thirst with this business of pulling the tongue out deliberately. That was all done to present a certain image, to put a certain idea into your head, to distract you from the real story about a gold merchant who came here to find a hidden treasure, something that, I would think, many people here knew. Why did they think that he came otherwise? No one would look for shellfish up by the Caher River. I think that Niall Martin was murdered because he found the gold and I think that he was murdered by someone here at Fanore.'

'I agree with you,' said Mara.

'So the sooner we get going the sooner we will return,' said Domhnall, rising to his feet. 'We could easily come and go on the same day, Brehon, if you wish.'

No, no,' said Mara firmly. 'Stay overnight with your father.'

Slevin was inclined, she saw, to argue, but Domhnall gave her a nod of comprehension, touched Slevin's arm and drew him towards the door, leaving Mara ruefully aware that this young grandson of hers could already read her like a book. It was her use of the words 'Stay with your father' which had betrayed her purpose. Oisín, she knew, as did his son, was a man who always knew what was going on in Galway, who always picked up the latest gossip, knew everyone's affairs almost as well as his own. Oisín would know if there had been any rumours about someone being involved with Niall Martin, he would know how to talk to the sellers at the fish market and find out who was ferrying the old man to and fro on his ceaseless quest after the gold of Fanore.

'Yes, you will know what to do and what questions to ask,' she said with a nod at Domhnall.

And then she went back out of the castle and down onto the beach. It was, she reckoned from the sun, about an hour before noon. The tide had already turned; a long curving line of cream-bubbled foam across the top of the beach and then a few feet of very wet sand showed that the fast ebb had begun. This was the best time for boats to go out and Brendan's splendid Galway hooker was among those. Etain was in it, but Brendan, Mara noticed, was standing on the pier, shouting detailed instructions and watching with anxiety as his sister manoeuvred the boat. Mara was not close enough to hear what he said, but she saw how he went right out as far as he possibly could on the line of rocks that formed the north side of the bay and how some of the other fishermen, catching his anxiety, made signs also to Etain, who was now hoisting a large brown sail to catch the freshening south wind. How would she manage without these instructions when she came to Galway City docks, Mara wondered. Perhaps it would be an easier task for the girl to land at Galway docks where she could follow in the wake of the other boats. And then something else occurred to her so she went in search of Art who was obediently helping Cormac to train Dullahán by handing him a sandal, allowing him to take it in his mouth and then commanding him to give it back. Dullahán had on his face the bored look of a dog who knew a much better game and despite herself Mara's lips twitched. She hastened to commend the effort, however, and Cormac looked pleased, though he said with gusty sigh: 'I just cannot believe that we had this perfect clue and now we've gone and lost it.'

'Never mind,' said Mara consolingly. 'There might be a chance that you will be able to find it at low tide tomorrow morning. You'll have to search the beach very thoroughly.'

'We can take Dulláhán now that he is trained and that will be a help,' said Cormac with the optimism of youth and Mara suppressed the first words that came into her head and said hurriedly, 'Did you see Etain take out that big boat of Brendan's, Art? How did you think she was doing?'

'Pretty well,' said Art judiciously. 'I think that's the first time that she's taken the hooker – she did well.'

'The first time!' exclaimed Mara. 'But how does she go to Galway then – I know she goes sometimes.'

'She takes their old boat,' said Art, who knew all about the fishing community here. 'If she does the morning run, then Brendan does the afternoon run and they come back together – they can tow the old boat so that's no trouble. She just wanted to take the hooker because she's late today and once the wind is behind it, it goes like a bird with those big sails.'

'Where do they keep the little old boat, then?' asked Mara. The pier was now completely empty and the very blue sea was dotted with boats of various sizes, though none of them as big as Brendan's splendid hooker. There was a fresh wind that whipped white caps from the rolling waves and most boats, big and small, had now hoisted sail and were moving rapidly out into the ocean. Brendan had gone back now and was engaged in laborious work of pulling the samphire from the rock pools and placing the plants in the loosely-woven willow baskets. She cast a look behind her, but there was no boat pulled up on the beach.

'She leaves it moored over in that little bay behind the rocks, just up by that old house, Murrough's place,' said Art knowledgeably.

'Murrough's place?'

'Yes,' said Art. 'That was the name of Michelóg's grandfather; you know that old house, Brehon, don't you?'

'Wish we could find another clue,' put in Cormac, not seeming to take much interest in this discussion about boats. 'Just like the one that you lost, birdbrain,' he said affectionately to his pet, rocking the great hairy head from side to side. H looked with a certain amount of unease at Mara and then back at Art. Mara was conscious of the looks that passed between them, but her brain was very busy, very intent and she allowed the pictures to flow through her mind, seeing each one as it formed itself.

'It's all your fault, Dullahán; you spoilt our clue,' said Cormac eventually, eyeing her anxiously.

'Don't scold Dullahán,' said Mara. 'You know I think that he has played a part in this and has helped me to come to understand what really happened.'

They both stood very still, watching her, and even the dog seemed to calm down and lay obediently at their feet. Mara looked across the rocks at the place where the old house stood precariously near the high-tide mark.

'Yes, of course!' She exclaimed the words aloud as suddenly the bits began to come together in her mind.

She would wait, she thought, until the return of Domhnall and Slevin tomorrow before taking any action. It was, she thought, a tricky legal point, but she was pretty sure she knew the solution. As to the other matter, well that would have to be sorted out also.

In the meantime there were a few questions in her mind so she went up the beach to find Cliona.

Cliona, when Mara first knew her properly, was a very young woman who had divorced her husband because he had not wanted her to have a baby. At the time of the court hearing, she had been suckling Art and after the divorce she had courageously worked her small sheep farm herself. Mara had given birth quite soon afterwards, and once she realized that she was unable to breastfeed Cormac, she had engaged Cliona to live with them and to suckle and care for Cormac as well as her own son. This had worked well, with Cumhal keeping an eye on the farm for her, while she lived with Mara. It had worked until Cliona and Setanta had fallen in love and wished to marry and live on Cliona's farm. Mara had been faced with the dilemma of finding another nurse for Cormac or allowing him to leave her house in order to remain with his little friend and almost twin-brother Art and with Cliona who had been a mother to him. The decision was made; Cliona and Setanta fostered the son of the Brehon and of King Turlough Donn and Cormac grew up devoted to them both.

And I probably did the right thing, thought Mara as she went up the beach in search of Cliona. No boy could have had a more affectionate foster-mother and Setanta, also, had been a father to Cormac. There had been feelings of jealousy when she had envied the love that Cormac showed his foster-mother; Mara acknowledged that to herself, but she had always trusted Cliona and had respected her judgement in all matters. What Cliona thought of her, she was not sure, but she noticed that Cliona was protective of Cormac and anxious that he should not be misjudged by his own mother. This made Mara slightly ill at ease with her on occasion so she began by making a laughing reference to Dullahán.

'He'll settle down – *the more cracked the pup, the better the dog*, did you ever hear that saying,' said Cliona reassuringly.

'Let's hope you're right – although I suppose he must be two years old now,' said Mara, and then she said, looking out to sea, 'Etain is managing that big boat of Brendan's well, isn't she? Art tells me that she usually sails the old boat, the one that they keep moored down by the old house.'

'That's right.' Cliona seemed relieved that the conversation was not going to be about Cormac. 'They work very hard, the pair of them. She'll have to slacken off now with a baby due at Christmas – so I hear.'

'I suppose that they have to work very hard because I don't suppose the samphire season goes on too long; just about up to the beginning of September, isn't that right,' said Mara. She had been thinking about that and wondering how Brendan got the money to buy that big boat. Had he, perhaps, been one of the lucky finders of a piece of gold on the early morning beach, had brought it to Galway and exchanged it for enough silver to buy a Galway hooker. It seemed very likely.

'Oh, they're not just reliant on the samphire,' said Cliona readily. 'Oysters are the main business. And of course the two things fit well together. The samphire plants are ready for picking from Bealtaine, right through Lughnasa, right to the end of that month, usually and then the oysters are finished spawning and ready to eat long before Michaelmas Day – and they go on right through the autumn and the spring, right around until the first samphire have come through again.'

'Of course,' said Mara. Oysters were something that she detested so she had not known that piece of information. It still all made sense to her, though.

'And when did Brendan get the new boat?' she asked, idly putting some more brittle, salt-encrusted, dried seaweed on to the fire.

'Just a few months ago, I think,' said Cliona. 'He must have had a bit of luck, Setanta says.'

Sixteen

Brecha im Gata
(Judgements about Thefts)

If a man steals an ox or a cow he must give back four oxen or four cows.

If he steals a horse, a pig or an inanimate object then he must return double its value. Every law-abiding man can take anything from a burning building, from a corpse on a battlefield, from a great depth at the bottom of the sea or of a lake, from a place of terror reputed to be haunted by monsters, or anything deep within the rocks which can only be reached by ropes.

Mara woke early and went downstairs. There would be no sign of Domhnall and Slevin bearing the letter from Valentine Blake for another few hours, but she was too restless and too full of ideas to spend any longer in bed.

The letter didn't really matter, she thought. She had asked Valentine certain questions, but now she was certain that she knew the answer to those questions – it would be good to get confirmation, but she was confident that she was right. There was no sign of either Fernandez or Etain so she poured some fresh milk into a carved goblet, sliced a wedge of the soda cake that had been left on the table and then went outside, looking first out to sea and then, when she walked out through the gate, turning and looking back over the mountain that rose up sheer behind her.

It was, she thought, a spectacular sunrise, almost the most stunning that she had ever watched. The colour of the sky was as though a translucent layer of soft red had been laid across a background of ever-changing blues, paling to pink at times and then turning a vivid red, then to a light purple. It had been a dry few days and in front of that spectacular sky the bare limestone of the mountain reared up in a glory of glistening silver, smooth walls, pointed crags, and long sloping shelves, all seeming as though some celestial power had designed them to be seen against the backdrop of that magnificent sunrise.

'Red sky in the morning; fishermen's warning!' The voice at her shoulder, amused and carefree was that of Etain. 'That's what we say, the farmers talk about shepherd's warning, but storms don't bother the shepherd as much as the fisherman, I can tell you that, Brehon. I don't like the look of that sky.'

'Do you fear the sea?' Mara asked the question, thinking that she knew how the dashing Etain would reply, but was surprised at the seriousness of the voice.

'Anyone who doesn't fear the sea dies young,' said Etain abruptly. 'You must never stop fearing the sea or else you are lost.'

'And Brendan?'

'Oh, he fears the sea, too! Why do you think he spent so much silver on buying that hooker – not for these summer runs, but in the winter to ferry the oysters across Galway Bay in a storm – that's not for a small boat. I pack the oysters for him so that he's not tired, but it's an anxious journey, I can tell you, Brehon, and I'm always glad to see him safely back.'

'And how is he going to manage without you this winter?'

'He'll have to hire some help. He can't afford to lose the market now that it has been set up. There should be plenty of fishermen who would do a morning's work, especially in weather too stormy for their little boats. He'll have to sort something out. I'll be too busy in the future to help him and I'm not having Síle do that work. She's not strong. She can help me to look after the baby and she'll have a home here with Fernandez and me.'

Mara had half-wondered whether she was supposed to know about this baby, but Etain looked and sounded quite unself-conscious. It was interesting that she did not appear to think there would be any difficulty for Brendan in paying a wage to a fisherman. There had been a time when Brigid had spoken with pity about the orphaned brother and sister, only seventeen and fifteen when their parents died, leaving them with the responsibility of a young sister and just a few acres of poor land and a small, disease-ridden herd of cows. Now, it appeared,

Brendan was wealthy enough to buy himself the best boat in the neighbourhood and also to employ labour.

'When did he buy the hooker?' she asked casually and was not surprised to hear that it was about eight months ago. Brendan had probably found a piece of gold at that time, taken it to Niall Martin and then bought himself a big boat to cope with the winter storms.

'Must have been expensive,' she commented, turning once more to look back at the sunrise. Now the dark red was streaked with pointed peaks of smoke-like black, seeming to replicate the jagged rocks that were now returning hues of the darkest dark grey. Mara looked back to the sea and was glad to find that the bows of those small boats that she could see dotted around the ocean were now turned towards the shore and she hoped the fleet of fishing boats would be back soon. She thought that they would. The sky would give them its message and all knew that if rain came it would douse the fires and the catch could be wasted. At the moment all was very still, rather ominously still, but the wind in these western parts could get up very quickly and come storming in from the Atlantic. Her scholars were not in the boats, she was glad to see, but were down on the beach and were being pressed into service by Fernandez to help to load his Spanish ship with the barrels. It would be a race against time and tide now, she knew as she watched the barrels being rolled down the sand and stacked up against the rocks, ready to be winched aboard with the sling which Fernandez had set up on his deck. Dullahán was acting as though the whole scene was set up for his amusement, barking wildly as he chased after the barrels and ignoring the shouts, commands and pleas to go away. Presumably he had not managed to find the lost, half-chewed map with the Greek writing, but the fact that Mara had advised a search at low tide might have prevented the scholars from going out with the boats this morning, so she was glad that she had thought of suggesting it. She counted heads. Cael was there, determined to prove the strength of her muscles by twirling a barrel over the strip of black limestone, Art and Cael were rolling another barrel across the sand, while Cormac tried to distract Dullahán by throwing a large flexible slimy stalk of kelp for him to retrieve. Finbar she saw, also, up to his knees in water, helping to tie the sling onto one of the casks.

Reassured that all were safe, Mara turned back to look at the sky again. Streaks of yellow were now imprinted across the fluffy red background, and as she watched the whole sky turned to a shade of dark orange that seemed to mirror, in soft glowing light, the expanse of sand on the beach. Even for the non-weather-wise, it looked as though settled weather could not be expected, despite the present calm.

'Are you going to Galway this morning, Etain?' asked Mara, turning reluctantly away from the sky and bringing her mind back to her task at hand.

'Not me; Brendan is going. There he is now. I've been up at dawn picking samphire and he was loading up as fast as I could pick,' said Etain. 'He'll do a second run in the big boat when as he comes back if all is well and the storm doesn't break.' She turned to look at Mara, saying, 'Did you want him? I'd say that he'll be back as soon as he can. That sky looks like as if it's brewing up a bad storm. Look at those clouds getting up. Amazing how quickly it can change, isn't it? One minute bright as an orange and now, look, it's all grey and black overlaying it– there's rain coming, I'd say. Your boys will get wet riding back from Galway. They should have gone with Brendan this morning in the hooker – the sea is quicker. Why didn't you send them with him? He'd have been glad of the company.'

And with that she left. And Mara was glad not to have had to reply. It would have been a difficult question to answer. Why had she not sent them with Brendan? That was not a question that she wanted to answer honestly to Brendan's sister. She cast another look at the sky, wished that she had Cumhal with her as he would undoubtedly be able to forecast when the rain would come. In his absence, she decided to be sure rather than sorry, as Brigid would say, and she went back indoors to fetch her cloak and went to walk up beside the Caher River until she reached the spot that she had identified from high on the mountain. There was something she wanted to check on and when she saw the rock formation she knew that her memory was right.

The rocks here were not flat slabs like in other places, but were slanted and sharp-edged. In most places those edges had been softened by a thick coating of springy grey-green lichen, but here and there the rim showed through, sharp as though they had been shaped by a whetting stone. Mara bent down to look, but there would, she thought, remembering Nuala's words about the lack of a wound, be nothing really to see – just a strong conviction that this was how the death had happened, here a couple of hundred yards further up from the sand dunes and the beach.

Domhnall and Slevin arrived back before the storm, triumphant at how fast they had come, but exhausted. They had set off before dawn and were both yawning heavily so Etain suggested that they pull a couple of mattresses in front of the fire in the hall and have a few hours' rest in peace away from all of the shouts and excitement on the beach. They handed over the letter from Valentine to Mara and she read it through, nodded at its confirmation of her guesses and put it into the pouch that hung from her waist. She did not share it with them, however, and left them to have their sleep and went back down onto the beach.

The hooker was back, moored to the pier, but there was no sign of Brendan. Setanta was pulling his boat up the strand with the help of Cormac, Art and Finbar. Dullahán tried to jump into the moving boat, but was roared at so fiercely that he for once desisted and stood with an uncertain and slightly hurt look on his face.

'Sorry for yelling at the dog like that, Brehon,' apologized Setanta hastily when he spotted her. 'It's just that I want to get this boat up onto the dunes as quickly as I can. We might have a bit of a storm this evening or even earlier and I don't like leaving them tied against that pier. The smaller boats can easily smash themselves to smithereens if the wind picks up enough.'

'Yell at him all you like if it makes him do what he's told. You'll have to tell Cormac your secret of making that dog behave,' said Mara and then was a little sorry when she saw her son look hurt, 'but he was doing some good training with him yesterday,' she added quickly and then, to distract attention from Cormac, she asked Setanta whether he had seen Brendan.

'I believe he's gone to have a look at the oyster beds, see how they're getting on, Brehon,' said Setanta, pointing an admonishing finger at Dullahán, who seemed to be about to recover from the shock of being addressed so harshly.

Mara left them. The oyster beds were over by the old house and she was anxious to inspect that. As she approached Murrough's place, as Art had called it, she could see that Brendan was quite some distance away and so, feeling thankful she was wearing a dark cloak, she slipped into the little old house.

Murrough's place was a small, cabin-like cottage with a gaping doorway. It had just one narrow window in the main room downstairs and another similar one high up in the gable on the southern end of the building. Mara came to the doorway, and saw that on the inner side of the three-foot-thick wall someone had hung a tarpaulin from a rod and weighed it down with beach stones inserted into a roughly sewn hem so that the wind would not blow it into the room. She pushed it aside and looked in. There was just one room downstairs and a solid and new-looking ladder leading up to a loft. With one backward glance at the distant figure of Brendan, Mara stepped inside. It had probably been used in the past to house animals – perhaps even Michelóg's notorious bull – there was a small lump of dried dung in one corner, but the stone flooring had otherwise been swept clean and the large empty fireplace had some charred lumps of turf lying in it as though someone had lit a fire there quite recently. There was an old bench, worm-eaten in places, drawn up in front of the fireplace and again that looked clean and able to be used as a seat by the fire. The house, in fact, was surprisingly dry and free from bad smells, with fresh lime-wash gleaming on the walls. She went to the ladder and climbed easily to the top of it and looked into the loft bedroom. Again it was reasonably clean, quite weather-proof, and with a large swathe of sweet-smelling hay thrown down in one corner – in summer weather like this a man could place a cloak over that hay and sleep the night comfortably, especially a man who was driven on by his lust for gold.

But this was not what she was looking for so she came back down again. From her early childhood she had been in and out of cottages like this and, one and all, they had their 'hidey-hole'. Without hesitation she dragged the bench over so that its back leaned against the chimney breast and climbed up on top of it, inserting her hand into the wood-lined cupboard that was built between the slope of the roof and the top of the wall.

And instantly her hand met the pliable osier rods of a basket. Carefully she drew it out. She had seen many of them during the last week, sometimes on the rocks where Etain worked, sometimes dripping sea water and filled with samphire, but this basket was quite dry and was stuffed with one of the short woollen jackets that fishermen wore over their *léinte*. She parted the folds and saw, by the sparse light that came through the window slit, a gleam come from within them.

And then the light increased. The tarpaulin was pulled across abruptly and the man came in. He stood there for a minute and then said harshly: 'That's mine; that's my property, Brehon, and this is my house.'

'Yes, of course, it is your house, Brendan,' said Mara, resting her spare hand on the back of the bench and climbing down. She carefully placed the basket on the seat before saying calmly: 'I should have listened more carefully when I was talking to Michelóg. I remember now that he said he had a word with you allowing the gold merchant to stay here. Of course he must have sold this old house belonging originally to his grandfather to you at some stage – it would be more use to you than to him. It touches on your land, doesn't it? And as for this gold; well, you know, you may be right. It could be that when I look into it, it will turn out to be your property. After all, your land has shore rights and the law says that *any goods found on the seashore belong to the owner of that shore unless it can be proved that they have come from beyond nine waves from the shore – in which case they will belong to the finder.*'

Mara left a few moments of silence after she had finished her quotation. 'And these rights have pertained to your family's land since time immemorial, have they not, Brendan?' she enquired in a matter-of-fact way.

'That's right, Brehon,' he said eagerly. 'I even remember my old grandfather talking about that. He used to tell me to keep an eye open for anything that we could find.'

'And then there were all those rumours of finds – the *sloping place of gold* – that was right, wasn't it?'

'Over the past few years,' said Brendan, his face darkening. 'I think I know who it was, too, but nothing would make them admit it. I found something myself, but I thought least said . . .'

Mara nodded. That had been enough to enable Brendan to buy his big new boat. It had been a lucky find for him, but she wished that he had come to her and shown her the gold and asked for a judgement. She had got a little out of touch with these people on the western fringes of the kingdom, she thought, but there was no good in regretting the past. The whole matter had now to be regulated and the facts laid in front of the people of the Burren. But first she had to settle the events of that night.

'And then the gold merchant started to come here,' she reminded him. 'You and Michelóg talked it over, you decided to allow him to stay overnight in this place, and, of course, you, with your regular journeys to and from Galway, were the obvious person to bring him. How many times was it?'

'This was the fourth time,' said Brendan. 'I watched him like a hawk the first time, but then I thought that he didn't know what he was doing, didn't know any more than the rest of us. I didn't think he had much of a hope, to be honest; people have been searching Fanore for gold ever since I was a child. No one knew who the gold belonged to and no one wanted to ask. There were rumours that it was the property of the man who owned Cathair Róis, that would be Fernandez's cousin – people used to say that it had been left to him in a will that had been stolen. There were all sorts of stories about this gold so when I found that arm ring, then I decided to say nothing and just to sell it off for as much as I could get for it.'

'You sold it to Niall Martin?'

Brendan nodded. 'And very inquisitive, he was, too.' His eyes had gone to the gold and then back again to Mara's.

His face had the look of man who wanted to appear cooperative.

'And then when you ferried him over on that day, that Monday after the storm, you decided to wait the night out of doors, you worked out that something might have been washed out the dunes, or out of the hillside after that terrible rainstorm on the Sunday. I suppose you noticed that the gold merchant usually came after a storm. So you dropped him off in this little harbour and you were there in the shadows, waiting to see what he would do.' Mara stopped and looked across at Brendan. She could see very well how it all occurred and a man like Brendan would be quick to seize an opportunity.

'That's right, Brehon, I thought that it was my rights that he was trying to make himself master of.' He sounded surer of himself now.

'So you kept an eye on him,' said Mara mildly.

Brendan shook his head in a display of self-disgust. 'I should have done. If God is my judge, that's what I should have been doing. I had it all planned. But you know what it's like, Brehon. I was up early in the morning, I'd been to Galway, had ferried Etain back, listened to all the grand talk about pie shops and delivery of samphire and the prospect for oysters in the future, all the plans for me to hire staff and perhaps two boats going, morning and evening – had gone back with the second load, well after all of that once I had dropped the gold merchant off in that little place, well, I took the boat over to the pier, moored it and then sat down to give him a bit of a start so that he wouldn't see me spying on him. And, you won't believe it, but I was so tired that once I sat down I went off to sleep – didn't mean to – I had resolved that I would keep an eye on him all night.'

'But you fell asleep,' said Mara, less by way of reproach than a means of getting back onto the story.

'That's right,' he said eagerly. 'I fell asleep and no one could have been more shocked than I was when I woke up and saw that dawn had come and realized that I might have wasted my chance.'

'And what did you do then?' Mara knew that he would have been immediately galvanized into action.

'Well, I went looking for him.' Brendan's face bore the look of one who is reliving the past.

'And you found him.'

Brendan made an impatient motion with his hand and Mara said no more. She guessed what had happened. She waited until he spoke again.

'There was no sign of him on the beach. The tide had turned, it was coming in, but the sands were still mostly uncovered. There was a gannet diving and feeding from the edge of the beach, the place where the river met the sea. He flew away when I came near so that I knew there had been no one else near – they scare easily, these birds.' He stopped and eyed Mara with a look of apprehension and she understood that the next part of his story was difficult for him to tell.

'Go on,' she said, trying to sound encouraging and not betraying her anxiety to hear what had happened next.

'Well, the morning that I found the gold – last winter – I reckoned then that it had been washed out of some place alongside the river – that made sense. I didn't think it had come in on the waves.'

Mara nodded. Brendan had thought like she had done.

'So I followed the river back up towards the mountain. I kept going until I came to that place where those pink flowers grow.'

'And you found him?'

'I found him, so as to speak,' said Brendan, his expression grim. 'But he was gone from this world. He was dead.'

Mara said nothing and he misread her silence. 'I know, I know! You don't believe me! No one would believe a story like that!' he said. He went and sat down on the wooden bench without a glance at the gold in the basket beside him. He buried his head in his hands.

'You're sure that he was dead; did you see blood?'

'No, no blood, but he was cooling. Not long dead, I'd say. For all I knew, he died because his heart stopped. There wasn't a mark on him.'

'You touched him?'

'Just to see if there was life in him; I'd have got help if there was any chance for him,' said Brendan piously.

'And what did you do then?'

Brendan inclined his head towards the basket beside him.

'I took the gold.'

'He was the one who had discovered the gold, you think?'

'Yes, he had it all piled up there. Piled up on the rock,' said Brendan.

'But not in a bag?' put in Mara.

'A bag?' He stared at her in a puzzled way and she thought she would leave that point. The bag, she thought, had been small enough to be unnoticed, might even, when folded, have been carried in the man's pouch.

'So what did you do next?' asked Mara.

'I didn't touch him again, just left him lying there and I put my jacket into my basket, and wrapped my gold in it and went off.' There had been a slight emphasis on the words *my gold* and Brendan looked at her hopefully.

'Had there been a fight?'

'Not with me, Brehon. I tell you that I didn't touch him. He was as dead as any stone when I came up to him. That's God's own truth.'

'So it wasn't you who killed him, was it?'

'That's right, Brehon. Not me. I swear it.' Brendan's tone was uneasy, but she felt that there was a note of truth in it.

'And you have no idea of who killed him?'

She thought that he hesitated for a second, but then he shook his head.

'No, Brehon,' he said firmly. 'I do not know who killed him or what happened to his body afterwards or how he came in on the tide three days later. Gave me a terrible shock, that. I couldn't understand the whole thing. How did the body disappear and then turn up again, that's what I was asking myself.'

Mara rose to her feet. 'I'll borrow your basket and your wrapping, Brendan,' she said. 'You'll get them back as soon as I have summoned my farm manager and some men to escort me back to Cahermacnaghten. This gold will be brought to Poulnabrone on one week from today and in that place of justice I will give the court's verdict on what happened to Niall Martin, the goldsmith from Galway, and also on who is the owner of the gold which he discovered.'

Seventeen

Bretho Crólinge
(Judgements of Blood-Letting)

A criminal who slays a man should not be fed or be protected. A law-abiding man must not give him any assistance to hide his crime or to evade justice.

On her return to the castle Mara went straight up to the room which had been allotted to her. She emptied her satchel of all that it contained and then placed the gold from Brendan's basket within it and turned the key on both locks. Etain was in the kitchen when she went down. She looked at Mara defensively and Mara looked sternly back, guessing that Etain's eyes had followed her when she had gone in search of Brendan. No doubt she was aware of all that had happened on that night.

'Could you fetch Setanta for me, Etain,' she said, coldly. She gave no reasons – she need not give any. As Brehon she was the King's representative and any command that she gave in the course of her duties was as binding on the members of the kingdom as if it had been given by the King himself.

Etain threw her a startled glance and slid out of the kitchen, immediately followed by Síle, who had stuck her thumb into her mouth. Neither returned and Mara went to wake up Domhnall and Slevin. They were old enough, trustworthy enough to do her bidding, and were both strong and well-grown for their age. Nevertheless, she was glad that she had thought of Setanta as an escort. When they came, she gave them her instructions, and handed the key to the enormous safe at the law school to Slevin, while Domhnall was entrusted with her leather satchel. When they came out of the castle enclosure Mara could see that her five younger scholars had come up from the beach and were standing beside Setanta, looking rather worried. Even Dullahán was quiet, for once, and stood panting with his tail drooping slightly. A few of the fishermen who had already secured their boats had followed them up and stood at some distance, as if anticipating an announcement. Etain was white-faced and held Síle's hand after making a vain effort to pull the thumb from the child's mouth.

'And, Domhnall, ask Cumhal to bring the cart and sufficient manpower back with him; he will know what to bring,' she said clearly and loudly, pitching her voice so that it would carry to the furthermost person in the little crowd around the enclosure wall. It would be just as well, if the story about the gold had got around, that they should suppose that she still had it with her in her room in the castle. In any case it would be handy to have the cart, as the scholars had accumulated a lot of belongings. Despite the lingering calm the weather was definitely going to break and she had a feeling that they would not be sorry to sleep in their own beds tonight. Perhaps, she thought to herself, she also would be glad to leave this place. The unravelling of the whole story could perhaps be left until the morning, until after their return, she told herself, but knew that was not satisfactory. She still might need to check on some details with Brendan. The matter had to be faced up to and dealt with now.

'Come inside, all of you, but first of all, Cormac, please shut Dullahán into one of the empty stables,' she said, knowing that her voice sounded grave. This matter was deadly serious and they all had to understand that. She didn't want any comic intervals with the unruly dog and so waited until that had been accomplished before leading the way back into the castle. She could hear the slap of the bare feet on the stone flags behind her, but she did not look back, just led the way in silence up into the room and sat down on the solitary chair while they ranged themselves on the floor before her.

'Where's Finbar?' she asked, looking around. He had, she knew, been with them up to the moment that they had gone indoors.

They looked surprised, looking over shoulders and Cormac, she noticed, looked concerned and began to get to his feet.

'Sit down, Cormac,' she said sternly and waited until he had obeyed. It was, she thought, just as well that Finbar had absented himself for the moment. She could manage better without his presence initially.

'Let me talk to you about this murder,' she said looking down at them very directly. 'I want to go back to that Sunday night of the storm. We came across to here on Monday morning and the sea was still very choppy, but Monday itself was fine and sunny. Brendan and Etain went across to Galway with their baskets of samphire and Etain went into Blake's Pie Shop to get an order for a daily delivery of samphire. By a coincidence – a coincidence pure and simple, I should say – by coincidence, Niall Martin was there and he was talking with a Greek sailor. I know,' said Mara looking steadily at them, 'from Nuala's examination of the body that the dead man ate apricots on that last day of his life and these were obtained from a pie in Blake's shop.' She saw Art wince and hurried on. She would not, she thought, mention the deliberate pulling out of the dead man's tongue. That would have been either Cian or Cormac, she thought, both of them a lot tougher than the sensitive Art.

'You all were invited to spend the night in this castle, Cael slept in one of the small wall chambers to keep Síle company and you boys were given mattresses on the floor in the hall. I believe that you three, and Finbar, decided initially to spend the night in the dungeon, but Domhnall and Slevin, sensibly, decided that the hall in front of the fire was more comfortable, that's true, isn't it?' She waited for the nods before she went on.

'So to go back to the story of Niall Martin, well he came over from Galway to Fanore on that same Monday and he went to sleep at Michelóg's house, got up at dawn on the Tuesday morning, went out, up along the bank of the Caher River, and, I believe, found the right place where the treasure had been buried but he found that someone else had been before him.' Mara heard her own voice recounting these much thought-over details and knew that it sounded dead and dull. She forced herself to be more brisk and continued: 'Someone was before him and that someone had found the treasure by accident – perhaps he got up at sunrise because he couldn't sleep, because, perhaps,' said Mara with regret, 'because he was deeply worried about something. He walked on the mountainside, looked down and saw a gleam of gold lit by the first rays of the sun. He went down hurriedly, and started to uncover the precious things, heaping them up on the rock face. He was,' and Mara's voice slowed again and she purposely deepened it, to avoid a quaver in it, 'he was,' she continued, 'a person who was needy, who perhaps suddenly saw these gold articles as a way out of a situation in which he should never have been placed.'

Mara looked around. Cael was looking interested, involved, the girl was pleased, perhaps, that a solution was in sight, but also a little puzzled by the atmosphere and the way that the other scholars were reacting. Cian, her twin, was wearing his tough face, Art looked miserable and Cormac stared at his mother through narrow eyes that challenged her to solve the mystery.

And Mara stopped and thought again. There was, she felt, no reason now why she should go into the matter of the death. That was for another hour, for another audience. Now there were other matters to clear up. There were words that had to be said to these law scholars, these lawyers and Brehons of the future.

'No one,' she began with solemnity, hoping to get through to them the seriousness of the matter, 'no one should interfere with the due processes of the law. In some this might be considered as ignorance, though ignorance is never a true excuse, but in this case, it certainly cannot be a plea. There was, in this case, a deliberate effort to mislead the King's representative, the Brehon. Not only was the body moved from the site of the murder, but it was stripped of its outer clothing, placed in a boat, a boat that had no oars, then launched on the river that took it down to the sea. I imagine that the perpetrators of this fraud waded in with it as far as they could go. And I'm afraid,' she added, looking straight ahead and not catching any eye, 'I'm afraid that they hoped never to see it again, but as we all know now, the body came ashore and the attempt to have it immediately buried, something that instinctively the fishing community here, who recognized this boat, wanted to do, something that almost all wanted done with no fuss; this was foiled by my two scholars, Domhnall and Slevin, who proved themselves worthy members of the Cahermacnaghten Law School and came to summon me.' She looked blandly at the faces below her, noted that Art crimsoned, that Cian looked uneasily at his twin sister and Cormac set his lips firmly together as if no form of torture was going to make him say a word.

'And that, of course, was not all,' said Mara gravely. 'There were more deliberate attempts to deceive me. First of all, it was important, once it was realized that the body had unexpectedly come ashore on the beach from where it was launched, that its presence was discovered by someone who would and could have had nothing to do with the killing or the concealment of the crime; the person chosen was eight-year-old Síle, younger sister of Etain and Brendan.' She thought back to Cormac's supposed kindness to the eight-year-old and told herself that she should have become suspicious sooner. 'And then,' she went on, 'there was the false trail, made by the boots of the dead man, leading to his clothes buried outside the outer wall of Michelóg's farm, and then the discovery by a dog . . .' Mara paused, wondered briefly where the clothes had been kept, remembered the underground room where the purple tassel from the dead man's hat had been found, then continued steadily, 'that discovery by the dog from Cahermacnaghten Law School of a map with perhaps the Greek work for "gold", no doubt you copied the letter "*xhee*" from Domhnall's *Iliad* – all of these were, I fear, all attempts to mislead the Brehon who was dealing with this case – to spread the suspicion far and wide so that eventually the case became unsolvable.' Her mention of the Greek sailor in the pie shop in Galway had been a stroke of luck for the conspirators, she thought, remembering the satchels, pens, inkhorns and vellum with which her scholars were provided in order to take down details from the fisherfolk. They would have had fun in doing a treasure map in Greek, she thought, repressing a feeling of amusement, and determining to bring home to them that evidence is sacred and must never be tampered with.

'I had nothing whatsoever to do with all of this, Brehon,' said Cael. Her disdainful face showed that she understood what had happened and how false trails had been laid. She gave a glance of scorn at the other three and she shifted away from the boys sitting beside her on the floor as if physically to mark her separation from their nefarious deeds.

'I know that, Cael,' said Mara. 'I hope that if you had been present, if you had not been sleeping in the wall chamber, looking after Síle, when this was all planned, I do believe that you would have been far too mature to try to throw dust over an enquiry into a death.' Her eyes met those of three boys, two pairs of eyes fell before hers but the third pair, pale green, fringed with gold eyelashes, looked at her steadily.

'My father, the King,' said Cormac, 'says that *the hinges of friendship should never grow rusty for the lack of the oil of assistance when help is needed.*'

Mara did not respond. Cormac had two parents, two very different parents, with different principles, different traditions, who surprisingly managed to be at ease with each other because each respected the other's point of view, but he was perhaps too young to understand what his mother felt about the law. The creed of a warrior was probably easier for an eleven-year-old boy to comprehend.

'How did you guess, Brehon?' asked Cael and the others looked at her with gratitude for asking the question that was on their lips.

'Easy,' said Mara, adopting the format of the question and answer volumes which taught the young to understand and memorize the tenets of the law which would become a life-long study for them. 'Easy,' she repeated. 'Who suggested to Síle that she might find some pretty shells in the cove where the boat with its body had come to rest? Who was with Cael when she found the tracks, very obvious tracks, leading to the place, outside a farmer's land, where the clothes of the dead man were buried? Why, if the goldsmith found the treasure, was it not placed inside his leather bag? Whose dog found the clue that seemed to point to the involvement of a Greek sailor – a man that I had mentioned a day previously – and above all, who had the legal knowledge to try to make the corpse look as though it was the result of a judgement of *fingal*?' There were other things that she could have cited. The pulling ou of the tongue to simulate death from thirst, the continual effe to lead her astray, to distract her from the real culprit and she remembered all the occasions when, looking back on them, the conversation had been manipulated to lead her away from the subject and she hoped that an involuntary smile was not going to come to her lips or her eyes to show amusement. This, she thought, was a serious matter, as lawyers-to-be they should not, they must not behave like this, though she was touched and moved by Cormac's words, and thought that his father would be proud of him. Turlough had a genius for friendship and his friends, going back over a period of sixty years, were numbered in legions.

'I'll leave you to think about these matters,' she said, rising to her feet and waiting until they stood up also. 'Now, Cael, would you please go and fetch Finbar. Bring him here to me.' Cael was the best choice, she thought. Officially, as far as Finbar was aware, she knew nothing, and she was sensible enough not to speak of what she would guess needed to remain secret for the moment. 'And you, others,' she went on, 'you will please get all your belongings together. We will be leaving here once Cumhal returns. Don't forget to thank Etain for her hospitality, oh, and perhaps you could write a letter to Fernandez – that I feel would be a good idea. Let's find a piece of vellum – one can write and the others can sign it afterwards.' She crossed over to the table by the window, sorted through the articles that she had emptied out of her satchel and talked on at length, appointing a scribe, discussing what should be said, talking, not only to bring back a feeling of normality to their relationship, but also to give Cael a chance to fetch Finbar. She would keep these three under her eye until Cael returned and then she would dismiss them to go back and help on the beach and she would speak to Finbar alone and in private.

Eighteen

Maccslecca

(Son Sections)

*A dependent child is classified as táid aithgena ('thief of restitution')
from the age of twelve to that of seventeen. Any offences below the
age of seventeen carry no fine, although restitution of stolen goods
must be made.*

The letter had been written, signed, left in Mara's possession for the signatures of the other scholars before being
placed prominently on the table for Fernandez to see when
he came back from Galway, but still there was no sign of Cael
or of Finbar, either. Mara peered out of the front door a few
times, noticing that the breathless calm had now gone. Suddenly
the air was fresh, the wind had risen strongly and the rain had
begun to fall. She looked out to sea and found that there was
no trace of the Aran Islands visible now, just mountain-high
waves, their top edges whipped to cream. The storm was
coming up from the south-west; she could see the rain
slanting across the seven-hundred-feet-high cliffs of Moher.
The large black-backed gulls were flying in from the sea, borne
aloft on the air currents, and their cries were carried across to
where she stood. She strained her eyes and then with relief
she heard the sound of voices. But it was just Etain who came
running up from the beach, dragging a soaking wet Síle by
the hand and then thrusting the child in through the door in
front of her.

'See to Síle, Brehon, will you, get her to change her clothes.
I must get Brendan's small boat up onto the dunes. That's a
hurricane wind getting up down there now. You can hardly
fight against it. Pray God that Fernandez and Brendan are safely
into Galway Bay by now and that they have the sense to wait
out the storm there.' And with that, she was off, running back

down to beach, her long brown legs, beneath the hitched-up *léine*, covering the distance easily.

'Síle, change your clothes; surely you're old enough to do that for yourself,' snapped Mara. 'You boys, see to it that she does so and all of you stay within the castle until I come back.' And she snatched her cloak from the top of the chest by the door and set off running after Etain down past the sand dunes. She spared a thought for her two eldest scholars, Domhnall and Slevin, but it was a sheltered passageway through the narrow valley between the mountains and they would be well inland by now. And the storm had only just hit the coast.

But where was Finbar, and why had Cael not returned?

She had gone halfway down the roadway to the beach when she heard running feet behind her. She turned and saw Cormac, his feet bare, his *léine* soaked, his green eyes blazing and rain dripping down from his bright gold hair.

'Go back, Cormac,' she said crossly.

'No,' he shouted, 'you must listen to me.' Despite the wind and the rain his voice rang out as though the blood of five hundred kingly ancestors had infused it with power. She turned back to him, trying to pull the heavy fur-lined hood of her cloak over her drenched hair.

'Listen to me,' he repeated furiously. 'You must listen. Finbar didn't mean to kill him. I judged him, I judged him not guilty.' His eyes were blazing with passion. 'Finbar found the gold. It was his gold. He saw it from the mountain. He was the one that found it. He thought it would save him from disgrace, from starving, if his father threw him out. And then that man from Galway, that *strainséir* who had no right to be in our kingdom, he tried to take the gold from Finbar. Finbar didn't mean to kill him, Brehon!' Cormac's voice rose almost to a scream and he grabbed at her arm as if to stop her walking away. His hand gripped her sleeve, holding her with a strength that she had not known that he possessed. 'He didn't mean to kill him, just to stun him and to escape with the gold, but the man hit his head on that rock, he hit his head and he was dead immediately. And Finbar came to us for help.'

'I know, Cormac. I guessed. You go back now. I'm not cross with Finbar. I want to help him too.' Mara had to say the words right into his ear to make herself heard over the wind that tore along the path, shrieking, from the Atlantic, but he shook his head firmly.

'I'm going to find him,' he yelled. 'You can't stop me, Brehon. He's my friend. When he sees me, he'll know that I'll keep him safe.'

'Very well,' said Mara. Her son, she thought, was probably right. His presence would help to reassure Finbar, help to make him feel that all was not lost. Together they would set his mind at rest. She made an inner resolution that whatever the Brehon of Cloyne might think, even if he considered her to be an interfering woman, father's rights, or no father's rights, nothing, she resolved, would stop her now from telling the frightened and guilty boy that a bright future in the busy city of Galway was opening out in front of him. He had lost the gold, removed by Brendan when Finbar had gone to summon help from his friends, but then he had no right to that gold. Let him honestly earn some silver from the merchants of Galway and build up his self-respect and his belief in himself.

But where was he? And where was Cael who had been sent to fetch him? Infused by the passionate fear, by the real anxiety in Cormac's voice, Mara began to run after him down the path worn smooth by the feet of the fishermen and their families. Even on this sheltered passageway, hemmed in by head-high dunes on either side, the wind tore the breath from her lips. On either side of the path there were clouds of sand dust, blowing and swirling around the stiff pale green clumps of marram grass. They looked as though they were whirling *sídhe gaoithe* and their presence made shudders of ill omen run through Mara. It seemed only minutes since she had observed that she could not see the Aran Islands and now with the driving rain in her face she could not even see the sea itself. All that she was conscious of was a giant wall of foaming white cloud-like spray rising up above the height of the sand dunes and the cliffs. The tide must be at about the halfway mark; by full tide the inhabitants of the beach camp would have all been forced to retreat to their inland homes, or to seek shelter within the hospitable walls of Cathair Róis.

They met a few men coming back with bundles of poles

and others were pulling the boats up even higher, but the
majority were frantically digging the dunes with their bare hands
and desperately throwing handfuls of sand onto the bottom
boards in order to weigh them down against the power of the
sea. There was an air of urgency and panic about the fishermen
and Mara decided against asking any questions. Her heart had
begun to thud with a heavy, insistent beat and her lips tasted
the bitter salt with a feeling of anguish

There was a figure ahead, a figure that came running back
up the path towards them, a figure that had black hair plastered
against her skull, coming up from the sea and passing Cormac
with a shrieked sentence. He shook his head, shaking the hair
from his eyes and kept on his course, but Mara narrowed her
eyes expectantly, trying to see through the rods of rain. It was
just Etain, coming back. But she was alone and had no boat
to drag up with her. Either Brendan had taken it and put
it over near to the old house or else he had already lodged it
among the sand dunes. Mara did not hesitate. She was beginning to get very frightened now. She had two children out
there on that terrible beach and she had to get them back.

'The boat's not there, it's gone!' screamed Etain, and then
she said something else, but the wind seemed to toss her words
aside. Mara did not stop. She felt that she had no interest in
Brendan or Etain's troubles – let them buy another boat, if
that one was destroyed in the storm. In any case eleven-year-
old Cormac was running ahead and she was determined to try
to keep up with him so she passed without a word, with not
even a backward glance.

Where had Finbar gone? He had been with the others
outside Cathair Róis, he had been with the others then and
by that stage Fernandez's ship and Brendan's hooker had already
gone swiftly out to sea. She remembered seeing the white sails
of the one and the dark brown sails of the other and the
south-westerly wind, already very strong, made them fly like
large birds over the surface of the sea towards Galway Bay.
Finbar could not have been with either of these. Where could
he have gone? He wasn't with the men in the sand dunes; she
would have seen his thin figure instantly.

But Cormac had seemed to startle at Etain's words; he had

bounded forward and was now completely out of sight. His ears might have been quicker than hers.

The wind caught her cloak when she came out from the shelter of the dunes and onto the beach. The hood was snapped from her head, filled with air, she felt it as a solid force dragging her back and then the cloak itself billowed out bringing her to a standstill on the edge of the beach. Without hesitation, she untied the string around her neck and let it sail backwards towards the cliff. She could just see, through the salt-tasting spray, a gleam of Cormac's white *léine* – that also was blowing back, but he battled on. He seemed to know where he was going, seemed to have some purpose, aiming directly across the beach to the place where the newly built pier jutted out into the sea. For a moment Mara thought that she saw someone there, but then a tremendous wave, the dreaded seventh wave came, almost in slow motion, rearing up, with menacingly curled and froth-fringed edge, coming nearer by the minute.

For a moment it appeared as if the tiny figure on the pier would be engulfed by that giant wave, but with incredible quickness it turned and seemed almost to fly as it was swept by the force of the wind up the grey, foam-besprinkled sand. It had got halfway up when it overbalanced and Mara heard herself scream, and in the maelstrom of wind and wave the sound was as thin and high as that of the soaring kittiwakes.

But the wave had done its worst. It had engulfed the figure but then had withdrawn; leaving it sprawled on the sands like an abandoned piece of prey. Cormac reached it first, pulling it to its feet, putting his arms around the sobbing figure. For a moment Mara could hardly make it out, but then as she came nearer she could see that it was Cael. The girl was soaked to the skin, her hair plastered against her skull, her starched white *léine* just a sodden rag hanging around her. She was crying bitterly, in great noisy sobs that somehow rose above the crash of the waves.

'Quick,' said Mara. She wanted to take the girl in her arms, but the danger was too great. She grabbed one arm and Cormac took the other and then they retreated up the beach and crouched into the shelter of the sand dunes. It was only then that Cael managed to stop crying, desperately scrubbing at her streaming eyes and determinedly holding her breath until the noisy sobs ceased. She did not look at Cormac but up at Mara.

'Brehon,' she said. 'Finbar is gone. I couldn't stop him. I kept shouting after him, but I couldn't stop him.'

'Gone,' said Cormac.

Suddenly Mara knew what had happened and knew, with a terrible stab of guilt, that she was responsible. Finbar had despaired, had felt himself to be disgraced, had been filled with a sense of sin and remorse. Why had she not talked to him first of all, why had she not realized how vulnerable he was?

'He took Brendan's small boat, was that it, Cael?' she said, steadying her voice as much as she could, but feeling overwhelmed with an enormous rush of contrition, almost as powerful as the gale that had battered them on the open beach.

'I couldn't stop him.' Cael resolutely bit back the sobs. 'He was in the boat before I got here, Brehon. I shouted to him, I told him that you were not angry, that you were just annoyed with Cormac and the others, I told him all that, Brehon, but he just didn't seem to be listening to me, he didn't even look at me, he just cast off and then the wind took the boat and I saw him just lie back in it.'

'He didn't raise the sail.' Cormac's voice was rough and broken. Cael shook her head. And then she leaned over and laid her face on Cormac's shoulder and began to cry.

'He didn't do anything,' she sobbed. 'He just got in, cast off, and then he lay down and faced up to the sky. It seemed as if he didn't want sails or oars.' She hesitated for a moment and then said, between broken sobs, 'It seemed as if he wanted God to judge him, Cormac, and I just can't bear to think of it.'

Mara sat there, helpless, looking out to sea, thinking about this boy, only fourteen years old, who had condemned himself to this lonely and terrible death. She judged herself mercilessly, judged, and condemned: her overwhelming desire for facts, for evidence, her need to have everything tidy and well-regulated. Why had she not foreseen this terrible and tragic ending to a case that seemed to be half-serious, half-farce? Over the years, she thought, I have become complacent, have felt that I was very clever, and that I always knew the right way to do things. No one should feel like that. Every case should be approached with due humility and with a tentative and sensitive way of interrogation. She had realized the truth, had known that she was being systematically misled, but that should not have had any weight with her. Her duty as an *ollamh*, as teacher in charge of a law school, should have, she admitted, taken precedence over her work as a Brehon, over her desire to be the one who always uncovers a solution. After all, she thought, as she stroked Cael's wet hair and tried to take the girl into her arms, after all, solving the murder of Niall Martin had led to no particular good. He had been a greedy man who had developed an obsession with finding the gold hoard of Fanore. Now his riches would go to enlarge the coffers of the wealthy city of Galway and a young life had been wasted.

Looking out through the wildly waving stems of marram grass at the tumultuous sea, at the almost sky-high waves, feeling the howl of the wind, she knew that no child could survive in a small boat out there.

'Come,' she said to Cael who was still clinging to Cormac. 'Come, Cael, let's get you indoors and dry. There is no more that anyone can do until this storm dies down.'

On the following morning Mara came to the sands at dawn. It would be just before the hour of six in the morning, she thought, looking back up at the pale sun looming in the sky over the mountains. The storm had blown itself out, culminating in a spectacular high tide at midnight and then subsiding gradually. By six o'clock the sands were bare and almost immaculate. Not completely immaculate because two bodies were swept ashore on the morning after the day of the great storm. One was that of a giant pilot whale and the other was the small thin body of a boy who had, thought Mara, as she knelt in tears beside him, been failed by all of the adults who should have cared for him. Why had she not given hope to him after that visit to Galway, why had she not taken him aside before she spoke to someone else, talked with him once the whole picture had become clear within in her mind? His crime was not a crime; not a crime in the way that the adults in his life had sinned against him. She tried to suppress her sobs, but they came and then she allowed them to come. It was the least that she could do for him now and her dignity did not matter to her. Her sins had been great and his, given his temperament and his dilemma, had been comparatively small.

Others had come down to the beach, also, but they stood apart, uneasy, unsure as to what to do. She would have to face them in a moment, she would have to tell them what had happened but she found it hard to move from beside the small thin body. If only time could have been rewound, if only the last week could have been relived and events differently handled.

And then she sensed someone who knelt down beside her. She felt a hand upon her shoulder and knew that it was time to stand up. The hand was firm and for a moment she almost thought that her husband, King Turlough, had returned unexpectedly, but a word was spoken: '*Muimme*,' said the voice and Mara reached out and put her arm around Cormac and for once he allowed himself to be held by her. She stretched the moment out, before releasing him and getting to her feet. Feeling that her son was still beside her, her courage flowed back and then she knew she would be able to tell the story. These people, the fishermen and shore-dwellers, deserved to hear the truth from her before the formal statement was made at Poulnabrone. She got to her feet and turned to face them.

'I have to announce to you all, who have been involved in this affair, what happened in the matter of Niall Martin, the goldsmith from Galway City,' she said steadily.

It was a very different environment from the usual judgement place at Poulnabrone where the enclosed space focused all attention on the ancient dolmen and on the figure of the Brehon handing down judgements from a law that was as old as that burial place itself. Here on these vast and level sands, bordered by the glittering sea and with the gulls shrieking overhead, she found simple words to tell the story of the boy who found the gold, accidentally killed the man who had been seeking it for months and then, bewildered and afraid, sought the help of his friends. Mara was moved to see her own sorrow, even her own tears reflected on many of the faces in front of her. No one asked about the gold and that was the way that it should be. That affair could await her judgement at Poulnabrone. Now, on the cliff top overlooking the vast Atlantic, she and her scholars, with the help of this compassionate community of fisherfolk, would bury the boy, Finbar, who had condemned himself to death, but who would live in all of their memories.